FAME & OTHER DISASTERS

MARIA P FRINO

Fame and Other Disasters

This is a work of fiction.

Title: Fame and Other Disasters

Author: Maria P. Frino

Cover Design: Mark Drolc - http://onthemarkdesign.com.au/

Visit the author's website at https://www.mariapfrino.com/

All inquiries to the author - mariapfrino@gmail.com

 Created with Vellum

QUOTE

What is friendship
but mutual respect
with a smattering of envy

Emma Beers Jones

PROLOGUE

Social Media. Two words that would soon strike fear into the hearts of television celebrities Molly Edwards and Emma Beers Jones. They were best friends, with an invisible thread of deep connection. But neither would predict that everything they cherished would disappear because of a stupid mistake.

TRANSCRIPT (PART) **of the first Podcast:**
"Hello, and welcome to *Social Mishaps*, a podcast about the dark side of social media and how to navigate its treacherous waters. I'm Molly Edwards, your co-founder and host, here with my best friend, Emma Beers Jones."

"That's right, I'm Emma. Welcome. We've learned the hard way what *not* to do on social media, and we're here to help you avoid the same mistakes."

It all began when they were besties.

Molly Edwards sits in the studio, her heart racing as the crew adjust her mic for her talk show, *Daytime*, airing on Channel 33-

Shine TV. She still couldn't believe it, this is her life, her dream job had seemingly dropped in her lap.

Molly is hosting a hit show on one of Australia's most-watched secondary networks, and all this with her loving partner David and their playful chocolate Labrador Bono waiting for her at home. Success, love, fulfilment - everything was perfect. Or so it seemed.

Across town, Emma Beers Jones, an award-winning journalist, was preparing for her own show, *Evening with Emma*, on Channel BBS12. Her climb had been methodical, hard-earned, and deserved. Both women had charted vastly different courses to reach the top.

When they met on a sun-soaked beach in Fiji, neither imagined this chance encounter would lead to the closest friendship of their lives. Despite their differences, they became inseparable.

Nothing, they believed, could come between them.

But lurking behind their perfect lives and shiny facades, something far more sinister was waiting to unravel it all. Something neither could see coming.

Social media.

It would twist their lives into a nightmare, and soon, they would both learn just how fragile success and friendship can be when the world is watching, waiting for you to fall.

This was the beginning of the end. The question now wasn't *if* it would all fall apart - but *when*.

ONE

Emma

THE MID-MORNING SUN BLAZES DOWN, her skin on fire, as beads of sweat race down Emma's body. She gulps down the cold, crisp water from the farm's freshwater spring, wiping her brow with the back of her hand. The intensity of farm life hits her hard again as it does whenever she is down here.

She watches Trevor, weathered yet strong, moving effortlessly as he works the sheep alongside their two border collies, Duke and Duchess. The dogs dart and weave, their barks sharp and commanding. Trevor's movements are precise, his body knows this farm well. Emma inhales deeply. Life as a farmer's wife may be tough, but when Trevor does most of the heavy lifting, she should not complain.

The heat is stifling, but here in Bowral nestled in the cooler Southern Highlands, it's bearable. It's nothing like the sweltering furnace that Sydney is today.

Standing outside in the open air feels liberating after being locked indoors for months. Thankfully, the restrictions have eased just in time for Christmas, allowing her to escape the city and join Trevor on the farm.

Emma Beers Jones may have been born in Bowral, but her heart belongs to Sydney. The city, with its endless energy, its social pulse, its constant hum, it's where she truly feels alive. Even in the oppressive heat, she prefers the chaos of city life to the slow rhythm of the countryside. Bowral, with its quiet charm, is Trevor's world, not hers. But for now, she's here balancing between the two lives she has come to know.

Gulping more water, she heads back to tending the garden before the sun really beats down. Her English Rose complexion suffers under the hot Australian sun, even with the protection of sunscreen, a large, floppy hat and a long-sleeved cotton shirt.

Walking into the country kitchen of the homestead, it's the size of a studio apartment, she places the hat, her garden gloves, and sunglasses on the granite bench. She washes her hands as she looks out through the bifold windows to their property. Trevor is the one who manages the farm, this is his job. She is here for the Christmas break and will return to her job at Channel BBS12 in late January. A month is as much as she can take on the farm whereas Trevor lives and breathes sheep farming. She is sure the animals think he is one of them. Trevor talks to them, has names for some of them, and definitely has his favourites.

Placing a pod in the Nespresso coffee machine, she presses the button. Harley, their golden two-year-old cocker spaniel pads into the kitchen, "It's too hot out there for you too," she says bending down to tickle Harley's chin. Standing up gingerly, her legs ache from bending over the garden beds reminding her to stretch more before gardening.

Her long black is ready and as she picks it up, she calls Harley to follow her to the lounge. "Time for a short break don't you think Harley? We've earned it." Harley's tail wags in fast circles as he watches her with large brown eyes. "You are too gorgeous," says Emma giving him another scratch under the chin.

He settles himself at her feet as she makes herself comfortable on the Chesterfield armchair. This is an heirloom from her grandparents, the whole lounge suite has occupied this room for a hundred years. The brown leather has faded to a burnt orange in parts and there are small cracks in places, but she can't imagine this room without it. Nothing else would be as comfortable. The eclectic mix of handmade cushions and crocheted throws add to the country charm.

Picking up her laptop next to her, she opens it. She checks emails and sends a few replies. Most of their friends and family are on holiday with all of Trevor's family in Bowral ready for the annual Christmas booze-up. She and Trevor host the lunch in their grand hall at the back of the homestead, and most times there will be an argument between two or more family members. Usually about politics and 'those idiots in Canberra' as one uncle always comments. It seems the Jones family know how to run the country better than any of our elected members. Although, with a long history of family members going back to colonial days and a few fighting in the *Rum Rebellion* of 1808, maybe they have a point.

She stops when she sees a news headline pop up, 'Christmas is cancelled due to Pandemic'.

Great. Trevor won't be pleased; he loves having his family round every Christmas and he's usually the one who coaxes everyone up for a backyard cricket match. She'll break this news to him when he comes in.

Continuing to scroll, she then opens her social media accounts. Of course, everyone is posting about yet another lockdown.

Emma brings up Molly on a chat to find out what she is missing in Sydney.

Morning, Molly. Looks like a quiet Christmas for everyone.

Hey you. Yes, I bet Trevor is devastated he won't be having his yearly booze-up.

Haven't told him yet. It will be just me, him and all the animals. Emma laughs as she types this. Am I missing anything being away?

No, I told you yesterday, this COVID thing has everyone locked indoors. We're all too scared to socialise. I'll be doing my show via video link if this keeps up.

Yeah, work is going to be very different. But I guess I'll be going into the studio when we start taping again, news never stops even though I'm on a break. Come on, spill some goss, I'm bored down here.

Ha, I wish I had some, but it's quiet up here too. David is pissed because he can't work as much, only emergency work is allowed. He's moping around our place like a lost soul.

I guess it's tough for many people, especially tradies like David, he's running a small business and needs to work. Have you spoken to Richard?

Yes, he said you called and whined about being stuck down there. You know you're lucky to be out of the city.

I know, it is beautiful countryside down here. And a bit cooler.

Concentrate on being with Trevor, he is your husband remember.

Thanks for making me feel guilty. Richard's a colleague, that's all.

Yeah, you keep telling yourself that. Gotta go, love you.

Bye, love you too.

Emma shuts her laptop and sighs. She hates it when Molly is right.

TREVOR OPENS the screen door and heads to the back of the homestead for a shower.

"I have some news you're not going to like."

"Great. But tell me after I've showered."

Emma and Trevor have been together since high school. Both their families have farming in their genes with Trevor's family also dating back to the Rum Rebellion. There are photos throughout the homestead of these colonial days, her family and Trevor's. Emma is an only child, her parents having her late in life, so her family consists of distant cousins she no longer keeps in touch with.

Their marriage is well respected in the community and they are deemed the perfect power couple. The fact that Emma lives in

Sydney most of the year doesn't bother the locals, they are pleased to have a celebrity in their midst. Although, some people do whisper gossip and cower away whenever Emma enters a room.

Whispers behind covered mouths can still be heard, you know. But what they think of her relationship is none of her business, she stays away from gossips because she doesn't want to waste her time on such nonsense.

Trevor meets her in the kitchen dressed in only a pair of shorts. His tanned body is lean from the farm work, the only thing aging him are his grey locks. He likes to say he has a distinguished look and is a younger version of George Clooney. His mates gave him hell after he had said that at a party a few years ago. Although Emma tends to agree, there is a resemblance to George, Trevor being the Aussie version.

"Well, what's the news?"

"Christmas is cancelled. We're all in lockdown again."

"Shit! I'd heard rumours about that. The mayor mentioned something about Canberra taking tougher measures. That means no one can come. It's just you and me."

"Yep, no visitors allowed. I guess we'll be having a romantic dinner for two."

He wraps his arms around her hips, kissing her cheek tenderly. "Well, that won't be so bad I guess."

Emma smiles and allows him to take her in his arms. He kisses her lips with passion then moves to her neck sending tingles throughout her body. Maybe this is a blessing, spending more time with Trevor before heading back to Sydney is a good idea.

TWO

Molly

THE STUDIO LIGHTS beam down with the intensity of a relentless summer sun, turning the set into a makeshift hothouse. Tropical plants would thrive here, but Molly is wilting. It's late January, and the studio air conditioning hasn't caught up with the early morning heat, leaving the room sweltering. Her makeup artist stands by, pointing a portable fan at her face, trying to keep the sweat from gathering on her brow and upper lip.

Molly's eyes flick to the director's face and then to the digital countdown ticking away on the camera. The fan moves out of sight, her makeup artist stepping off set as Molly takes a deep breath. It won't be long now. The first recording of her show for the new year is just seconds away.

She waits for the show's logo and tagline, *'Brighten Your Day with Daytime'* to fade out.

Her face beams as the camera zooms in with the air around her beginning to cool finally. "Welcome to the new year and another fantastic season of *Daytime*, your daily hit of celebrity and all things social, fun, and fabulous. I'm your host, Molly Edwards, and my promise for this year is that this ...," she waves her hand over the set, "is a COVID-free zone." Loud claps and cheers from her audience, only half of her usual and all wearing masks, stop her mid sentence. She waits until it all dies down. Her heart drops at the sea of masked faces, some colourful, some drab. The eyes peering over them wary of being in public even though they are all spaced apart.

"You heard me, *Daytime* is not the show to hear any more awful news about the pandemic. If you want stats and information about what we have all endured and are still enduring, then you have the wrong show." She pauses as the audience erupts again and doesn't speak until there is silence. "I'm glad you all agree with me. Now, it's time to introduce our first guest who as a first-time author ..."

Chatting to the author amicably putting him at ease, she is oblivious to the cameras, the crew and the murmurs she can hear from the studio control room. Molly is now a seasoned professional and is able to put her interviewees in a comfortable space, they trust her. The author has settled into the conversation well, a good choice as a first guest.

When the interview ends, she accepts a copy of the book from the author. This is a perk of the industry, all the freebies, and even though she won't have time to read this book for a while, she still appreciates receiving gifts.

The first show is done. Molly sits and waits while the audio technician unhooks her microphone. The crew is milling around happy that this first show of the season is complete. The shows are produced over four days and it can be intense at times. Molly keeps things upbeat and uses her humour to appease any ripples when her crew becomes fatigued. Mostly, they are professionals, and the shows go to air without any hint of anger, animosity or mistakes. Working with professionals like Harold, the floor manager, who keeps an eye on everything and anticipating what the director and producer need, is a big plus in this industry. The crew is the cog that keeps the show on-air.

"Ok, one down, four to go."

"Thanks, Harold. How long's this break?" Molly asks adjusting her mask.

"Half an hour. Just enough time to change the set."

Molly nods and heads back to makeup to change and check her running sheet. They have all been back on deck since early January planning and setting up for the new season. One guest is allowed in person, so, apart from guests being interviewed via video in their homes, the show's format has remained the same for the past two years since Molly took over hosting. She reflects on how she became an accidental television star.

Molly had been the production assistant on the show when its host went AWOL after a huge disagreement with the producer, Sophia Adamson. This happened mid-show and they desperately needed someone to stand in. Molly was chosen because she had shown an interest in hosting one day, and that day had unexpectedly happened.

The host didn't come back, he became a recluse and Molly has been the host ever since.

DAY two of taping ends with Molly and the last guest, a celebrity chef, doing a cook-off to see who could bake the best chocolate cake.

"I knew you couldn't bake, Molly."

"We all know it, Sophia, but viewers love the fact that I can laugh at myself and Jamie, the trouper that he is, played along."

"Yes, he's good value and a great chef to boot. Are you coming to celebrate the beginning of another season?"

"Sure am. I have a couple of things to finish in the office and I'll meet you all in the boardroom." Molly smiles as the crew makes its way out of the studio. Once the first five shows are done, they go to air in February. Their season runs from February to November and taping five shows a week is tiring but she loves being a television host, it is intoxicating. Heading to her office she adjusts her mask again wondering when these things will be a thing of the past.

When she looks up from her desk, she has been working for an hour. Pushing up and out of her chair, she heads to the boardroom, knowing they will have already started on the food and drinks.

The boardroom has floor to ceiling glass windows overlooking the harbour. This is the best area of their television station and has seen many functions, albeit smaller since lockdowns, but many, none-theless. Those seated had masks off with drinks in hand, the people standing were getting their drinks and nibbles with masks on. Molly, adjusting her mask yet again, is heading to get her drink when Sophia starts speaking.

"Welcome back to season ten everyone. Good to see you all safe although I know some of you have caught COVID over the break. And that's the last I'll say about that. Like Molly, apart from our masks, this is a pandemic-free discussion zone."

"Yes, let's keep it that way." The current production assistant raises her glass.

"We'll do our best. Now, as always, your ideas are welcome, and Molly is ready for another year of games and challenges."

"As long as they're not dangerous guys. The bungee jump challenge last year scared the hell out of me. You all forgot that I'm scared of heights and conned me into doing it anyway." Molly stands a safe distance from Sophia who acknowledges her.

"I'm hearing you, Molly, we don't want to lose another host."

Everyone laughs but Molly can see the strain on Sophia's face because Molly knows she misses Robbie. He was the host who argued with her about a particular stunt he refused to do, and he just happened to be her ex-husband as well. This was one of many fights they had endured, Robbie was opinionated and rubbed people the wrong way at times.

But given all this, they were the most amicable ex-partners Molly had ever known having worked together for ten years and only married for two of those years. As far as Molly knew, Sophia had not seen Robbie since that incident, he had taken himself off to some remote part of the outback and no one knows where. Sophia doesn't talk about him saying she has moved on because after Robbie's disappearing stunt their relationship stopped being so amicable.

THREE

Fiji

MOLLY AND EMMA are drunk and twirling on the beach like two wayward dancers. The music gave up hours ago, but thanks to an ample amount of vodka and a solemn vow to see the sunrise, they're still partying. They stumble into each other, limbs flailing, and collapse onto the sand in a tangle of giggles. Their beach shoes, having abandoned ship, fly from their hands - one smacks Molly square in the forehead.

"Ow!" she yelps.

"You'll survive," Emma slurs, barely able to form the words, "No one's ever died from a flip-flop to the head."

Molly glanced at her new friend, Emma, whom she'd met just a week ago while waiting to register for tours. Emma, a stunning brunette with striking brown eyes, could easily pass for a model. But when Molly had suggested it, Emma scoffed, insisting, "No way, I'm a journalism student - I'm going to host a hard-hitting news show."

Molly immediately knew Emma would make it happen; her determination was written all over her face.

Emma had arrived in Fiji with friends, but now, with them gone, it was just the two of them. Though Molly had enjoyed the group, she'd grown closest to Emma, her kindred spirit.

"Aww, look how beautiful ..."

Molly looks towards where Emma is focusing on the horizon. A pearl of sun is skimming its edges, the glow of their last day in Fiji coming to life. "Wow. And it's our last day here. That's a bit sad," says Molly standing up unsteadily to have a better look. "Woah, sand and being drunk don't mix."

"Here, I'll hold you up." Emma moves towards Molly and instead of helping her she missteps and they fall over again.

Bursts of laughter and shrieks come from both of them. This has been the norm for the past week. "Best holiday ever," says Emma with Molly joining her in even more laughter.

FOUR

Molly

SHE PARKS HER CAR, the carport shielding her from the summer shower. After a productive week, Molly is hoping to enjoy the weekend by doing as little as possible. The past two years since becoming host, Molly's following on social media has exploded. This meant she hired someone to keep up the engagement. Evan Gidgeon had come into her life via her niece, Samantha. "He'll save your arse and grow your audience to new heights," she had said chuffed she was able to help her famous aunt.

And saved her he had. Evan took over managing her Instagram, Twitter and Facebook accounts then added a TikTok account, which she had dabbled with briefly. This meant her weekends were now her own, much to the delight of her partner, David.

She enters their Federation semi to find, Bono, their two-year-old chocolate Labrador bounding towards her with tail wagging, his face beaming. Giving him a quick pat, she sees David further down the hall, he is up a ladder heading into the roof cavity. 'What are you up to now?" she asks. David is hands-on whenever something needs fixing around their home, as a sparky he seems to know a lot about repairing just about anything.

"Oh, hi you. We seem to have sprung a leak. I'm going to see what's going on up here."

"Uh huh. Take it easy on that ladder." Although she needn't worry because David had done even more dangerous things since they moved in together. One blistering hot day soon after he'd moved in, he was on the roof replacing a tile that had broken. No safety equipment, no hat, no sunscreen, and wearing only a tattered t-shirt and old gym shorts. At least he had worn rubber-soled boots. When he finally came down, his face was beetroot and the back of his neck and legs matched his face. "You're crazy you know that?"

"Ah Molly, I'll have a nice tan tomorrow," he had laughed as he headed for the shower.

That was her easy-going David, nothing fazed him, and he kept her grounded. Her fame didn't interest him, he preferred to stay out of the limelight.

Bono followed her as she walked into her home office that they had set up in a room off the kitchen. Molly places her bag on the bench then bends down to give Bono a hug. "How are you boy? Have you had an easier day than me?" With a swift move, Bono licks her face and bounds around the small room with his tail whirling like a fan. She laughs wiping her cheek as she turns to where her laptop sits. Sitting down, she checks her emails, socials and messages from her personal groups, replying to the ones she needs to address.

She has three different groups – family, friends, and colleagues. The family one is mainly for keeping in touch with her brother, Tim, and Samantha, his daughter. There is a message from Samantha but not on the same group chat they usually use -

Need to speak to you about Dad's birthday bash, give me a call when you can. I'll add people to this group but obviously not Dad, I want to surprise him.

Molly adds a reminder on her phone to call Samantha at some

stage, but there is plenty of time, Tim isn't forty until next year. She wonders why Samantha wants to discuss it so early, but then again, she is an event manager and knows what she is doing. She opens her friends' group messages next, and Emma had sent another message, she was still in Bowral.

When are you back?

End January. Can't wait. We start taping first week of Feb.

Ok, we can catch up when you're back. Maybe Feb 1?

Sounds great, lock it in. I'll call you that morning.

Molly snaps the lid of her laptop down then goes into the kitchen to rustle something up for dinner.

An hour later she and David are sitting at the kitchen bench they use as a dining table. Their semi-detached home doesn't have a dining room. Not that they miss it, their life is busy, and they don't entertain much, so the extra space would probably have been a waste.

"It was a small leak that I patched. I've placed a container under the spot and will check it every now and then in case it springs again."

"Well done as usual."

David smiles at her, his deep brown eyes always loving. "These old Federations need work, but there are a few more years in this old one yet."

"I hope so, our mortgage tells me we'll be here for some time."

"Well, you wanted to live close to work," he smiles. Listen, want to go to the beach tomorrow, maybe Bronte? You look like you need a break."

"Sure, but let's go north to Avalon and see if anything has changed in my home suburb."

"Ok, then we should head out early, you know what Saturday traffic is like."

She's happy David has suggested a day out. Although, they still need to be careful as another lockdown may be imminent. These days they go out whenever an opportunity arises.

After dinner, they sit quietly on the lounge watching the news.

David is engrossed in the sport and isn't aware of Molly looking at him. She loves David with his Aussie bronzed looks and he is the normal person in this relationship, he stabilises her feisty personality.

PLACING a few bottles of beer in the Esky, David adds ice packs and closes it. "Right, I'll put this in the car, are you ready?"

"I'll meet you out there." She was checking her phone for messages, but nothing is urgent so she walks out to the car wearing a huge floppy sunhat and dark sunglasses. Apart from sun protection, she is trying to go incognito because sometimes her fans can be a bit overzealous.

"When was the last time we went to Avalon?"

"It's been years, David. I felt like a change of scenery and wanted to see what's happening up north."

David turns the key in the ignition and they start their trip feeling great to be leaving the city behind. Inner city living suits their life-style but at times Molly misses the carefree days of walking to the beach to meet up with friends. She smirks quietly and wonders what they're all up to now, she had lost touch with all of them years ago.

The Harbour Bridge traffic is flowing but there are bottlenecks along the way. They arrive at Avalon Beach almost two hours later, but it is worth it. The beach is scattered with a few people, with the northern end deserted and that is where they are headed.

"You, ok? You seem far away."

"Oh, I'm reminiscing. Tim and I had many good times down here. All our friends, we all knew each other and most of us went to the same schools. It's sad I haven't kept in touch with some of them."

David places his arm about her shoulders, "Ah Molly, you senti-mental old thing. They haven't exactly made an effort either. How about this spot here, it's not too far from the steps?"

Molly nods and places her beach bag down, pulling out her towel while David sets up the pop-up tent. David's skin tans easily but Molly needs to be out of the sun during the hottest part of the day.

The tent is mainly for her use. She puts her bag in the shade of the tent when David's finished. She thanks her lucky stars again at having a partner who is handy, she would have taken twice as long to put up this small tent.

"I'm off, you joining me?"

"I will once I warm up." She watches as he walks towards the waves, which are calm for now. In the afternoon they can become choppier when the wind picks up. Breathing in the sea air, Molly looks over towards the pool and the south end. This is where families tend to be. Looking across the sparkling water there are a few surfers out, some older people on long boards, always a feature at this beach because they consider this beach one of Sydney's safest. Surfing was something she never tried although she can body surf. Looking towards the blue ocean it is inviting but she isn't ready for a swim, she isn't that hot yet.

Her mind drifts back to those wild teenage years - so many beach parties, endless weekends spent with friends. The air always smelled like salt and sunscreen, the nights full of laughter and the crash of waves. It was all so carefree, the kind of fun that felt like it would last forever. Those were the days when mornings blurred into afternoons, and the only thing that mattered was squeezing every bit of joy out of each day.

The shrieks of children playing in the distance brings her back. Securing her hat under the tent, she adjusts her sunglasses and lies down to catch a little sun after applying sunscreen again. She breathes deeply and relaxes into the sand, adjusting her body where she needs too. The warming sun is fine for now, but soon she'll need to move under the tent.

She wakes from her nap as cool, wet drops kiss her skin.

"What happened to coming in?"

"I must have dozed off," she says blinking at him. "How's the water? Those drops feel freezing."

"It's cool at first," he says puffing slightly after his swim, "but once you're in, it's perfect."

She sits up with a shiver. "I'll go in soon. Maybe."

"You can't come to the beach and not swim," he teases, offering his hand. "Come on."

Reluctantly, she lets him pull her to the water's edge, her feet meeting the gentle lap of the waves. "Woah, it's cold." The sea is calm though, perfect for a dip. She hesitates only a second longer before diving into the next wave, surfacing with a gasp.

"You'll warm up," David laughs, wrapping her in his arms as they float together. The water swirls around them, their bodies moving in sync with the rhythm of the waves, the ocean wrapping itself around them too. Molly feels safe in David's arms, his strength as he hugs her is reassuring of his love for her. Her love for him is just as strong.

Back on the beach, David dries himself off, pops on his bucket hat and settles into the seat he brought with him. He starts to read his latest book, the second one of a science fiction epic series.

Molly remembers that day in the bookstore, five years ago, just after she returned from setting up the orphanage in India. She had been browsing the shelves when a book caught her eye, and as she held it in her hand, a deep voice interrupted her thoughts.

"You have to read that one," he said, flashing a grin. "I highly recommend it."

She had looked behind her to find where the voice came from. She remembers how her heart fluttered at the idea of being *picked up* in a bookshop. A man who loved books was a keeper.

David had introduced himself, slightly shy. "Sorry, I didn't mean to intrude. Only buy it if you want to."

She'd smiled. "No, it's fine. I was going to buy it anyway. I'm Molly."

Their conversation flowed naturally, so easy that it didn't feel strange at all being approached among the book shelves. David, tanned and fit, was handsome in a rugged way. He had that tradesman look - strong arms and sun-kissed skin. She guessed he might be a tradie, and he later confirmed he was an electrician.

"Hey, why don't we take this chat to a café?" he asked, with a smile that made her heart skip.

"Sure," she replied, feeling an unexpected warmth. "Let me just pay for this book."

At the café, their conversation deepened. David was fascinated as she told him about her time in Mumbai, fundraising and helping build an orphanage. She laughed, brushing off the admiration in his eyes. "It wasn't all me, I didn't exactly plan to spend five years of my gap year there," she joked, stealing glances at his strong arms, his t-shirt sleeves straining over his muscles.

Feeling the heat rise to her cheeks as he looked at her intently, Molly nervously pulled out her phone, fumbling to show him photos of the orphanage on her Instagram. Anything to distract him from noticing the blush that had bloomed across her face. But his gaze never wavered, and in that moment, she felt something shift - something new, and something good.

Continuing to show him her posts, videos and photos she had regularly posted of the progress at the orphanage, she told him these helped her to raise funds and she was so pleased to help these beautiful children who were left orphaned by sickness, accidents and parents disappearing without a word. She felt the most sorrow for the kids whose parents disappeared without explanation because they all lived in hope that maybe their parents would return some day.

"It was this account that helped me find my job in television at Shine Channel 33. Even before I started work at the station, I had made the evening news with my work in India. Now I host my own show and consider myself lucky."

"Sounds like you enjoy what you do," David had said then looked at his watch. "I'm sorry I have to go and do a quote, it was great meeting you. I'd rather spend more time with you, but sorry." He stretched out his hand and Molly had shaken it. She felt something in her hand and looked up as David was on his way out of the café looking back at her smiling. He had left her his number on a piece of napkin. How old school and adorable, she looked forward to seeing him again soon.

FIVE

Richard

HIS PHONE TRILLS and his son's name appears on the screen. "What's up?" He listens then says, "I'll be home at seven-thirty, we can discuss it then."

"Problem?" asks his makeup artist.

"Not really, my son needs some help with his assignment."

"Is that the one who is following in your footsteps? Wants to be a journalist?"

"The very one. Although, why in this era of fake news and low pay for the whole industry, I'm not sure why he wants to."

"Oh Richard, he might become a news anchor just like you. All your kids have the looks to be on television."

He smiles but she is right. He is proud of his children, each one model material. Married twice and twice divorced, Richard Penser, has four children – two girls, two boys. His girls had moved out two years before his first divorce. The boys lived with him after their mother remarried and moved to Italy. They didn't get on with the younger Italian hothead their mother had married.

Richard had married his childhood sweetheart first and she left him after finding out he was having an affair with someone at the station, Channel BBS12, the top news channel in Sydney. He was a rookie journalist at the time. They had two girls who he rarely sees now. Vowing never to remarry, he met and fell very much in love with the boys' mother five years later. Again, he strayed, and she left him as well.

With makeup done, Richard makes his way to the studio to host the nightly six o'clock news. He hosts with Liana Trivetto, his sometimes squeeze. They were friends with benefits, but mainly friends. It was more for Liana's benefit, he had someone else he adored more.

Liana had gone against her father's wishes and left her husband two years ago, he was abusive. "My father wasn't worried about me, all he cared about was what would people think." She had told Richard this early on in their friendship and he wondered what kind of father does that to his daughter. After that conversation he had called both his girls telling them to call him whenever they needed to.

Walking to the studio, he sees his co-host and walks towards her.

"Hi Richard, how was your weekend?"

"Fine Liana, a bit quiet without you around."

"How sweet, you missed me. Byron Bay was nice except my father was at the wedding."

"Your cousin invited him knowing how you feel about him?"

"He probably had to because my father is his dad's brother. Blood runs thick in Italian families."

"Ah, family, what would we do without them?"

"My life would be easier without my father at least."

"Ten minutes everyone," comes the instruction from their floor manager.

Richard and Liana take their seats behind the news desk ready to be miked up. Both their makeup artists come to check their faces before they go to air. Ready, they look at the camera and start the bulletin after they are counted in. The nightly news is one hour long with fifteen minutes of current affairs, sports news, and weather. Richard had been at the helm for ten years, Liana joined him three years ago.

"... and that's the news this Monday, from me Richard Penser, enjoy your evening ..."

"And from me, Liana Trivetto, have a great night."

HIS PENTHOUSE APARTMENT in Kirribilli overlooks the harbour, a prime view looking straight at the Sydney Opera House with its sails glistening on sunny days and when you look right towards the imposing Harbour Bridge, the steel arch sprouting from the pylons, spans the skyline. Richard had purchased this penthouse after his first divorce with money inherited from his parents, both passing away within a year of each other. He missed them more than he thought he would. With four children and two ex-wives, he was grateful his parents had saved and owned two houses. The inheritance helped with looking after his family, especially with having his children in private schools.

"Dad, in here."

"Hi Scott, what do you need help with?" asks Richard as he walks into his son's room. The acrid smell of marijuana hit his nostrils. "Really? Do you have to smoke in your room?"

"Sorry Dad, but I'm so stressed about all this work and especially this essay."

"Not an excuse, what do we have a balcony for? Anyway, let me look at it for you." Richard is annoyed but doesn't push it further because Scott needs him to be the cool dad right now. Scott is his eldest. Mark, his youngest is up in the Northern Territory. He is studying to be a marine biologist and is on an early internship with a Territory government body. He is a smart one, but all of Richard's children have made him proud. Scott went off the rails after the divorce, which was hard on everyone. Luckily, he pulled himself together and went back to university. This is his last year. Richard is looking forward to the graduation because this means only one more to go. Mark had another two years and would probably stay up in the Territory.

THEY ARE SITTING in front of the television watching some sports channel after a late dinner. Richard had helped Scott for over an hour, then they ordered takeout, both too exhausted to cook.

Richard is on his iPad chatting to three different friends, one of them Emma. He and Emma have been having a long-term affair, they see each other often when she isn't in Bowral with her husband. Their affair had started soon after he took on the news role, Emma had instigated it by inviting him to dinner at her apartment, only a two-minute walk down the road. Whether Trevor, Emma's husband, knows about the affair, he had never let on. He did come to Sydney occasionally and Richard had met him a few times. Luckily for Richard and Emma, Trevor preferred the farm.

Missing you, when are you back in Sydney?

Molly already asked me that, end of January.

Good, not long now. Call me when you arrive at your apartment.

Will do. How are you anyway? I haven't heard from you much during this break.

Fine, just busy. I'm preparing an investigative show with Liana for Sunday nights but can't say much about it yet. May or may not go ahead. How's the farm?

Same as always. You know country life bores me. Trevor lives and breathes farming, and he looks after the place well. Less for me to worry about.

They keep chatting until late with Richard hoping the next week passes quickly. Liana is lovely but she isn't Emma.

SIX

Molly

SHE IS CHECKING emails while sitting in her home office. Clicking on one from Evan, it's his monthly report with her statistics for her social accounts. She brings up his document and skims over the follower numbers.

Facebook – 1 million
Instagram – 3.3 million
Twitter – 951,000
TikTok – 100,000

Instagram has always been her best account due to *Tulip Treasures*, the orphanage she helped set up. The name came from the shape of a rock formation on the block of land they purchased, it resembled a tulip in full bloom if you used your imagination. The formation now stands in the centre of the front garden, which, unfortunately doesn't feature tulips due to the climate in Mumbai. Instead, the front door has an inlay of the tulip shape and the logo for the orphanage incorporates a tulip. Molly finds this flower fills her with a feeling of peace and hopes this is what the orphans find when they arrive.

Her followers had tripled since she became a television host and Evan had taken over the admin for her accounts. She enjoys answering the messages and comments occasionally, but it's Evan who does most of that now. But Molly likes to keep an eye on what he posts making sure it's always appropriate.

Flicking through her accounts, everything seems fine until she finds something strange on TikTok. An account, @MeandYou, has liked everything Evan has posted on her account, @DaytimeShow, and added several comments.

Love your show

Best host eva!

Looking hot today Molly

Molly's the bestest

Television's hot host

I'm watching you

Hello, you stunner!

Scrolling through there were more. Is it normal for someone to be liking and commenting this often? She flicks an email to Evan. Continuing to browse through emails, she sees Evan's reply come in straight away.

I wouldn't worry about this, Molly. You obviously have a fan, enjoy your moment, TikTok can be brutal. You have to manage it, that's all. No different to the other platforms.

Quickly replying, Molly writes - Then why am I on this platform if it's brutal? I'll see how it goes. Not sure I like what's happening here.

Whatevs, comes Evan's reply almost instantly. What is it with young people and their insouciant way of looking at life? She decides to discuss this with David because she wants a second opinion from an adult, Evan is young and doesn't know how the world works yet. Samantha had told Molly of his upbringing with a lawyer father and a mother who runs her own marketing firm. It seems Evan only knows the good things in life.

Standing up, she goes looking for David. She finds him sitting watching his beloved cricket. When he looks up, she tells him how she feels.

"Sorry, Molly, I'm not sure of the workings of tok ... what did you call it? Anyway, it doesn't matter because if you're uncomfortable then that's all that matters. Get Evan to shut down that account."

"I'm used to people commenting on my socials, David. This seems to be a bit much with multiple comments per post or video. They're all complimentary but in a sleazy way and it feels weird. It's almost like I'm being stalked."

"All the more reason to shut down the account. Come here babe, you look like you need a hug."

She drops into his lap as he gives her a warm hug. He kisses her gently while rubbing her back. "Thanks David, what you've said helps. I'll go back and have Evan delete that one." David keeps a hold of her hand as she tries to leave. "I have a better idea. Come with me," he says as he leads her to their bedroom.

Molly smiles, this is probably a good idea, she needs some stress release.

As they enter the room, she pauses, breathless, saying, "Wait one second," as she digs through the drawer for matches. Her heart races as she lights the three candles on the dresser, their soft glow casting dancing shadows across the walls. A quick spritz of her favourite perfume lingers in the air as she turns around, only to find David already naked, waiting for her.

His body, all ripped with muscle, radiates raw desire. He is sprawled out on the bed, his fit, bronzed body commanding the space, driving her wild. Every inch of him exudes heat, making her pulse quicken. His eyes are on her, and the tension between them is undeniable, thick with anticipation. She feels the pull of him, his body calling to hers, and she can barely contain herself.

Her dress scatters onto the floor, she moves over to him and straddles his waist. The essential oil bottle is on her dresser, she rubs a few drops into her hands. Massaging it onto David's chest, he moans as she works her way down his body. He bites his lip as she keeps massaging until the oil seeps into his skin, then she allows him to roll her over. He takes one of her breasts, caressing it passionately, as she breathes in the oil. He is caressing her neck now, a sensitive spot for her and she feels the wetness between her legs. His fingers move into her as she arches her back craving more. Breathing deeply she arches higher, her body reacting as she climaxes. Clasping her hands over his taut butt, she pushes him over so he's laying on his front. Adding more oil to her hands, she massages his shoulders as he moans with pleasure.

Even before she is finished, he turns over pulling her towards him kissing her with fury, putting her body on fire. She is ready for him. "Now, David. Now." He does as he is told and they move as one, both of them are in the heady space of lovemaking that is both familiar and still exciting at the same time.

They lie together, spent, the warm glow of the candles flickering softly around them. The room is filled with the lingering scent of the candles and the oil. His arm drapes lazily over her, skin still hot from the intensity of it all, and she can feel the steady beat of his heart against her. All that matters in this moment is the feeling of his body against hers, the soft warmth of the afternoon wrapping them up in the aftermath of their passion.

Lying together, they both doze.

Molly wakes first. She manoeuvres herself from under him with David turning over not waking. She pulls the sheet over him smiling. Her body stirs with love as she looks at his taut body, she still finds him attractive and desirable ... her sexy tradie.

Walking back into her home office after a quick shower, she opens her laptop with another message popping up from Samantha.

Dad and I are going for a drink at the Whale Inn, want to join us? We'll be there at 8.30.

Without asking David, she answers 'yes' because she is always up to seeing her brother and niece.

. . .

THE LAST SHOW of the first week has aired and they have started filming more shows. Molly, eyes straight at the camera, begins talking after the footage of the indoor skydiving challenge ends, the first challenge of this season. "That was a lot of fun. Do you know indoor skydiving is suitable for ages three and up? One of the safest challenges I've done, thanks to Deborah Embers for sending in that suggestion, your merchandise pack is on its way. And remember, if you want to give me a challenge, then go to our website and fill in the challenge form ... And we'll be right back after this break."

"That sounds awesome. I'm going to try it this weekend."

"You'll enjoy it, Harold. Floating way up there looking down is exhilarating and relaxing at the same time. And my fear of heights didn't bother me, I felt safe the whole time."

"Ok, I'll book a session this weekend. Now, back to more mundane things, your next guest is a little nervous so go gently. She hasn't been on television before. We're on again in ten minutes."

Molly had met the guest in the makeup room and knew she was nervous. She ran an adventure tour company for disadvantaged kids and had a special camp set for the April school holidays. For someone who loves adventure, there is no need to be nervous. As the guest sits down, Molly assures her everything will be fine. "Take a deep breath and think of me as if you're chatting to a friend, ignore the camera."

She hears the director and watches Harold as he counts her down, "Welcome back to Daytime. My next guest is Jennifer ..." Right from this moment Molly knows this interview is not going to be an easy one. As much as Molly tries to appease the young woman, she stutters and keeps staring into the camera. It is one of Molly's more excruciating interviews and she is glad when it is over.

"Well, that was fucking horrible," she says when her guest is out of earshot. Saying this to no one in particular, she sees Harold and Sophia laughing.

"You were warned," says Harold.

"I know, but let's keep guests like that to a minimum. It was bad for her and for us."

"True," agrees Sophia, "not very professional, she should have done some media training beforehand. I'll make sure it doesn't happen again."

"You're a gem," says Molly as the three of them leave the studio chatting about what they've been up to. Molly fills them in on how she and David had met up with Tim, her brother and her niece, Samantha. "She is looking after her dad with so much love, Tim isn't doing well since ... well, you know." Molly's eyes well with tears.

"Come on, Molly, maybe it's time for another drink," says Harold leading her away from her office to the pub instead. "This is not the time to be brooding, we need you to focus on the show."

Molly smiles at Harold being so thoughtful albeit more about the show that her own wellbeing. She wipes her eyes as thoughts of the accident come to her, she still misses her late sister-in-law.

SEVEN

Emma

EMMA'S TEAM wrapped up the first episode of *Evening with Emma*, set to air tomorrow night. They film on Thursdays, keeping the content fresh, but the real chaos starts if breaking news hits before the show goes live. When that happens, they scramble to tape a special segment, pushing a pre-recorded filler story out of the lineup. It's a delicate balancing act - filler stories are like safety nets, always ready to be swapped in when a segment collapses last-minute, which, much to their frustration, happens more often than they'd like. It's the unpredictable nature of live news, but this is exactly what Emma thrives on, the adrenaline is addictive.

When the tagline, '*Spend your evening with Emma*', fades out she walks off the set and out of the studio. As she is walking back to her office, Richard is in the hallway speaking with his PA. The PA walks back into Richard's office as Emma approaches.

"Oh hey, welcome back." He bends to kiss her cheek.

She feels his warmth and is comfortable in his bear-like presence, although Emma blushes slightly, having been with Trevor recently, a pang of guilt ushers into her body. "Thanks. Sorry I didn't call you, but I caught up with Molly and she filled me in on all the gossip. I didn't miss much, did I?"

"No. We were all still confined to our homes mostly. How was Bowral?"

"As I told you on our chat, I'm not much of a country person but it ended up being quiet and enjoyable. It was only Trevor and I on Christmas Day."

"Same here, very quiet, only Scott and me. Although, I didn't mind the peace."

"Hmm, I'm a bit over it to tell you the truth, had enough of talking about lockdowns too. Will I see you tonight?"

"Sure, apparently we're allowed five visitors now."

"Yes, I heard that too. I'll be home at seven, see you then."

"You will," he answered and allowed her to walk past him into her office.

As she enters the office, she thinks of Richard. It was instant attraction for her when they first met, she knew she would have sex with him. He is tall at well over six feet, she likes the fact he is taller than her but not by much. Her height can intimidate some males, but she considers herself lucky to have both Trevor and Richard who are taller than her. Short men are not her thing.

Flicking on her desktop computer, she brings up emails and there are a pile of them to go through. Mostly news stories she has to consider for the next few shows. Maybe Bowral wasn't so bad after all? It had definitely been more carefree than work.

RICHARD FILLS their wine glasses again as she places hers on the kitchen bench. They had been chatting since she arrived and were about to eat some Thai takeaway.

"Let's sit on the balcony. It's a pleasant night."

They sit and eat while discussing work, family and anything

other than the pandemic. Emma remembers how she pursued Richard. He had said no to a few invitations from her before finally agreeing. Not wanting to become involved due to her being married, with two failed marriages under his belt, he was wary. And there was the fact they were colleagues. That was five years ago and somehow, they had managed to keep their affair relatively secret and make it work for them.

Emma knows Richard goes out with other women, but this was as a coverup for their affair. Nothing serious happens with the others, although with the younger ones, Emma does feel a jealous streak occasionally. When she had mentioned this to Richard he had laughed and told her it was a ploy to take the scent of their affair, something she already knew. Emma accepted this but the feelings still surfaced when someone prettier and younger came along.

Richard is different to Trevor in so many ways. Where Trevor is down to earth, Richard has an ego; where Trevor is quiet, Richard is opinionated, speaking about anything and everything, where Trevor is a homebody, Richard loved adventure and travel. She loves them both in different ways. Trevor keeps her grounded with Richard giving her the excitement and the rush her body and mind craves.

She watches Richard as he fills her glass again, smiling inwardly. He is classically handsome with a chiselled jaw and dark, brooding eyes. His hair, that he is so proud of, is full and always perfectly styled. His height gives him an air of 'don't mess with me' and he uses it to his advantage if needed. He has had to fend off many a drunken fan.

After sitting contemplating their own thoughts for some time, Emma breaks the silence, "I will never tire of this view," she says as the sky pigments towards a night sky. The city lights shimmer across the water, the bridge lights twinkling.

"It is a magnificent harbour, and it never gets old for me either." Richard stands up and offers his hand, "now, shall we have some fun, the first for the year."

She stands and takes his hand. Sex with Richard is another exhilarating thing she adores about him, he makes her feel special each time they make love.

EMMA FINISHES the news and stats on COVID and moves onto a more light-hearted piece about a kitten being rescued and the fire-fighter who saved it. After this interview, she completes the next two segments, and another show is done.

"Thanks everyone, see you all at the production meeting."

The PA hands her two more running sheets and she scans them. Nothing too interesting going on for the next two shows except for an interview with the Prime Minister. Emma has every intention of putting him on the spot and asking him to give his assurances he is listening to the medical professionals. Although she is tired of talking about the pandemic, her show is news based and viewers expect to be informed. Flicking to the second run sheet, she smiles because her producer, Jack Briten, has scheduled an interview with Kate Bidwall, a star of movies, television dramas and sitcoms, who happens to be a friend to both of them.

"Jack, seeing as Kate's coming, how about we go out for dinner? It's been ages since we caught up?" Jack, Kate and Emma had gone to university together until Kate left her law degree to pursue acting. She went to NIDA and had never looked back.

"Sure, I'll book Elio's," he agreed as they walk into the production meeting.

The taping of Kate's interview is done, meaning this show is complete and ready to air. The audience is clapping as Kate walks off the set to sign autographs. Emma smiles at how easy Kate makes it look, how she chats with her fans and treats them like equals. There is no hint of diva-isms from her. Kate looks back towards her when she's finished and says, "See you at dinner. Jack is picking me up." Emma nods and waves as she exits the studio.

A few audience stragglers come over to speak to Emma, she obliges for a little, but she is not as comfortable talking to strangers as

Kate. She makes an excuse to leave as soon as she can. Looking through a camera doesn't faze her but being around fans makes her uncomfortable. Not that she lets on how she feels but does avoid having to speak to fans where possible.

Walking into her office she collects her bag and heads home to change for dinner. She is looking forward to relaxing with Kate and Jack.

WAITSTAFF ARE MILLING around serving their dishes, refilling their glasses, and asking whether they want dessert. The three of them reply they are fine and resume their conversation once they're alone again.

"That was lovely, but no more, I am so full."

"You're not the only one Emma," says Kate stretching and patting her stomach. "The place hasn't changed. Thanks for bringing us here, Jack."

"It's nice we can afford it now, right? Remember how we wanted to eat here during our university days?" This restaurant has been an institution in Sydney.

They all laugh and keep talking about how broke they were back then. "Oh, and when we were thrown out of that pub for inciting a fight. That was your fault, Jack."

"Me? I seem to recall you wanting me to step in when some guy accosted you after he recognised you from that ad, Kate? Umm, I know you were running along the beach but don't remember the product."

Kate laughs, "I think it was a soft drink. I cringe when I think about how they made me run in a bikini on a freezing cold June morning. And we did so many takes because the wind kept blowing my hair in my face."

"You always had unruly locks, Kate. Mind you, the bob suits you now."

"Yes, I had hair down to my waist back then, remember Emma? You were always finding blonde strands all over the apartment."

"Yes, I bloody well did. I hated that, and you never seemed to notice. You flitted in and out of the place going to this or that audition leaving a trail of stray hairs. And don't get me started on the bathroom."

Continuing this vein of ribbing each other for things said and done in the past, they drink and talk until Elio flicks the lights indicating it's time for them to leave.

Once outside, there are fans milling around asking Kate for autographs. Again, she obliges willingly and Emma is in awe of her friend who embraces fame easily.

Emma and Jack wait for Kate at the end of the lane. She is only a few minutes and apologises when she meets up with them.

"It's fine. You're so good with your fans," says Jack.

"They wanted to know about my latest movie, it's being shot in Morocco."

"Yes, you mentioned it to us before your interview. Are you excited about shooting there?"

"I guess so, but you know what it's like Emma, there isn't much time to see the sights because you're working the whole time. My life might sound glamorous but it really isn't. Lots of lonely nights in hotels and in places where I don't know anyone other than my cast and crew. Still, I can't complain, it pays well."

Emma can because as a junior roving reporter, she spent many a lonely night in hotels in towns she had never heard of.

They are walking toward's Jack's car. He had picked Emma up as well as Kate, so they continue talking about old times as they drive home.

After being dropped off at home, Emma isn't tired and decides to text Richard.

I'm home, are you up for some company?

Sure. Your place though, I'll walk down. Scott is home.

Ok, see you soon.

. . .

RICHARD ARRIVES and Emma hands him a cold beer. "Thanks, it's unseasonably warm tonight, so this is perfect. I was happy to hear from you, was only scrolling through YouTube."

"Good. I'm still hyped from seeing Kate. We reminisced and laughed all night." She clinks her scotch glass to his bottle, "I need you to calm me down."

"With pleasure," he replies moving towards her. Emma raises her head to meet his lips, her body responding as it always does with Richard, with lust and want.

He moves her towards the lounge and takes her glass and his bottle placing them on the coffee table. She is wearing a kimono that he slips off her shoulders revealing her naked body. He gasps and cusps her breasts to his face as he guides her onto the lounge. Emma moans feeling her want for him increase. She guides his face down her body. He arouses her even more with his fingers as well as his mouth. Her moans grow louder as she feels her body respond to his touch.

"Richard," she whispers mainly to herself. His shirt was already on the floor and he adds his pants there. He looks at Emma with passion as he enters, pleasure washing over his face. Thrusting in, he grabs her arse squeezing further into her. Emma is digging her nails into his back then grabs his butt, arching her back as they moan with pleasure. They are both familiar with each other's body, which respond easily to each other's touch. Both breathing heavily, they writhe together in heady lovemaking.

After, they are spent and lying together breathless, his head on her shoulder. Sweat covering their bodies. After a few minutes, she wriggles from under him and sits up. She takes a swig of what is left of her scotch giving Richard his beer. He drinks what's left looking down at her with a broad smile, "Thanks, this was a pleasant surprise to what was going to be another ordinary night."

Emma smiles back knowing she will sleep soundly tonight with

Richard staying over, something they both enjoy, but she especially likes it when it's in her own bed.

EIGHT

Molly and David

SHE IS LISTENING to Samantha talking about Tim's birthday plans wondering again why they are discussing it so soon.

"Dad doesn't want anything, he says he wants to forget he's turning forty. This is why I think we should surprise him. The reason for starting to organise it now is I want his friends who live in Bali and the States to come."

"If they are able to, Samantha. But sure, we can start sending 'Save The Date' emails to everyone. I think maybe we should keep it on the smaller side, given your dad is not keen."

"Well, that will be determined by who can make it and any restrictions, of course."

They keep discussing the logistics and Samantha tells Molly she will add details to the group chat as necessary. She emphasises the fact that they use this chat to communicate rather than phoning or emailing because she wants to minimise her dad finding out. Molly agrees and adds that the odd phone call like this one between the two of them should be fine. She ends the call as she ambles over to where David is sitting and lets out a sigh.

"A bit early to be discussing Tim's 40th, isn't it?"

"Yes, but she's keen to have people from overseas at the party, so is giving them plenty of time."

"Fair enough, hopefully parties are allowed by then. Come and sit down. Anything you're interested in watching?"

"Not really, I might take Bono for a walk, I need to stretch my legs." Bono overhears and is by her feet within seconds. "Ok Bono, let me get your lead first," she laughs patting his head. As they walk out the front door, the sun is low but there is still heat in the air being late spring.

Arriving at the dog park, she takes off Bono's leash and he bounds off to be with his doggie friends. The dog café, *Pupspresso*, is closed but there are still a few dog walkers in this park, a little haven for dog lovers with its small, sometimes dry creek and mature trees.

"Nice to see you, Molly. We usually see David with Bono at this time."

She answers her neighbour, "Yes he usually does the evening walks, but I wanted to get out tonight because I needed some air." A few other dog owners join them. They chat as they watch their dogs interact and play. Molly loves owning a dog, apart from the exercise and unconditional love they give, she also enjoys talking to other dog owners. Bono runs up to her and jumps up wanting a pat.

"You can tell he's still a puppy, he has so much energy."

"Too much actually, and he eats and eats. He's growing every day," she answers another dog owner.

"Be careful, Labradors tend to gain weight easily and become lazy."

Molly had heard this and hoped that with both David and her keeping up the twice daily walks this won't happen to Bono.

After half an hour, the group starts to head back to their respective houses and Molly heads to hers, darkness having descended, daylight saving had not yet started. As she walks with the only light coming from the sparse streetlights, her neck prickles when she feels someone behind her. Bono starts barking but is silenced quickly by a swift kick from the stranger.

Molly screams, "Hey, how dare you hurt my dog." She attempts to run pulling on Bono's lead but he's not moving. "Bono, come on boy."

The man, with dark sunglasses and a tattered overcoat too heavy for a night like this, grabs her by the arm and places his hand over her mouth, "Shut it, Molly."

Her eyes widen like a frightened animal caught in headlights, this man is going to hurt her as well. She gags at his smell, her nose prickles at his body odour. Wanting to see if Bono is ok, she tries to bend down but he stops her. "Your dog will be fine. Now, I want the hottest television host on Australian TV to come with me."

Molly tries to scream with hopes someone will see what's happening but he stops her with a chilling look. He drags her to an old beaten-up black sedan and pushes her inside. The car reeks of him, not only his body odour, but stale smoke and alcohol as well. She starts to scream again.

"If you want your dog to stay alive, I'd shut that mouth if I were you."

She stifles her crying and cranes her neck to see if Bono is moving but the man speeds off in the opposite direction. *Bono please be ok and go and alert David.*

ONE OF THE two police officers, the smaller of the two, is taking notes as David explains Bono had returned home without Molly at around 8pm.

"Do you think she hurt herself?"

"I don't know, but why would Bono come home, wouldn't he stay with her until someone found them? No, something else has happened."

"Has she any enemies, someone who would want to hurt her?"

"I, ah ... I don't think so." David's face shows concern then he remembers the conversation they had about that social account and how Molly was worried by all the comments. He tells the police officers about that.

"Are you able to show us that account?"

David rubs his chin, tears beginning to well in his eyes. Did Molly cancel that account? What if this person is dangerous? "I'll have to find it, I need to speak with ... umm, let me make a call, excuse me." He walks to the office with Bono whimpering behind him, his front leg limp. Calling Evan, he confirms he deleted Molly's TikTok account and then says, "David, you're not thinking that the dude who commented has something to do with this?"

"Possibly, but look, we can discuss this later, I need to get back to the police." With his head bowed, David walks back to the lounge where the police are discussing what may have happened. "The account was deleted, it was on something called TikTok."

"That's fine, we'll be able to retrieve it. Can you find us the login details?"

David hopes Evan remembers them, "I'll try."

"Mr Talan," says the smaller policeman, "I know this is distressing, but we will get to the bottom of it. In the meantime, you might want to have your dog's leg checked."

"Ah, yes, I will, thanks. Please keep me ..."

"Don't worry, we'll keep in touch."

"Thanks," whispers David as he sees them out.

THE NEXT MORNING, David rolls out of bed having slept only a little. He tossed and turned due to nightmares of finding Molly dead or worse, dismembered. Shuffling to the bathroom, Bono is following him still hobbling on his left foot. David had taken Bono to the vet hospital after the police left. The vet had said there was nothing broken, Bono was favouring it because there was bruising from the kick, this should subside in a few days he had been told.

"Hey mate," says David giving Bono's head a scratch, "you going to help me find Molly today?" He had called his tradie mates and told them he won't be on the job until Molly is found. They were fine with this and even offered to help. "No, you guys keep my business going, thanks for offering though." He had said this with the words catching in his throat. What if Molly was already dead?

NINE

Molly and David

SHE WAKES UP. Groggy and disoriented, she tries to focus her eyes. In the dimness, the pungent smell of petrol attacks her nose. Raising her head, it's heavy and hurts. Placing her hand to her forehead she feels a bump remembering what has happened. *That weirdo hit me.*

Her eyes now focused; she takes in her surroundings. It's a tin shed or garage full of rusted parts and other junk. Her left arm is tied to a corner timber beam. Sitting on an old mattress she cringes on what might be lurking in or on this thing. Now fully awake, Molly screams, "Hey, get me out of here. Somebody help me."

Nothing. So, she tries screaming again, "Hey, help me." Again, nothing. Padding herself she is looking for her phone in the hope her attacker might have forgotten to take it off her. No such luck, he didn't forget. Surprisingly, she isn't too scared. If anything, she is angry and wonders what the hell this idiot wants with her.

Footsteps approach.

She hears a door open but can't see it, it's on the other side of the shed. The footsteps come closer, he has dark sunglasses on and this time, a cap. Apart from his mouth, she can't make out his face. "I've brought you breakfast Miss Molly, I assume you like corn flakes."

"What do you want with me?" she asks her anger seeping up through her and spilling out of her mouth.

"I have my reasons and you are not in danger as long as you don't scream for help again. Now have your breakfast like a good girl."

"People will be looking for me. I'm supposed to be at work by nine."

"You won't be going to work today." He says this as he ambles out of the shed. She notices he has a slight limp.

What the hell? Who is this nutter?

Molly works on the rope that has her left arm tied. It's thick and her wrist is now red raw from her trying to pull it off. She looks around for anything she can use to cut the rope. There are tools on a workbench, but they are out of her reach. Suddenly she screams when she feels something crawling on her foot. *Where are her shoes?* "Get off, ugh how gross!" A cockroach scurries off the mattress.

Her eyes begin to tear up and she sniffles. She needs to keep it together. If he senses she is scared, who knows what he will do? No, she will not allow herself to be scared, she'll concentrate on remaining angry and use this energy to find a way out of this mess. Wondering why this is happening, she tries to think of a way to escape. But unless she can cut this rope, she has no hope.

WHEN HER ABDUCTOR comes back to collect the breakfast bowl that she hadn't touched, he walks up close to her, his nose right in her face. "My lovely, I am going to cut you loose and you are not gonna do something stupid are you? You are my special girl and I'm gonna look after you."

Molly gags at his stale breath. His body odour attacks her senses yet again. Doesn't this guy know how to shower? She notices his stained teeth, yellowed by tobacco and who knows what else he chews. "What do you want from me?"

He is busy at the tool desk and comes back with a saw that is way too big to cut the rope. She retracts back wondering what the hell he is about to do to her. *Don't show him you're scared.* This is easier said than done.

When he goes straight towards the rope, she lets out a sigh. "Did you think I was going to hurt you with this?" he asks pointing to the rusty saw. "I love you, Molly. I already told you I'm not going to do anything to you, I'm looking after you."

Molly is officially creeped out but decides to let this nutter do what he is planning, she'll think about her own plan of attack as he goes about his. As he is cutting into the thick rope, it rubs against her wrist. "Ow, take it easy."

He doesn't answer, he just stares at her with a wry, wicked smile. Holding onto the rope that is still tied to her wrist, he tells her to stand up. "I'm taking you into my home. This is where we will be together and look after each other."

This is becoming creepier by the minute. *He thinks I'm going to look after him. Not bloody likely.*

After he locks the garage, she allows him to drag her into the house, he has left a length of rope on her arm so she can't run off. And where are her shoes? She asks him but he doesn't answer. The stale smell of alcohol, wet tobacco and cat pee travels up her nose when they enter the house. She sneezes. Where are the cats? Two bowls of stale food sit near the fridge, untouched. She gags.

"Bless you, my darling." He leads her to an antiquated wooden table with what look like axe marks cut into it. He ties her to a battered chair with a rattan base sunken with age, using the remaining rope. "Now, if you behave yourself and do as you're told, I'll untie you. Then we'll be a couple."

"What! Are you crazy? You and I will never be a couple." The thought of this creep touching her sexually makes her gag again.

His face is on hers again, so close. And he whispers, "We are already. You are in my home, you are mine and you will do as you're told or I will make you suffer. I don't want to hurt you but I will if you make me angry." Tingles ripple down her neck as he moves away from her.

"People will be looking for me, you know that right? I'm sure they're scouring the suburbs right now."

"No one was around last night to see us leave in my car. They don't know where I live. You will remain in this house, I'll go out for what we need and you have no reason to see anyone other than me."

His face has a contended smirk making Molly feel sick, her stomach churning as she stifles a vomit. She knows David will have called the police by now and they are all out looking for her. She has to keep thinking this and being positive, maybe even play along with her abductor so she remains safe.

"Now, you didn't eat breakfast. I'll make you some eggs and coffee. Do you drink coffee? How do you like it?"

"Umm, just coffee, I'm not hungry. Milk no sugar." How can she eat when she is so disgusted by her surroundings. The musty smell of this place, his body smells, everything is making her squirm.

"Suit yourself." He turns to the hob placing a kettle that has seen better days on it. He then pulls a mug from the rusting tray on the sink. He even runs it under hot water. This makes Molly feel a little better, who knows what she is going to catch in this filthy place.

Taking this opportunity while he is distracted, she says, "Look, I need the toilet. How can I go if I'm tied up?" She can't believe she hasn't needed to before now, but then she hadn't eaten or had anything to drink since dinner last night.

He sighs and turns towards her. He holds the rope and unties it saying, "Follow me."

"What? You're not coming into the toilet. Are you crazy?"

"Calm down, my love," he whispers eerily, "I'll be standing outside the door waiting for you." She takes a breath allowing the fearful shivers down her spine to dissipate hoping like hell she will have a chance of escaping soon. When she comes out of the toilet, where there was no chance of escape because of bars on the filthy, web-covered window, he is standing there with her runners.

DAVID IS at the Marrickville police station. The taller officer is explaining to him that Molly is probably not too far from home.

"That's good but how do you know this?"

"We were able to check her TikTok account and saw the many comments came from one person. I take it this is the person she was concerned about?"

"Maybe, I don't know much about that account."

"Well, we have an address and are going to check it out today."

"Oh, great. I'm coming with you."

"There's no need ..."

"I'm coming. I want to see the bastard who hurt my dog and is possibly hurting Molly too. I'm bringing Bono with me, he'll know if she's there."

"It's fine for you to come but leave Bono home, we have our own dog, she'll be more helpful because she's trained. And don't put yourself in danger. We don't know what this guy is capable of."

David is sitting in his car and doesn't start it until he sees the two officers drive out. His phone pings with a message from Tim. He answers telling Tim they are close to finding Molly and he'll call him later. Placing his phone back in his pocket, David follows the officers.

They come to a stop only minutes later at a derelict house in Tempe. The two officers get out of the car, but no dog. What happened to them bringing a dog along?

An aeroplane roars overhead making the house shake like a rattle as the smaller officer comes over to David's car. Indicating David wind down his window, he says, "Stay in the car. Let us deal with this." The officer joins the other one before David can query where the dog is. They knock on the front door. Nothing happens for quite a few minutes and David breathes heavily, hoping Molly is ok. If something has happened, if that dick has hurt her ... David's anger surges.

The front door opens. The taller officer speaks to a man wearing dark sunglasses and a cap. They are ushered in.

David waits for some time but then can't sit in the car any longer, he needs to know what is happening. He heads towards the house and steps onto the rickety front porch. His foot falls into a crevice as the timber gives way. "Ouch." The timber catches his ankle and scrapes it as he pulls it out. Limping to the front door, he places his ear to it hoping to hear something. But there is silence. Opening the door slowly, he peeks in. The gloomy hallway is littered with peeling wallpaper and the once burgundy hall runner is faded and ripped. Then he hears the officer.

"Thank you for your time. We'll be going now, sorry to have bothered you."

David attempts to run back to his car, limping on his sore ankle. He sees the officers come out and return to their car. His phone pings.

No luck here. This man hasn't been out of his house for weeks. He's a recluse. This is a dead end, sorry.

David can't explain why, but he thinks this man does have something to do with Molly's disappearance. He answers the officer -

I'm sure this guy has Molly, he has a record of bothering celebrities.

He watches as the three dots do their dance.

We're looking into that and will keep you informed.

He begins to drive home fuming that the officers believed what the guy said. *A recluse, my arse. He's been seen around town many times.* He'll do some research on him but first he'll attend to his ankle, which is stinging with pain.

MOLLY STRETCHES. She is back in the kitchen chair after he had brought her out of the disgusting bedroom he'd put her in for hours. When he had heard cars out the front, he taped her mouth and dragged her to the bedroom warning her to keep quiet. When she had heard voices she had tried to scream and reach for the locked door, but her hand was tied to the bedpost. Later in the afternoon, he dragged her back to the kitchen.

Pulling off the tape, he said, "This will go back on if you try to scream again." His voice is low and menacing, he keeps mumbling as he walks out the back door.

Her limbs are sore from sitting and trying to sleep on this chair next to the axe-damaged table. She is wondering why the axe marks are there and tries not to think about what they mean. Still no cats around and the stale cat food reeks. This whole place is rife for her to catch some weird virus.

She had kept talking back to her abductor yesterday trying to find out his reasoning for bringing her here, so her *penance* (as he had said) was to stay tied to the chair. He seems harmless, in that he hasn't tried to harm her again since knocking her out, so she has decided to play along with him, this may help her to find an escape. Thankfully, he hasn't made a move on her yet, the thought of him trying makes her queasy.

He comes back into the kitchen at sunset and places the kettle on the burner. The old gas hob hisses again as he turns it on.

"Hey, what do you want? Is it money?"

He turns and gives her a wry smile, "I'm happy you're here with me Molly. That's all I want."

She shivers, her body quivering with fear at that smile, a smile that says anything can happen.

HE HEARS THE FRONT DOOR. "Fu ... again. Just a minute," he yells. "You ...," turning to Molly with a scowl, "Keep quiet and stay in the shed." He undoes the rope and drags her to the shed while yelling towards the front door, "Be with you in a minute."

"I'm warning you, if you so much as whimper, I will hurt you." He throws her in and runs back to the house.

She hears him latch the side door where they had entered. Looking around, the windows are barred, and the roller door is secured. The hairs on her neck stand on end again at how low and chilling his voice was. She shudders. Thoughts run through her mind as she tries to make sense of this. She is a celebrity, yes, but not that famous. What the hell does he want with her? *Arrrrgh, somebody help me.*

TEN

David

HE IS on the phone to Tim. Both Tim and Samantha had called him while he was with the police. Tim is angry, frightened and ready to help out. "No, they didn't find anything. But they said they were taking a dog with them and turned up without one. I should have taken Bono with me, he would have smelled Molly, I'm sure."

"Did they check out the place?" asks Tim his voice gruff and concerned.

"They were out quicker than I thought, which annoyed the shit out of me. I don't think they looked around the place. Who knows what that idiot abductor told them."

"So, what makes you think she is there?"

"I have a hunch, that's all. Or maybe I'm hoping she is so we can bring her home before he does something stupid." David can hear Samantha asking questions and understands how concerned she and Tim are.

"Is the media still out the front?" This is one of the questions from Samantha.

"Yes. I have given an interview, it will be on tonight's news. Basically, I'm appealing to anyone to come forward with anything they might know. Maybe someone saw Bono being kicked and Molly taken."

"This is bloody awful," says Tim, "I'm so worried and wish I could do something."

"The police assure me they have it in hand. This person of interest is known to them, they're not discounting it's him." David listens as Tim asks him to keep them informed and to call if he needs any help. "Will do, you and Samantha stay calm and don't talk to the press or media, we don't want Molly's abductor thinking he's famous." He clicks off the call and walks to the fridge grabbing a beer. He's not as confident that Molly is in that awful house as he was when he was sitting in his car parked out the front, but he's hoping like hell the police know what they're doing.

Next, he calls Emma who had left many messages. She is just as concerned as Molly's brother and niece. David tries to calm her down too appeasing her with assurances he will call if he needs help. Exhausted, he downs the beer throwing the empty bottle in the recycling and shuffles over to the lounge. He sleeps for hours.

WAKING, he fumbles around for the remote. Finding it he turns on the television to find the news has started. More talk about lockdowns easing, vaccinations and then the story of Molly's abduction. David presses the volume button up ...

"Much-loved TV host, Molly Edwards has not been seen since being abducted two days ago. This alleged abduction happened when the television presenter, host of 'Daytime' on Channel 33-Shine, was walking home after taking her dog to the local dog park. We speak with David, Molly's partner about what the police are doing about this."

David watches himself being interviewed, this is all so surreal.

He's a tradie, how the hell is he on TV and involved with trying to find his partner? He really can't understand what Molly sees in being famous, even if she denies that she is. If she wasn't famous then she would not have been abducted.

He clicks the television off, having had enough. When was the last time he ate? His stomach grumbles and gurgles, obviously it was a long time ago. The same goes for Bono who is now standing in front of him with expectant eyes. "I suppose we should eat, hey mate. We need our strength the find this bad man."

When he finishes the meal he had heated up and Bono is fed, David sits in front of the television again but doesn't concentrate on it, instead he texts the police officers wondering if they have any further information. They both report back that they are following leads but nothing major to report yet. David grunts knowing he wasn't expecting anything more. He then texts Tim, Samantha and Emma telling them there is no further news. David's shoulders droop as he hopes this nightmare ends soon.

THE NEXT MORNING, rain is smashing the bedroom window. A storm is rumbling through the city and this suits David's mood. Sleep had eluded him again because he kept having more nightmares of finding Molly hurt, or worse, finding her dead. Shaking his head, he walks to the kitchen to feed Bono. "Hope you slept better than I did," he says as he places food in front of Bono. He thinks about going to the Tempe house with Bono, then shakes this thought off, he should leave the detective work to the police.

In Molly's office, he sends a couple of emails to his tradie mates asking them to cover for him again. They acknowledge he won't be around until Molly is found and again, they to offer help if he needs it. Thanking them, he closes his laptop and places it away in the drawer, he doesn't use his as often as Molly uses hers. He touches her laptop wondering when she'll be using it next and he wants it to be soon. If that bastard hurts her, he will bash the fuck out of him. David's anger grows with every passing day since he last saw Molly.

ELEVEN

Molly

FOUR DAYS later Molly has been upgraded to sleeping on the lounge with her abductor sleeping on the floor. He has something hidden in his pocket and says he will use it if she tries to escape. Molly isn't sure what it is, but it could be a gun. She will have to think carefully and plan her escape, she wants to make it out of here safely.

The lounge is lumpy and sags, only marginally better than sleeping in the chair. Whenever her abductor goes out, he ties her up to the chair, which she had discovered, is bolted to the floor. Has this guy planned this, or worse, done it before? She had thought of a few ways to escape but each one was thwarted by him always being around when she was not tethered to the chair. The bars on the windows and the double locks on the front and back doors don't help either.

He has hidden her phone and there seems to be no internet, he doesn't even have a working TV anymore and he had told her the only thing he missed was watching her show. She has no idea what is happening. *Is anyone actually looking for her?* She scoffs at this thought. Of course they are, it's just that they were thrown the other day because they couldn't search the property. Her worry now is, will they come back to search the place? She needs them to do this, but what will make them come back?

She lies there listening to his snoring trying to think of ways to escape. She could try now. Without thinking too much about it, she lifts herself up and goes over the end of the couch. She is barefoot as he has hidden her runners again, so she is barely making any noise. Heading towards the front door, she is about to reach the handle when she feels a thud to the back of her head.

MOLLY IS COMING TOO and hears his voice. "That was stupid of you. And you made me hurt you again. This isn't what I want from our relationship, you are a bad girl."

Molly is shaking her head and the pain sears through her making her feel faint. She is tied to the chair again. "What the hell, my head is thumping. What did you hit me with?"

"I told you I had something in my pocket. And you were naughty so I had to use it. Please don't do that again, I don't like hurting you."

Is that supposed to make her feel better? She rubs the back of her head, what the hell does he have in his pocket? "Do you have any pain killers?"

"No, I don't keep drugs in the house. You'll have to live with what you've done wrong, it will stop you doing it again." He walks off and disappears towards the back of the house.

Shit, what was she thinking. If she's going to escape, she has to put more thought into it. And what the hell are the police up to? Is David helping them? Molly is beside herself with frustration, she isn't scared of her abductor but she is frustrated and doesn't want to spend any more time here. She rubs her wrist that is now red-raw due to him tying her up whenever he isn't around.

When he comes back, she asks where her runners are.

"Why, what do you need them for? You're not going anywhere. They're my treasure now."

His *treasure*, what the fuck is this guy on? Does he have a fetish with feet? "I notice you limp, what happened?"

"Born with it, don't know anything different. Stop asking so many questions. Stay here and behave, I'm going out to buy food for us."

"Hey, my wrist is sore and looks about to bleed. Please untie me, I'm hurting."

He scowls at first but loosens the rope mumbling as he leaves locking the front door behind him. Hearing a scraping sound she assumes he has placed something in front of the door.

She is able to wriggle her wrist out of the rope so she walks around the house again looking for an escape route, finding everything is still barred and locked. Then she tries searching for a phone again, any phone. Nothing in the house, so she walks to the garage finding it locked, the windows are no use either, they're all barred.

Anger surges through her because she is sure she is not his first victim, this place is set up so on one can escape.

TWELVE

Emma

SHE WATCHES David and Bono both limp as she walks into their home. Following them into the kitchen, she asks David if anything else has happened. He nods his head whispering, "No." She hears the frustration in his voice and wants to give him a hug but decides against it. As much as she wants to, she knows Molly better than David and she doesn't want to make him uncomfortable. "What happened to your ankle?"

David fills her in on the details of how he hurt his ankle on the alleged abductor's porch as well as his feeling Molly is at the house in Tempe.

"Poor Molly, I do hope he hasn't hurt her as well. But the police went in, wouldn't they have seen her?"

"They were supposed to have a dog with them, but they said they would take a dog when they had a search warrant. They didn't want to intimidate the alleged perpetrator. He obviously had her hidden. All the police did was question him. I know he's suspicious because they said he was wearing dark sunglasses and a cap. And I saw some of the inside of that house, it's dark in there. What does he need sunglasses and a cap for?"

"Maybe he has issues with his eyes? That doesn't make him suspicious."

"I think it does. This is all too weird, I just want Molly back and safe." David hands Emma the coffee he has made and sits on the kitchen stool next to her. He continues explaining his feelings, Molly is hidden somewhere in that house, he is sure of it. He had explained all this to the police as well. "So, they have agreed to go inside again but this time with a search warrant. This guy has a history of bothering famous people and is known to the police and I'm not sure why he hasn't already been put away."

"The police know he's done this before and are letting him get away with it?"

"Well, not this time, I hope. Would you like an exclusive on this story? I know Molly is there and I intend to rescue her."

"Oh, how very gallant of you, David." Overstepping boundaries because he needs her to, she kisses his cheek as worry seeps into his face. He doesn't pull away or seem uncomfortable. "But what if she isn't there and you're accusing an innocent man?"

Finishing off his coffee, he says, "As I said, the police know this man, he has pestered other well-known people before. You know the judge who lives in the old mansion two streets away? Well, apparently this lunatic harassed him a few months ago."

"Oh right, we did a piece on that. It's the same guy then. Ok, we'll certainly do an exclusive. When is it all happening?"

"Tomorrow morning at six."

"I'll have a camera crew ready. But I'm warning you David, if Molly isn't there, I'll have some explaining to do. Jack won't be happy."

"I'm certain I'm right, Emma. You'll get your story."

Placing her hand on David's knee, she stands as Bono limps towards her. She looks down at the dog she loves as much as her own,

"Don't worry, Molly will be home soon." She rubs his chin and Bono whimpers almost as if he knows what Emma has said.

Walking out towards her car, Emma wonders how being famous can place you in dangerous situations like this one. The stupid thing is, it's a job like any other. But there are people like this idiot who think they know you because they see you on television or on social media. Emma squirms at the thought. She already hates it when fans approach her, let alone being stalked or abducted.

THREE POLICE CARS are parked in the street. The two officers head to the front door of the abductor's house. David is with Emma and her crew. It's cool, the sun low in the sky and Emma shivers despite wearing a jacket. She hopes David is right about Molly being here.

The officers are let into the house as the camera whirrs out of sight. Emma can see the man, he's wearing a heavy coat, sunglasses and a cap. He certainly looks dodgy, maybe David's hunch is right.

"That's him," whispers David, "make sure you get a clear shot of him with your cameras."

Emma and her crew stay out of sight as the police have asked but then a gunshot rings out. David runs into the house. "David no," yells Emma. The camera keeps whirring as her crew follows her.

Minutes pass but it feels like hours before David walks out towards Emma, he is crying.

"What, no, she's not ..."

"Molly is fine, he sniffs, the man has been shot in the leg because he tried to jump the fence and escape. But you should see where he had Molly, she was tied to a chair with a rope in a filthy kitchen. Bowls of stale cat food and no cats in sight? What a weirdo. And the chair is bolted to the floor!" David is shaking.

Emma places her arm around him, "Oh god, that's disgusting but as long as Molly is ok. Now, you stay here." She indicates to her crew to follow her. They are about to enter the house when one of the police officers comes out holding Molly.

"Molly," says Emma with her voice full of concern. Molly is barefoot, dirty and weak but otherwise seems ok. Her eyes look up at Emma trying to assure her.

David is behind Emma pushing his way towards her. Molly collapses into his arms.

"IN A SPECIAL REPORT TONIGHT, we bring you the story of Molly Edwards of the *Daytime* show on *Channel* 33-*Shine TV* and her abduction. We speak exclusively to Molly about her ordeal and why she was abducted in the first place. That's tonight on *Evening with Emma* at 9pm."

Emma walks out of the booth when she finishes recording the promo. With the script in her hands, she enters the studio to finish filming the story.

THIRTEEN

Richard

HE IS SIPPING his morning coffee and waiting at his apartment for Emma. Scott is out and will be staying at a friend's place. They have the apartment to themselves and his body reacts to the fact he is spending the weekend with Emma.

She walks in plonking onto the couch next to him, giving him a light kiss on the lips. "What a week. Did you see the show last night?"

"Yep. Good exclusive for you. How is Molly doing?"

"She's shaken up. David is looking after her, so she'll be fine. Ch33 has given her a week off, so they still have a stand-in host for the show."

"Yes, I heard. That host is ok but she isn't Molly. It's good she wasn't physically hurt but emotionally she'll be shaken for some time."

"He did hit her a couple of times, once on her forehead, the other at the back of her head. Enough to knock her out, but those bumps will heal." Emma fills him in on why she was abducted and how Bono had been hurt as well. "He took her shoes as a souvenir; she was bare-foot most of the time. How creepy is that? But you know what? Molly is taking it better than I thought. David seems angrier than her."

"What a jerk, kicking a dog like that. And yes, the shoe thing is creepy. It sucks how a fan can think they are your friend and don't realise how dangerous they are."

"I've never been stalked or harassed, thankfully." Emma shakes her head, "social media doesn't help either. Her abductor was able to find out all about Molly by following her on the socials, especially her TikTok page, which Evan had only set up a few months prior. The police were able to find out about the abductor even though Molly had asked Evan to close the account."

"You know Liana my co-host? She was stalked at the beginning of her career. She was traumatised for years and needed therapy."

"Liana is such a professional, I had no idea she was traumatised at the time. I remember her going on-air as if nothing was happening."

Richard agreed with Emma stating that everyone dealt with the dark side of fame in different ways. He then moves on to tell her what he has planned for the weekend, which is not too much given the current restrictions.

"Fine by me, I'm happy to chill here with you. There'll be some-thing worthwhile on Netflix."

He moves towards her, slipping a strand of her hair behind her ear, "More time to spend in bed with you too." He kisses her as she starts to unbutton his shirt and his hand moves up her leg under her dress. She allows the stress of the week to disappear as they move to his bedroom.

LATER THAT DAY, they are sitting up in bed each with their laptops open. The wind is whipping up waves on the harbour and whistling through the open window in Richard's bedroom. Emma places her laptop down and pads over in bare feet to close the window. She shivers in her nakedness. Richard admires her and he knows she feels validated in their relationship. They both know this is convenient for both of them, neither ever mentioning being in love with the other.

As she climbs back into bed pulling up the doona, her email pings. Picking up her laptop again, she reads and sees it's from Harold. "Ha, I've been invited to a house party at Harold's place next month. You know him, Molly's floor manager."

"Oh yeah. Are you going?"

"I guess so, I haven't been to a house party for ages. Restrictions should be eased even more by then. You know what, maybe Molly will come along, if she feels up to being with people?"

"Hmm, maybe. It could lift her spirits. What's the party in aid of?"

"Nothing. Harold doesn't need an excuse other than wanting to splash out and have his friends over. He loves having parties when he looks after his parents' house." Emma finishes reading the email, "Oh and he says to bring a plus one or two, would you like to come?"

"Me? I hardly know Harold. Thanks, I'll pass on this one."

"Ok, that's fine by me. I'll send Molly an email, she can be my plus one and I can be hers, it'll be fun to spend some girl time together."

Richard nods and is happy not to go to this party, the less he and Emma are seen in public, the better.

FOURTEEN

Molly

BONO HAS his head on her lap and she is scratching it absently.
Molly is bored, it's been three days of being stuck at home after being
rescued and David isn't letting her do anything, not even cook. She
had told him she was fine, but he wanted her to rest and recover from
her injuries. What injuries? The bumps on her head had healed and
her wrist is still a bit red and sore, but that was it! Actually, she had
had a medical examination and the paramedic said she was lucky her
wrist hadn't festered. Another few days of captivity and things could
have been a lot worse.

She feels anger rather than anything else. Overall, her abductor
was harmless having allowed her to roam the house once she played
along with his plan. She cleaned the areas where she was sleeping
and sitting, more for her benefit than his. It helped to pass the time
too. Five days of wondering what was going to happen to her now
seems like a distant nightmare. Or was it seven? Some of her memory
is foggy. He was only violent twice, once when he took her into his

car, and the other time when she tried to escape. Things could certainly have been a lot worse.

She has been offered counselling but doesn't feel she needs it. The offer stands if she feels the need to talk to someone and she might if her emotions become shaky with post-traumatic stress. She knows that the aftereffects of trauma take time to manifest.

With her laptop open she browses her socials as well as news feeds. There are fans' messages and comments saying they are glad she is home and safe. She answers as many as she can, although Evan had kept up with most. She decides to give him a call and discuss her feelings about being stalked due to social media.

"Molly, you're blaming this on you having social media accounts. He's a stalker, he would have found you no matter what. Social media is not the culprit here. Celebrities have been stalked long before social media came along."

"But they are used for this type of crime, why don't these platforms have better regulations. These nutters should be stopped before something happens. I was lucky to be found quickly and my abductor didn't harm me too much, but someone else may not be so lucky." She shudders at how lucky she is to be alive.

"I am not going to advise you to take your accounts down, but if you feel strongly then you have every right. Up until now your accounts have given you positive feedback, your fans love you and don't forget the money you've raised for the orphanage with your Instagram account."

Molly thinks about what Evan is saying and decides to take his advice. For now, she will leave her accounts as they are. The TikTok one has been cancelled already and she has asked Evan to keep an eye on any other suspicious activity. He agreed to this and asked her not to worry, her social media status has increased since her stalker acted out his fantasy. This was another reason for Evan to keep posting on her behalf.

As she keeps scrolling, the talk of the pandemic is still a feature on all the news networks, so she changes to Glitz and catches up on celebrity gossip. This site is a magazine-style gossip-fest and is the go-to for anyone in the entertainment business. She bookmarks a few stories and sends emails to Sophia, her producer, as well as her researchers to follow up on them. One of them she particularly wants to focus on is about two celebrities who were once engaged, then broke up and are now having a baby together. But they are not a couple, she just wants to have his baby. This is a good one to feature on her show and the gossip press is having a field day with it, there's a lot of material they can use. Shutting her laptop because she is beyond tired now, she heads to the kitchen deciding to have a coffee.

As the caffeine kicks in, she is reminded of her dream last night, it felt so real.

She and Richard were at a café chatting and next thing his lips are on hers and she welcomes his advances. He guides her to the café floor with Molly wondering where everyone else is, can they see what's happening? She attempts to stop Richard but finds herself enjoying him, wanting more. Richard is not her type but he is handsome and cultured. She has admired him from a distance. Given he is Emma's squeeze, she would never dare. But then why is she having sex with Richard now?

She had woken in a sweat. This was not the first time she had a dream involving Richard and her in a compromising position. She shakes off these weird feelings of her good friend's lover.

Thinking about something totally different, Harold has invited her to a party, and she is considering going. Given her fantasising about Richard, she needs to get that out of her head. Emma had asked they go together. It's a few weeks away and this abduction ordeal (and Richard) will hopefully not be on her mind as much, so why not? It'll be fun and Harold will probably do one of his routines, he's good at comedy having performed at a few clubs before live acts were cancelled. Harold is good value when you want your spirits lifted and this party will be good for her.

She hears the front door, "Hi, it's me. I'm home early."

"You are," she says kissing David as he walks into the kitchen.

"I'm off to have a shower, we're going out tonight." David walks past Bono patting him and heads towards the bathroom.

"We are?" asks Molly, raising her voice so he can hear.

"Yes, I've booked us dinner at that Mexican you like with Tim and Samantha."

Molly smiles, that will be a nice distraction from this boredom (and her fantasies). Seeing her brother and niece will definitely perk her up.

THE FOLLOWING week she is in her office at the station, finally back to doing what she loves and reading scripts for today's recording. It will be great to be in front of the cameras again, interviewing people and generally being back in the real world. She had become so restless being home but had received many messages, flowers, and gifts from well-wishers. Her fans were loyal and helped her to see how much she is loved. This had made her feel special and she was grateful yet again that nothing worse had happened.

Her abductor was sent to a psychiatric facility, and she didn't press charges because of his mental state. And he hadn't made any sexual advances, thankfully. The poor man will be in there for a long time along with his delusional thoughts of being in love with Molly. He told the police he was friends with many celebrities, but Molly was his favourite. She shivers and decides not to think about him anymore. Work brings her joy, and she will concentrate on this. Looking down at the scripts, she picks them up heading to the studio.

"Welcome back." "Hey, Molly." "Glad you're back." These are the voices of her crew ... oh how she has missed them. "Thanks every-one, it's good to be back."

"That was some ordeal, eh?"

"Yes, but I'd like to put it behind me, thanks Harold. Tell me, what have I missed?"

Harold fills her in on the shows of the previous week, which she had watched in the post-production studio. Asking Sophia to make a few changes, she was happy with the stand-in host but a few things she said were not in keeping with the show. Sophia had agreed and had them edited out.

"So, how are you?"

"I'm fine. Honestly, I wish everyone would stop worrying. I know I was in that awful house for days and hoping like hell I would be found before anything happened, but as you can see, I'm in one piece."

"Sure, but what a horrible time for you. I hear he fed you and didn't hurt you."

"Well, he gave me food, but it wasn't edible. Other than breakfast, I didn't bother eating much. He did hit me in the head when I tried to escape, with a small hammer by the way. My fear of being hurt took away my appetite, especially the first few days. This is why I was weak when the police found me."

"A hammer? What the hell. Still, I'm glad you've had a week off, but is it enough?"

"It was a mechanics' hammer, so not big thankfully. A week away is enough, I'm not going to play the victim, Sophia. This is what these weirdos want, they want to rattle you. I'm stronger than that. Plus being back at work will help. My abductor is in the right place to get help and hopefully won't be bothering anyone again."

"I like your attitude, Molly. Many celebrities could learn from your wisdom."

"Everyone has their breaking point. Being in that filthy house hasn't broken me. My yoga and meditation help too. Thanks for your concern, Sophia, it helps to know who cares about me."

Harold walks toward her and discusses the interviews with her. He rattles off that a cricketer is coming in as well as a celebrity gardener and the live music is from a local band of young kids with disabilities. "Another jam-packed show."

"Sure is, umm fill me in on the cricketer please? I googled him but couldn't find him?"

"What? Did you spell the name right? It's Charli Wagner, she's a female cricketer."

"Oh right, that name did come up, but I was expecting a male."

"Molly, maybe you need another week off, the stress of what happened has gotten to you." She gives Harold the finger and he laughs. "No, you're just fine. I can see you have recovered."

She walks onto the set and wonders if Harold and Sophia are right, does she need more time off? But she quickly dismisses this thought, she is strong and refuses to let the abduction bother her any longer.

FIFTEEN

Emma

AN AUTUMN CHILL is in the air and Emma's light coat isn't helping much as she walks through the city's wind tunnel laneways. She is meeting Molly for lunch at their favourite Thai place, and she is running late. The restaurant is full when she arrives and sees Molly towards the back waving at her. "I'm sorry, the production meeting went over time. I ran here as fast as I could. And I'm still freezing." She takes off her coat and mask after she sits ignoring two men who are staring at both of them.

"Don't worry, I only arrived a few minutes ago. Here, I ordered wine, I thought you might need it." Molly hands her a glass.

"Thanks," says Emma taking a sip, "you know me too well. Are they still staring?"

"No, they've gone back to talking to each other. Relax."

"Ok, you know how much I hate being recognised."

Molly nods and tells her a waiter coming. "Enjoy lunch, we don't have much time."

The waiter comes up and asks if they would like their usual. They both nod. They come to this little Thai place often when short on time and always order the same dishes. This way they are served quickly and leave with enough time to arrive back at work ready for their respective shows.

"How are you? I'm still worried you haven't taken time to heal."

"Oh Emma, it's been months since it happened, I'm fine. Honestly, I had forgotten all about that man until you mentioned it."

Emma hadn't seen Molly much since the abduction and the subsequent interview on *Evening with Emma*. Even though they have spoken often since the incident, Emma wasn't convinced Molly is telling the truth. "It was an ordeal and you seem to have bounced back prematurely. I'm worried, that's all."

Molly places her hand on Emma's, "I love that you are concerned. You really are a good friend, but honestly, after being rescued and with that week I had off I came to terms with the fact that fame has a dark side, and I certainly won't be the last celebrity to be bothered by a stalker."

"Ok, as long as you're fine. But you know I'm always available if you need me." Their food is placed in front of them. "Oh, did I tell you, another charity gala has asked me to be host."

"Good for you, which one this time?"

Emma thinks about how many charity dinners, galas and awards she has hosted as well as attended. She is feeling weary of them, maybe she has done too many? "This one is for kids' cancer research, a worthy cause and I'm happy to do it. But I've done so many maybe I need to give them a break. Like, well ... maybe it's a bit of overkill?"

"That's for you to decide. Worthy causes are always looking for celebrities to give their time and it does wonders for your career."

"I agree, at the beginning it was great. Helping these organisations made me feel good. Now, not so much. I'm tired of being the go-to for any charity who wants something for nothing."

"It's all part of being famous, I guess. Everyone wants a piece of you." She shivers as she thinks of her abductor but quickly dismisses this thought. Instead she smiles at her friend. "Harold's party is on Saturday, let's enjoy that and I know it will help all of us to loosen up."

"You know what? You're right," replies Emma.

They tuck into their food and discuss everything other than Molly's abduction for the next hour.

THEY ARRIVE at Harold's home, or his parent's home actually. He is looking after the house while his parents are on holiday. Stark white painted bricks with slate grey tiles and green aluminium windows, this double-garage monstrosity is a reminder of the 1980s style of gauche. Harold now lives in a federation semi-detached not far from Molly and has more style than any of them.

"Welcome my lovelies, come on in." He greets us holding a bottle of beer and wearing a BBQ apron with 'Australia's best BBQ-er' on the front.

"Glad to see you're using some of our Australia Day merchandise," laughs Molly.

"Well, I am the best at barbecuing, so this came in handy."

He takes them down the long, dark hallway to the backyard. Everyone is milling around the pool with their coats on and wave hello as they walk towards them.

"Hi, you two. Emma, always good to see you," says Sophia.

Emma smiles and takes in Sophia's beautiful Armani coat. The navy-blue wool, or more likely cashmere, screams class. Sophia's trips to Italy mean she shops at the best stores in Milan and Rome. "I buy a few good pieces, keep them for years and wear them often," she had told Emma during one of their shopping expeditions in Sydney. She had helped Emma buy a few classic pieces over the years.

She looks over to Molly who hands her a champagne. Molly has a totally different style to both Sophia and Emma. She is more boho chic, and this afternoon she is wearing a tan and floral swing dress with a ruched hem. The back is longer than the front allowing her to show off her beige boots that match the oversized felt hat she is wearing. A long overcoat in rust is keeping her warm. She too looks amazing, but this is a style only Molly can pull off.

Harold hits a bottle with a knife, loudly. He is asking for everyone's attention, "Hello everyone, thanks for coming to my 'we need to party' party. It's been too fucking long between drinks. Now, take your seats, the food is ready.

"Woo hoo, looking forward to this," yells someone behind Emma and Molly. Emma realises she is starving having not eaten since breakfast, it's now 4 o'clock.

Once seated, Emma and Molly chat with Sophia until they have to go over to the smorgasbord once it's laid out. Harold has outdone himself with a mix of Asian and Australian dishes to suit everyone – vegetarians, vegans, gluten free, and even seafood for the pescatarians. The spicy smells are enticing.

Back at their table, they eat while listening to the music mix Harold is playing over the outdoor speakers. Emma taps her foot as she listens. "Molly, how are things with the orphanage?"

"As good as could be expected with the current situation. I haven't been able to travel over to India obviously, due to the travel restrictions, but the management is doing their job and the children are safe."

Sophia pipes up, "It is amazing that you managed to set up the orphanage during your gap year. A wonderful thing to do for those poor kids and you were young yourself."

"I was twenty-three and felt I needed to do something worthy, to give my gap year a meaning. I hadn't planned on going to India when Emma and I met at that resort in Fiji. We were having a blast. But three months into the year, I felt empty and after speaking with an Indian waiter in London about his country, something drew me to go. I saved my money and flew to Mumbai. Five years of hard work, raising funds and schmoozing many rich people, *Tulip Treasures*, a safe haven for children, was opened."

"Five years, I didn't realise. How was it living in India?"

"Oh, it is a beautiful country with people who are willing to help. They are kind, industrious and they all have family with skills that helped us out and didn't ask for anything in return. Many of them have fathers, uncles and brothers who were good with their hands. It didn't matter what I asked for, when they heard about the project, they were all willing to help. I was lucky to have generous people around me."

The conversation continues with Molly telling them of her dreams for the orphanage going forward. They are heavily immersed in the conversation when Harold starts his comedy skit.

"Ladies and gentlemen, Harold Zheng here to entertain you." He begins his jokes and it isn't long before everyone is laughing and heckling him. He gives back as good as he receives and they all revel in each other's laughter - "Fuck you, Jake. Who says the pandemic hasn't been good for some? You're at a party aren't you. Now chill and enjoy yourself."

When he finishes, Harold comes to sit down with them all again. "Well, that was a bit of fun. Now, who would like to try some of my latest weed? Believe me, it will blow your mind."

"Na, I brought my own," yells out one of the crew sitting opposite them. "Come and join me in the bathroom if you want something better." He jumps out of his chair and a few people follow him.

Emma says, "I'll try yours, thanks Harold."

THE TWINKLING NIGHT sky sparkles with stars as they all assemble onto the upstairs balcony. The suburban view of light-filled windows in nearby homes stretches before them. Harold has outdoor heaters and turns them on keeping everyone comfortable. He is laughing and telling more jokes, although these are cruder than his skit earlier this afternoon. A few people laugh through their stoned fog, but Emma isn't finding this funny, she is infatuated with the darkening sky. "Whoa, look at those stars. How pretty are all those twinkles?"

"Yeah," says Molly looking up slurring her words. They had both drunk copious amounts of wine and the weed was working its magic. "Little puffs of twinkling sparkles." They both fall about laughing and go to find some chairs.

They sit on the balcony until late. All of them chilled and happy, their drug of choice doing its job. It's after midnight when people start to leave and Emma, Molly and Sophia decide to share a cab.

"This has been great, Harold. Just what we all needed," says Emma.

"Yeah, I'm glad you enjoyed yourselves," he says his eyes glazed from everything in his body. "See you at work Molly. And Sophia. Emma, always good to catch up with you."

SIXTEEN

Molly

SHE IS CONSIDERING whether she should say no to this latest challenge, a fan has suggested she lie in a box filled with cockroaches, when Sophia walks into her office. "Hi, I'm not too sure about this one. I hate cockroaches," says Molly her face cringing, "they're so creepy and ugly." Memories of the cockroach scurrying off that filthy mattress make her squirm.

"That's the point, Molly. It's all about facing your fears. The viewing public lap up this sort of stunt. The audience will love it. You'll have good publicity from it too."

"Oh, I know it rates well but ..." Even thinking the word *cockroaches* makes her cringe.

"It's not scheduled for another few weeks, there is time to decide. Are you ready to go into make-up? We're taping half an hour early today."

"Right, yes, the crew has that workshop to attend." She jumps up from her chair and follows Sophia.

Along the way, they chat about things in general, both happy that the pandemic is easing. "Life is getting back to some sort of normal, at least for most of us."

"It's a good thing, those lockdowns were brutal," says Molly. Changing the subject, she asks, "Is the rumour true about Two Shot and his latest squeeze splitting?" She is talking about a hot celebrity couple who feature on Instagram and TikTok. Two Shot is a rapper and Evie is an influencer of make-up products with her own line. "I read about it on the Glitz website but they didn't confirm it."

Sophia sighs, "Yet another celebrity bust-up story. We're on it, the researchers are trying to tie up an interview with Evie."

"Awesome, our younger viewers will be interested to know, I hope she agrees to an interview. Our usual audience wouldn't know about these two, right?"

"Evie is better known than Two Shot, she is the business brain of the relationship. If kids are following her then some of their parents will have heard of her. Anyway, it will be a good interview, especially if she spills some juicy stuff on Two Shot."

Molly already begins formulating questions she will ask Evie. Who doesn't love a juicy celebrity bust-up interview?

LATER, she arrives home to wonderful smells coming from the kitchen. Kissing David hello, he places some curry on a spoon and asks her to try it. "Woah, spicy. But yum."

"It's nearly ready," says David.

"Ok, let me put my stuff down and I'll be back to help."

By the time she returns, David has served the meal and poured her a glass of wine. They both sit on the stools and she proceeds to tell him about the stunt.

"Really? That's gross. I see lots of cockroaches when I'm rewiring old houses. And what a subject to be talking about over dinner," her laughs. "You're not going to do it are you?"

"I haven't decided yet. It's brought back memories of that filthy mattress, but Sophia says publicity from it will be good. Also, it has something to do with facing your fears. But I'm not interested in facing my fears, I already faced them in that filthy house. Maybe that's my answer, I'm not interested?"

"Sounds good to me. Your show gets enough publicity, doesn't it? Why do you have to face your fears? What, to get a few more likes on social media? And you don't need to be reminded of that incident. Neither of us do."

"I know. Thanks, you've helped me decide, I won't do it. End of that disgusting subject. By the way, you won't know who this couple is, but I may be interviewing Evie, of Evie and Two Shot fame."

"Who? What?"

She laughs as David mimics a look of disinterest, shrugging his shoulders. "She's an influencer and he's a rapper. Apparently, they have split up and things are awful."

"Big deal. Celebrities are always splitting up, what's different about this one."

"There are rumours going around that he slept with her sister and has spent most of their money on cocaine and prostitutes. Something about a sex fetish. The thing is, nothing is confirmed yet so I'm waiting until my researchers find out more."

"He sounds like a keeper," laughs David, "don't these celebrities know how easy it is to get caught with today's technology?"

"Maybe that level of fame makes you immune or clouds your mind. Who knows what he has been putting into his system?"

"Hmm, yeah, I guess having too much money can put a lot of goodies in front of you. Anyway, she'd be smart to have left him."

"Yes, I agree. She is the one with more fame anyway, it won't hurt her career. Hun, this was delicious, thanks. Want to take Bono for a walk and discuss more about the virtues of celebrity and fame." David laughs and nods yes.

When they're out walking Molly finds she prefers to walk with someone ever since the abduction incident. Rugged up, they find the park busy and let Bono off his leash.

Their neighbours are there and greet them warmly. "Hey, good to see you both. Molly, you're looking well since the ordeal."

"I'm fine, thanks. He is in the right place to get help, so I guess it has ended well for him. I've moved on," she lies. The incident is still on her mind, but she doesn't let on as she wants to deal with it in her own way.

SEVENTEEN

Richard

THEY ARE LYING in bed and chatting about work when there's a knock at the door. "Come in."

"Dad ... oh hi Emma," Scott says awkwardly, "sorry I didn't know you were here."

"Hi Scott, I came over late last night, you weren't home yet. No need to apologise."

"Ok, umm Dad, can I speak to you for a minute?" Emma notices Scott's face is as red as hot coals, and she smiles wondering why he still gets embarrassed when he's around her. Scott is not as outgoing as his father.

Richard rolls off the bed and places his robe on before walking out to see Scott. "What's up that you couldn't say in front of Emma?"

"I need to borrow $200 please?"

"Everything ok?"

"Yeah, I need it for a dinner. I'm taking a girl out and my credit card is maxed out."

Richard wonders where Scott is taking this girl, $200 is a lot to spend on dinner at his age. But he decides not to question his son. "Well, don't let me stand in the way of love," laughs Richard, "I'll send it to your account when I can. Do I know this girl?"

"She's the daughter of Judge Stephenson, you know the one who has had a few high-profile cocaine cases."

"Oh yes, she's a good tennis player. Bronte, right? And the judge was stalked by the same idiot as Molly."

"Oh right, I didn't know it was the same guy. And yes, that's her and I want to make an impression. Dad, I really like her."

"Good for you. I'll transfer that money asap. See you later."

"Thanks Dad," says Scott as he heads for his own bedroom.

Richard stands for a minute wondering how this happened? When did Scott grow up and become a man? He smiles as he walks back into the bedroom.

"Everything alright with Scott?"

"It sure is. My boy is in love and I'll never see that money he borrowed again." Laughing, he proceeds to tell Emma what Scott had told him.

"Oh, Bronte Stephenson, she's lovely. Her father is a tough one though, he'll be hard to impress."

"The other person who will be hard to impress is Scott's mother. She may live in another country, but she will want to vet anyone he goes out with."

Emma doesn't answer and Richard knows it is because she doesn't want to engage in talk about his ex-wife. Emma had heard of his ex's jealous streak and how she wouldn't think kindly of Richard having an affair with a married woman, even though he is no longer her husband. He decides to drop the subject and leave it to Scott to deal with if he ever needs to.

While Emma is engaged with her phone, he thinks about his ex, Caroline. She was a stunning woman when they had met and was an accomplished businesswoman too. Her long blonde hair is now a close crop after suffering breast cancer soon after they split. He sometimes blamed himself for causing the stress that brought on her illness. Unfortunately, she blamed him too. Everything had been his fault during their marriage, which was the reason he strayed. Caroline believed she was never wrong. He scoffs at how arrogant she had been and he was glad she lived overseas, the less he had to do with her, the better. Their boys, who were teens at the time, had been happy to live with him and he was grateful to be able to see them become adults. They had many good times together.

"What are you smiling at?"

"Oh nothing. Just reminiscing about my boys." He turns to her and asks her to put her phone down, he wants to be with a woman who appreciates him and puts any thoughts of his ex out of his mind.

EIGHTEEN

Trevor

HE CHECKS the stock market and shakes his head. His stocks have taken a hit in the last few years and the pandemic had made things worse. He stands up stretching his considerable frame as he heads to the bathroom. He smiles as he's thinking of Emma, how she loves the fact he is a gentle bear of a man, all six feet four inches of him. Sitting on the toilet he thinks of what he needs to do around the farm when he hears a low, hungry grunt. "Ester, is that you?"

His pet pig comes into the bathroom and cocks her head towards him. "Good morning, are you hungry?" She snorts and he takes this as a yes. Her huge frame just fits in the doorway with her pink skin with dark spots randomly spread on her back urging him to give her a gentle pat. Ester lost her mother when she was born and both he and Emma thought she saw herself as human since they had brought her up. She spent more time with them and other humans than in her pen with the rest of the pigs.

At the kitchen window, he sees the sun had not long risen, and it would soon be obscured by the clouds. He eyes his pride and joy. This farm has been in his family since colonial days, the country life-style is in his blood. At 250 hectares, *Blusters Gap* is one of the larger farms in Bowral. He thinks of Emma again, and even though she was born in Bowral, she doesn't love the farm like he does. Looking out over the barns, the fields are a rich dark green with recent rain and the few cows they own are happily grazing through them.

Picking up the bowls of various pet foods, he calls Ester, and she plods behind him. Outside, the two cattle dogs and Emma's cocker spaniel, Harley, run towards him. The chickens follow behind and the two alpacas in the pen put their faces over their fence. "Every-one's hungry this lovely morning," says Trevor as he feeds them their various food.

Looking up he sees the lovely morning will not be around for long as dark, foreboding clouds are coming, rain and a possible storm are forecast again. The rain they need, but hopefully a damaging storm doesn't eventuate.

The animals had wolfed their food down so he collects their empty bowls leaving them on the porch for now. He whistles to Duke and Duchess, his cattle dogs, to jump in the truck, he needs to herd the cattle to be milked. The cows are only a hobby, this farm is all about the sheep and it's their wool that keeps his finances afloat. Emma had thought he was mad when you bought the six cows, but for him all farm animals were a delight, it was in his blood to look after them.

Once the cows are in the milking shed, he proceeds to milk them, this milk will be used for the next meeting he is organising with other farmers. Some he will set aside to make his favourite Farmers cheese, similar to ricotta only firmer.

He and Emma had spoken last night, as they always do on a Friday. He had accepted the fact that she lived in Sydney a long time ago. He also accepted she was having a long-term affair with her colleague. He feels a lump in his throat at this thought, the hurt starts there ready to ruin his day, but the fact she needs another man in her life is on her conscience and he has never mentioned it her. Her life in the city was her own as was his in the country. He is an old-fashioned bloke and likes the solitary life. Had they lived together on the farm for longer than they had, which was only the first few years of their marriage, they probably would not have stayed together. Emma bought her apartment in Kirribilli when she landed her first job at the city station.

She probably still thinks he doesn't know about Richard, or maybe she does, but for Trevor it no longer matters. When she is in Bowral, they are a couple in every sense of the word. Their social life in this country hamlet is strong and all their friends run farms, they have a lot in common. Some of Emma's friends judged her when she moved to the city, needless to say she doesn't speak to them any longer. The ones who are proud of her career have stuck by her decision. These are the friends they see often when Emma comes home.

With the animals all attended to and the crops checked Trevor heads back indoors. He is inside for an hour before the rain hits. The three dogs and Ester pad their way into the homestead, the rain too heavy for them to endure. "Nice to have your company, did you wipe your feet before coming inside?" Harley comes up to him and Trevor bends his long body to give him a pat. Duke and Duchess follow Harley for their pats too as they nudge their way towards him. "Wait your turn, will you," laughs Trevor giving the cattle dogs some love as well. They all settle in their respective beds satiated.

Sitting at his desk, he opens his laptop to send emails to everyone that is participating in the local agricultural shows, these are huge events and bring many city slickers to town. He is the MC at both shows and is on the committee with six other people. This is the first time the shows will happen in three years, and he is looking forward to both of them being bigger than ever.

Within minutes, he receives answers to his questions and spends the next three hours speaking with other members of the committee. He then asks the secretary to send the minutes of the last meeting for him to read. There is still much to do, but he can feel the adrenaline rushing through him as he begins forming ideas of what they can do better this show season.

As he is working, an email comes in from Emma. She has sent him an invite for a New Year's party at her boss's home in Rose Bay, an uber-posh suburb in Sydney's east. Trevor sighs, he's uncomfortable going to Emma's apartment let alone be around a bunch of her colleagues who all think they're smarter than him. He sends back a thank you but doesn't answer yes or no, there is plenty of time before he has to decide. Although right now, his answer is no.

Standing up he feels a sharp stab in his chest. Placing his hand to it, he takes a deep, gasping breath. When the stabs become sharper he steadies himself against the desk. Breathing deeply, the pain subsides as he walks to the kitchen. While making a tea he decides he will speak to his doctor soon, he's had this pain more than once lately.

NINETEEN

Emma

IT'S mid-morning and she's sitting in her office talking to Molly on her phone about the invitation to the New Year's party. They both enjoy these parties at the house of the CEO of Channel BBS 12.

"I wonder who's going to make a fool of themselves this time?" laughs Molly.

"Ha, yes, someone always does, right? I've sent the invitation to Trevor but all he sent back was a thank you. Not surprising, he won't decide until the last minute."

"Hmm, a bit like David. He says he has nothing in common with my colleagues and complains that they're not interested in a tradie who has no interest in television types."

"That's Trevor too," laughs Emma.

"Is Richard coming?"

"I can't stop him and there is no reason for him not to come. Trevor doesn't know about us."

"Do you really think that is the case? You and Richard have been having an affair for a long time."

"He's never mentioned it and is always happy to see me when I'm down there. I love them both in different ways and don't want to give either of them up."

"Well, I guess it's worked for you for this long, why change things now?"

"Exactly, why spoil the fun?" Emma does feel a twinge of guilt whenever this subject is broached, but it's usually only Molly ribbing her about having two men in her life. Deciding not to think about this any longer, she continues discussing the party knowing the invitations have been sent out early to ensure the overseas correspondents can make it. Some of them have not been home for three years.

"Thanks for the chat, Molly. I'm heading into taping now, see you on the weekend?"

"Yes, after yoga ... unless you're joining me?" Molly jokes.

Emma laughs, "No, I'll see you after your yoga session, thanks anyway."

EMMA IS TAKING a short break from taping as her make-up artist is fiddling with her face and hair. Opposite her the same thing is happening for the Minister for the Environment. They will be discussing the current climate change debate and what this government has planned. It's a hot topic, and with climate protests happening in the city, Emma is keen to hear the minister's perspective on the disruption they are causing.

"Two minutes," yells the floor manager.

Emma and the minister ready themselves for taping to begin again as Emma focuses on the digital countdown. The autocue begins to scroll down the screen as she begins the interview. She has some hard-hitting questions ready for the minister. She sees her moving uncomfortably in the chair, the minister knows what is coming. But she settles in and answers Emma's question diplomatically. This minister is a seasoned professional and Emma enjoys interviewing her.

Before she knows it, the interview is over. The minister was professional and had good knowledge of the subjects discussed.

"Minister, thank you for your time." Emma looks into the camera, "And we'll be right back with more."

The minister keeping her cool made for a great interview. She answered Emma's questions intelligently while adding a positive spin on what the government has planned. The interview ran smoothly, Emma is pleased with the outcome. She is also pleased with the minister's attitude, if only more politicians were as smart.

Taping ends and Emma looks forward to heading home to walk Harley. Before leaving the studio, she continues speaking with the minister about the interview discussing the protestors and their cause.

"I understand what the protesters are trying to do but they are going the wrong way about it. The public doesn't take kindly to their lives being disrupted. Who wants to be stuck in peak hour traffic due to protests? There will be change Emma and we in government know it needs to happen. We are already putting plans in place, or we won't have a planet suitable for humans to live a sustainable life. The protestors know this, but they continue to disrupt and it's frustrating for everybody."

Emma agrees with the minister and sees her out of the studio. She is about to leave but turns around when she hears her name.

"Hey Emma, wait up."

She turns to the familiar voice, it's her floor manager. "Hey, Jonathan."

"That was a great interview. You allowed her to open up about both sides of the debate."

"Thanks. She makes it easy because she is knowledgeable and knows how to express her thoughts."

"You know who's coming in next week, right?"

"Yes, the leader of the *Australia Owns* party. Oh, I'm so looking forward to that." She sighs, her sarcasm obvious. Emma is not fond of the politics of this party, but she gives everyone in politics a voice on her show, she wants to be impartial and that's how she wants the show to be viewed. Still, the leader is a larger-than-life character and viewers tend to like watching him babble on and stumble over his words. See smiles to herself, he is worth interviewing even just to lighten the mood of the show.

"I'll keep a close watch on that interview, and we can always cancel it if he becomes too controversial."

"Thanks Jonathan, but maybe a bit of controversy will help ratings. I appreciate you looking out for me though. We can discuss it with Jack at the production meeting."

"Ok, sure. Hey, are you going to the boss' party? I'm definitely not missing out!"

"Of course, I'm going. There will be a who's who of industry types there. We all need to network and keep ourselves relevant. You have a lot of years ahead of you so it's important you go to as many of these events as you can."

"You betcha. I do get a little starstruck at these things being a newbie, but I make the most of it. I haven't made a fool of myself yet."

"Right," she laughs, "best to keep it that way. See you at the meeting."

A WEEK LATER, Emma's phone pings just before she begins taping. Looking at her phone, there is a message from Trevor's brother. When she opens it, her hand rushes to her mouth and her face pales.

Jack notices, "Emma, are you ok?"

Emma stands up and asks for audio to disconnect her microphone. "It's Trevor, I have to go."

"Wait, calm down. Tell me what's going on." She sees the concern on her producer's face.

"The message is from Trevor's brother. He's had a heart attack. I have to go to Wollongong Hospital; they've taken him there."

Jack is stunned into silence and Emma is grateful not to have to continue the conversation. She runs out of the studio leaving Jack to deal with finding another host for this taping session. Richard might have time to step in but it's not her problem, her problem is getting to Wollongong Hospital before anything grave happens.

SHE IS SEATED NEXT to him. His face etched with sunken lines and his skin is tainted a bland grey. The sterile atmosphere of the room is depressing. Trevor is hooked up to monitors that beep, and even though these machines are keeping him alive, she hates the sound as she wishes her ears could block it out.

Arriving yesterday afternoon, she had relieved Trevor's brother who had been at the hospital with Trevor since he was brought in. He was exhausted and explained how he found Trevor slumped over his desk at the homestead. "He ..." Barry stopped and cleared his throat as tears formed in his eyes. "Umm, when he didn't answer his phone after I called twice, I went to the farm. That's when I found him."

Emma knew why Barry had rushed over, Trevor always answered after the second ring. He had continued telling Emma he called triple-o and the paramedics stabilised him. Trevor's condition was serious, so he was brought straight to the hospital. "The drive here was the longest and worst time of my life. Seeing his body limp like that ..."

Emma had hugged Barry until he stopped crying. "It's ok, Barry. He's in the right place now."

"He's too young for this. He's fit, how can he have a heart attack?"

Emma had known about Trevor's heart condition; he had been a heavy smoker and dabbled in drugs in his younger years. Having stopped smoking on his fortieth birthday, his doctors were hoping this would help. His cardiologist had told them, "The damage to his arteries is significant, but with bypass surgery, he should be ok."

Trevor had that surgery and up until this incident, he had been well. Or had he kept things from her and Barry?

They both sat for a minute, Emma allowing Barry to compose himself. His face showed his lack of sleep. "Look, you go home, I'm here now."

"I'm too tired to drive, need to rest first. I'll stay at Clark's place for a few days. This way you and I can take turns," he had said to her. Clark is a cousin, Emma liked him and was sure he would help Barry.

The next few days are a blur of spending time with Trevor remaining unresponsive and her taking turns with Barry. They wear full protective gear to protect themselves and Trevor from the virus. Even though things with the pandemic have improved, hospitals were still hotspots. They had listened to the doctors' diagnosis – "He's had a massive heart attack and we're doing everything we can, but don't get your hopes up.

Her heart shatters with this news. She sheds tears and sorrow clasps her body - Trevor is too young to die.

TWENTY

Molly

SHE HAD STOOD her ground and the cockroach stunt was shelved, just the thought of those gross things made her cringe, the vision of that cockroach scurrying across her foot ... "I'm not doing it. Ever," she had exclaimed at the production meeting. "Find me something that's not so foul and a bit more fun." Sophia's face showed frustration, but Molly is the host and she meant what she said, from now on it was fun challenges only.

Walking into her office after the meeting, she sits with a thud allowing a long sigh to escape. Trevor's death had rattled her. This, on top of her abduction by that crazy nutter had left her nerves on edge and this is a feeling she isn't familiar with. Molly is a confident person who prides herself on being able to take on anything, but seeing Emma so devastated at the funeral, Molly had lost her control. She wept huge tears then and now, her body shaken to her core.

She had not seen Emma since she had left for the hospital, nor spoken to her. It wasn't until the funeral that they managed to talk.

After it, at the wake, Molly had hugged Emma for so long, it felt like an eternity. Neither wanted to let go. They finally pulled apart and stood looking at each other, their faces smeared with sloppy mascara and tears.

Emma had lain low in Bowral wanting to remain with family who were helping each other to manage their grief. She had not even returned Molly's calls or texts. This had flustered Molly; didn't she need her friend? Molly had certainly wanted to hear from Emma.

Emma spoke once she pulled away from Molly, "I'm sorry I didn't call you. I was ... it was too hard for me to speak, especially over the phone."

"No need to apologise, Emma, you had a lot on your mind," Molly had lied wiping away tears with her fingers. She wished she could have done more for her, been with her at her time of need.

Family and close friends had returned to the homestead for the wake. There were people mingling in the lounge while Molly and Emma retreated to Emma's bedroom. Emma sat heavily on the bed. Molly stood not knowing what to do.

"He was fit and young. Why did this happen?" Again, Molly was at a loss. She remained quiet hoping the question was rhetorical.

"Apparently there is a history of heart disease in his family. He had never wanted to mention his condition to anyone other than me. I then convinced him to at least tell Barry."

Molly sits next to Emma. Gingerly, she looks at her friend not wanting to upset her more. "Maybe he didn't want to worry everyone."

"Maybe. Oh Molly, it hasn't hit me yet. How can Trevor be gone? And this farm, I can't run it on my own."

"You have a lot to deal with but don't think about it all now, I'm sure Trevor's family will help you sort things out."

Emma began sobbing again, and Molly placed her hand on Emma's knee, "Come on, let's head back where the others are. You need a drink and so do I."

The day of Trevor's funeral had been the saddest in Molly's life so far. Even the death of her parents had not rattled her to this extent. Both being very ill, it had been a blessing when they passed. Trevor dying was sudden, and Trevor was young. It was so horribly tragic.

Molly had remained in Bowral overnight and had gone back to the farm to say goodbye to Emma. Upon seeing her friend shuffle to the front door in her dressing gown, Molly had cried, and they both hugged each other for the longest time again.

Tears keep falling as she remembers. She rips more tissues from the box on her desk wiping her eyes and blowing her nose. Emma had returned to Sydney only two days ago and still wasn't up to seeing Molly, or anyone for that matter. She had said she would contact Molly when she felt like socialising again. This had rattled Molly. She wanted to be with Emma in her time of need, but she had to accept that her friend was processing this loss by herself. Was it Molly who was the one who needed to be consoled? Her nerves were making her feel that way. This was the reason she wanted to see Emma, to console herself as much as Emma.

Death is never easy but having lost her parents when she and Tim were in their early twenties, Molly knew Emma would bounce back. How long before she did is anyone's guess. She will be there when Emma needs her and is ready for Emma to reach out.

MOLLY IS TRAVELLING to Canberra at the ungodly hour of three in the morning. Although, she is looking forward to this challenge, it's not a hard one. She is doing a hot air balloon flight, which isn't really a challenge other than having to leave this early. Having to be up at two this morning was definitely the challenge, but at least she can rest in the back seat, Sophia is in the front with Harold.

"When we arrive, you'll be briefed on the safety drill and meet the other couple going up with you."

"Oh yes, the proposal. What a lovely thing to have on the show. I hear they are fans."

"They are, which is why they applied to come up with you."

"I'm honoured that they want me to witness this wonderful occasion." Molly uses a posh tone, a *full plum in her mouth* voice.

Sophia laughs, "Don't be too honoured, we're the fourth show the guy contacted, he really wants to do this on television."

"Did you have to tell me that? I was having a moment," answers Molly her ego deflating. Continuing to discuss what will happen, Molly isn't worried, this challenge is going to be enjoyable.

When they arrive at the office of *HighUP Ballooning,* the young couple is already there. Molly is introduced to them and is struck at how young they are. They're not far from being teenagers. "They are childhood sweethearts," Sophia had explained in the car, and both are still at university.

Molly takes in his size, he is a Sasquatch, she is as petite as a fairy in comparison. Molly has an image of him smothering her in bed. She shifts this silly thought and thinks about the upcoming interview. She wonders why some people commit so young, she had travelled extensively and started to set up the orphanage all by the time she was twenty-five. She and David had been together for five years and neither had even mentioned taking it further. Still, each to their own.

After the briefing, the three of them plus the camera operator, who happens to be Harold, walk towards the balloon area. Molly pulls her parka zipper up closer to her neck. Although it's October, the cool Canberra air seeps in. The day before had rained so the grass is wet, and they had to step around puddles. And a few cow paddies as well, the acrid smell is overwhelming as it attacks their noses.

They are introduced to the pilot and are asked to wait as the balloon is filled with hot air. Molly looks around, the morning light gives the horizon a honey glow. The day will warm up, but probably well after they finish this flight.

Finally, they are off. Molly is surprised at how gentle and light it is, the flames warming the air and its passengers. She takes off her parka and Harold mikes her up. She is ready.

"Well, here I am in Australia's capital, Canberra, flying in this magnificent hot air balloon with these lovely people. Say hi everyone."

The couple and pilot smile into the camera.

"I can't tell you how amazing the view is from up here. The sun – Harold takes a shot of the rising sun – is beginning to peak through. Look at that orange glow across the horizon, how spectacular. But the main reason we are here this morning is to talk to Frederick and his lovely girlfriend, Jessica. So, what brings you two on this flight?"

Frederick answers as he is the more confident of the two. "Apart from wanting to meet you, Molly – we're huge fans of your show – I have something I want to ask Jessica." He turns to Jessica whose face is aglow with surprise, "Jessica, you are my childhood sweetheart and I have loved you with all my heart for years ... Jessica," he says his voice trembling, "will you marry me."

Jessica brings her hand to her mouth as tears stream down her face. "Oh my ... oh Frederick, yes, of course I'll marry you." Her voice is as petite as she is.

There is a pop of a champagne bottle and Molly, Harold and the pilot let off some party crackers.

"Congratulations," yells Molly, "we're so happy for you. Everyone ... look she said *yes*." Molly surprises herself at how pleased she is for them. This has certainly been a challenge she has enjoyed.

Once down on the ground, she signs the couple's shirts and gives them a signed promotional photo of her sitting on set.

"Thanks so much for agreeing to this, Molly. Many celebrities wouldn't go out of their way for fans, but you're different." Frederick's face blushes almost matching his hair.

"I'm glad I was able to help you out with this, and Jessica, you have a catch here, don't let him go." Jessica blushes too without saying a word, she is definitely the quiet one in this relationship. Frederick keeps talking to Molly as they walk back to the cars, theirs taking them to the airport and hers taking her to the studio to finish the show.

Harold is driving and asks Molly how she is feeling, "Are you ready for the taping of the rest of the show? You've been up for hours."

"Me? I'm fine, Harold. That couple made me feel special and even though we all had to wake at that stupid hour, I have enough adrenalin to power me through the rest of the show."

"That's my girl," says Sophia, "professional as always."

"What did you expect? If I don't perform, we don't have a show. You guys want to have a job, right?"

Both Harold and Sophia laugh, "We sure do."

TWENTY-ONE

Emma

IT'S THE CHRISTMAS HOLIDAYS, her first without Trevor. The family had been over for the day on Christmas Eve, knowing she wanted to be on her own Christmas Day. She was pleased they respected her wishes and found she didn't feel lonely once they all left. Trevor's presence is everywhere – his aftershave filled the bathroom with musky smells, his clothes strewn over the bedroom floor on his side of the bed, his shoes on the stoop outside. But the thing making his presence all too real was his computer, it still had the webpage of the agricultural show he had been working on. A heaviness had come over her when she had booted it up. This farm belonged to Trevor, his spirit was all over the place.

It's now Boxing Day and Emma is stroking Harley's golden fur; he hasn't left her side ever since Trevor left them. Whenever Emma is in Bowral, her cocker spaniel is her constant companion, but now even more so. He makes it bearable to be in the homestead on her own. All the animals seem to know she is sad, and she is sure they miss Trevor too. The two cattle dogs, Duke and Duchess as well as Ester the pig have been unusually quiet and lethargic since their master died. Whoever buys the farm will inherit these animals, who were essentially like family to Trevor and Emma. All of them will stay on the farm. Except Harley. She is planning on buying a terrace or duplex in Sydney so he can come with her. She is on her computer searching real estate websites now, while also looking for an agent to rent her apartment.

Richard had been respectful of her time, as had Molly. A thought comes to her mind, *what is friendship but a mutual respect with a smattering of envy.* She is envious of her friends whose lives haven't been torn apart like hers. Trevor was her first love, and even though Richard had come into her life, Trevor was always first. They had history together. And family, their lives had intertwined for years. Her friends were there for her when she needed them, but right now that envy coursing through her body is keeping her from wanting to be with anyone. She knows they are worried about her and want to see her. Especially Richard. He had texted when she left for Bowral hoping that she had arrived safely and said to contact him if she needed to. She hadn't yet. He had also hinted they move in together, but that was never going to happen, she wanted her space and had lived on her own in Sydney for too long. Richard was a lovely distraction, she felt comfortable with him, and their shared work helped with the relationship. Trevor had never understood her love of the limelight.

Molly had sent beautiful messages every day that Emma was in Bowral. She was appreciative of this but had not answered her either. She and Molly had been friends since meeting in Fiji. It was Emma's first trip away without her parents, but Molly had been travelling for some time. This had been Molly's third trip to Fiji. They had connected through their love of music, all things celebrity, and movies. Emma was fascinated by Molly's adventurous lifestyle, her boho dress sense, and her fabulous sense of humour. She couldn't imagine her life without Molly, she is the sister she always wanted.

Looking towards her computer screen again, there are a couple of properties she is interested in and sends emails to the respective real estate agents. Stretching, she gasps in air as she slumps her head, her chin hitting her chest, then slamming down the lid of her laptop. Her forehead lands on the table. Slowly blowing out air, she begins to cry. A full, grieving weep filled with sadness and loss.

THE INTERVIEW with the Prime Minister goes well. She is feeling confident about being back on-air after the Christmas break. Emma wants to pour herself into work to help her cope with the chasm left by Trevor's death. Having this interview recorded is a good start to this season, with the virus easing its hold, the Prime Minister had a lot to say. People are sick of lockdowns and his assurance that they will no longer happen will please many.

Back in her office, sitting at her desk, Richard walks in.

"Welcome back."

"Hi Richard, thanks. And to you, too." She makes no effort in moving and he remains on the other side of her desk.

"Are you coming over tonight?"

"Yes, I'm back and want to resume my normal life. That includes you, I guess." She gives him a cheeky smile, although she doesn't feel the mood she's projecting.

"Well I should hope so. What's with 'I guess'? He's taken aback by her nonchalant tone to their relationship.

She looks back up at him. "Sorry, it's all still raw. I didn't mean anything by it."

He turns to walk out still feeling dejected, "So, I'll see you tonight then?"

"Yes, you will." She watches as he walks out and wonders why they had been so formal with each other. But her attitude had not helped. Maybe Richard changed his attitude to their relationship as well? Did he really mean it when he asked her to move in and was now brooding? Still, she was adamant to remain living on her own.

All she wants is Harley for company and to be with Richard on her terms. This might be harsh after all the years they have been together, but it is necessary to protect herself from more harm. What if she did agree to move in with him ... and he died? She stops herself thinking of this awful scenario and turns to her computer.

A few hours later, after finishing checking her scripts, she texts Richard and asks if he felt like going out for dinner. His reply is swift – Sure, I'll book our usual. That was easier than she thought. Going out for dinner gave her an out if she didn't feel like going back to his apartment. The grief of losing Trevor is still too fresh for her to resume a full-on relationship with Richard.

She prints out what she had been working on and decides to call Molly later. It's time they had a coffee together because Emma needs her girlfriend now more than she does Richard.

HE OPENS the door to the seafood restaurant Richard booked and allows Emma to walk in. He has always been a gentleman, but he is upping his game. The few times she has seen him socially, only three times so far, Richard has treated her gingerly giving her his full attention.

As they walk in, people stop and look. A few whisper and both Emma and Richard smile towards the other diners. They're used to being recognised and at times accosted by fans, but Emma will never get used to it. Richard takes it in his stride.

This being a local restaurant, they know they will be left alone tonight, their privacy will be respected. This is one of the reasons they stay local, Emma especially doesn't like dealing with overzealous fans and Richard knows this.

They have an amicable dinner with Emma being quieter than usual. She knows Richard is doing his best to keep the conversation going, but she is still raw with grief and now wishes she hadn't agreed to see him so soon. She makes a mental note to give herself more time, she needs to take care of herself and not rush back into this relationship.

After dinner, she tells Richard she won't be going to his apartment and asks him not to come to hers, she explains she needs time by herself. He agrees but she knows he is not pleased. Well, that's his problem, she has her own problems to worry about.

AS SHE WALKS into the apartment foyer, she sees the moving boxes had arrived and begins carrying them to her apartment. She is going to start packing on the weekend and move into the townhouse she bought in Wollstonecraft, not far from Kirribilli. She is looking forward to bringing Harley up from the farm, he will be good for her soul.

TWENTY-TWO

Molly

IT'S late afternoon and they are seated on the balcony of a café at Balmoral, the sun blazing down with its final remaining heat. The beach below teems with life — families, teens, singles all basking in the heat, but up here, the air feels thick with unsaid things.

After signing autographs with their practiced smiles, they had retreated to the corner table by the window, where the view of the ocean is stunning, yet Emma's words deny them the enjoyment of the scenery.

Her voice, normally so composed, cracks slightly as she tells Molly how she feels about Richard — what she needs, what she's missing. It's raw, exposed, as Emma is fragile in a way Molly's never seen before. But Molly doesn't respond right away. Not because she doesn't care, but because the waiter breaks the tension by placing their lunch in front of them. The plates clatter lightly on the table, but the real noise is in the silence between them.

Molly breaks the silence, "You need to feel right, Emma. Have you spoken to Richard and told him how you feel?"

"Not really. I've kept my distance, which is causing the tension between us. I just ... it's hard for me to know how I feel about him now."

"Try not to put pressure on yourself. You're still grieving, that's obvious to me, and probably to him too."

"You know me too well, Molly. I haven't spoken to anyone about this, but I trust you not to blurt it to out."

"No reason for me to do that. I cherish these chats between us. You know we can tell each other anything." Emma smiles before she chomps down a mouthful of her salad, half of it falling back in her plate. Emma isn't usually this sloppy with her food, she is feeling that bad she's not caring.

They sit in silence again as they eat. Molly thinks about Richard and how he must be feeling about all this. She understands what Emma sees in him; he is a handsome man. Even Molly fantasises about him, especially when she and David fight. She wouldn't say no to him if pushed. There is an aura about him that gives her tingles, almost like she's a teenager again. She shudders at this thought wondering why she thinks of him in this way when she's already in a committed relationship. And he's Emma's lover.

Trying to stop thinking of Richard in this way, especially with Emma in such a state, she says, "Maybe you should talk to Richard and find out what he's feeling."

"Probably. I'm not being fair to him, am I?"

"You need to be fair to yourself first, which you are doing. When you're ready and feel right, that is the time to have the conversation with him."

Emma turns away from Molly and stares out through the sea haze and Molly knows she is processing her advice. There is no more to say, Emma has to decide when she is ready.

"I'm here whenever you need me."

When Emma turns to face Molly, fat tears are running down her face. Molly takes Emma's hand and gives it a squeeze.

BONO BOUNDS towards her as she opens the front door. Placing her bag over her shoulder, she holds onto his paws and eases him off her chest. "Hi, baby. I'm home and very happy to see you too." Her voice is an octave higher, excitable making Bono's tail wag faster than an electric fan.

"Hey, how was the beach?" David is in the lounge watching the cricket.

Molly plops herself next to him and sighs. "She's down. Poor Emma, she is still in shock and it's affecting her relationship with Richard."

"I guess that was bound to happen. I'm sure you gave her some good advice."

"Well yes, but am I the love guru? Both Richard and Emma are my friends, and it will be sad if they break up. She needs more time, but I think Richard's patience may be running out."

David looks at her with a curious look. "That bad, huh? I guess Emma loved Trevor more than we knew."

"I guess so. If Emma had lived in Bowral full time, I don't think she would have had an affair. She loved Trevor, she never said she didn't."

"Still, I never understood why she bothered with Richard, he's a bit of a tool."

Molly laughs, "Oh, he's ok on a good day. His ego does get in the way, so I get what you mean."

"Too often for me."

Molly knows David is not a fan of Richard and decides to drop the conversation. She is about to stand up to go to her bedroom when her phone pings with several messages. "Oh, shit! The paps saw us. There's a less than flattering photo of Emma crying doing the rounds. And the captions are horrid." She shows David her phone.

The gossip columnists had posted a photo of Emma crying.

'Looking haggard, Emma Bears Jones still deflated', 'Grieving Emma was seen at Balmoral recently', 'Bears Jones is still missing her husband', 'Molly isn't helping Emma Bear Jones, she is still crying'.

"Those bastards, she is a grieving widow."

"I know. And it was a private moment between us at Balmoral. Well, am I giving those gossip mongers a piece of my mind." Molly jumps off the lounge and heads to the bedroom to change into her trackies then sits on the edge of the bed all the while posting comments on the various sites Emma had sent her. She will call Emma soon and calm her down. Bono plods along behind her. She sighs as Bono puts his snout on her knees. "Human love is so complicated, and the paparazzi don't help, you're lucky you're a dog." Bono barks in agreement.

"Hey Emma, are you ok?" Molly is still sitting comfortably on her bed having changed into her house fleecies and a t-shirt.

"The fuck I am, what the hell are those paps thinking? Trevor was a very private person and I never put him on the socials. FUCK THEM!" These celebrity sites had broken an unwritten rule about using photos to hurt family and everyone in the industry knew it.

This was true, Emma never discussed her private life with Trevor, in fact, apart from a few rumours about her and Richard, she kept it all to herself. "Ok, calm down, you know they've done this to rile you and obviously it has worked. Don't let them get to you."

"He's dead, Molly. Do they think it's ok to *talk* about him now that he's not around? Yes, I'm grieving, and I miss him every day. This is fucking devastating."

"Ok, you need a plan of attack here. I've already commented and see you have too. Let's leave it at that and let this settle. You need to post some happy snaps of yourself, maybe some with Harley to take the focus off this."

"I'm already looking through photos, send me some you have please. Poor Trevor, he'd be so disappointed in me."

"Emma, try to forget this and move on. Trevor knew you loved him and that is the important thing. And remember, this is not your fault."

"I know and I still love Trevor. Why did he have to die? My life has been turned upside down. Those paps need to fuck off and go back into the hole they came from."

"Ha, ok, let it all out Emma. Gotta go, love you." Emma clicks off saying *'love you too'* and Molly wonders whether the paps are going to escalate this. She decides to post some happy snaps of her and Emma together, having asked Emma to do the same. Between the two of them posting, it might discourage more awful photos of Emma being used by the gossip sites.

SHE'S in the studio looking at her phone when a text arrives from the CEO. Looking up, she sees everyone is on their phone. Sophia is the first to speak about it. "An Australia Day party at Rose Bay. The New Year's Eve party was postponed so this is the new date. That's something to look forward too."

"What the fuck. What's with the short notice?" asks Harold.

"Is that a problem? Do you have something better planned?"

"No ... Australia Day is next Thursday, Sophia. Eight days' notice is unusual."

"Still can't see what the problem is mate. RSVP yes or no, it's not that hard." This from one of the crew.

Harold doesn't answer and Sophia and Molly can see he's embarrassed. Although, it is unusual for their boss to do this, maybe it was a last-minute decision given restrictions have eased. She is looking forward to a party, the last one was at Harold's place, which seems like eons ago.

"Ok everyone, places. Let's get this one finished so we can all go home."

Molly's make-up is being touched up and her mike is fitted. She's ready to film this episode and is looking forward to meeting her guests, two porn stars who work together and have an interesting open relationship. She watches as they enter the studio hand in hand. A more mismatched couple you wouldn't find – he is shorter and stumpier than her, she is a stunner with height on her side. Molly introduces them with their porn names, which produces a laugh from the audience. "Oh behave, we're all adults here." She proceeds to ask them questions and then allows questions from the audience. It's one of the most hilarious and seductive interviews Molly has done, she had to reign them in at times due to a few too many risqué comments from both of them. But they will get some great take-outs for publicity from this.

Once they finish filming, Molly chats with her guests and thanks them for joining her today. As they leave, Harold laughs.

"What?"

"Your face was priceless when they talked about their actual sex life. I didn't think you were a prude."

"I'm not, you know I have an interest in tantric sex. But they took it to an extreme, I think they are living vicariously through their movies. And not too appropriate for our time slot."

"Huh, maybe, but I found them both interesting, I might have to check out their movies. I could learn a thing or two."

Molly laughs. Maybe she and David should watch one too.

TWENTY-THREE

The Party

MOLLY IS STANDING on the balcony looking towards the Royal Sydney Yacht Club. This is another world. So much old money is in this area. The leafy, tree-lined streets and large period homes hark to another era when society lived large in Sydney's eastern suburbs. She imagines having this lifestyle of parties, influence and mansions. And backstabbing, gossips and paps. *No, thanks.* She dismisses this thought, it's not her thing.

"Magnificent, isn't it?"

Molly turns to see Emma. "Oh, hi, I didn't know you were coming." Emma was still pissed with the paparazzi and things with Richard were still strained.

"Last minute decision. I took your advice and spoke to Richard. We're taking things slow, and he understands I need some space. I'm looking forward to seeing him here."

"That's brilliant, I'm happy for you both." Molly is pleased they are at least looking at being a couple again. Although Richard is probably the keener of the two.

"Yeah, I guess I am looking forward to seeing him." Emma takes a swig of the bubbly she's holding with a distant look on her face. Molly isn't convinced Emma is fully onboard with reconciling but decides to remain out of it, she had done her bit.

They chat about the pap photos and Emma tells Molly the strategy of posting happy snaps of them both seemed to have scared them off. No other unpleasant photos of Emma had surfaced, maybe these people had a conscience after all. Molly is grateful because she didn't think Emma would have handled being dragged through social media as the grieving widow well at all.

They are called into the lounge area where the CEO is about to speak. Richard joins them and affectionally kisses Emma on the cheek. Then, "Molly, nice to see you," he says reaching out to shake her hand. She awkwardly goes to shake his hand then remembers the virus and gives him her elbow. "Oh yes, sorry. Old habits die hard." There is a scuffle as more people come into the room and then they all settle down to listen. Some find a seat, others stand. Some people keep their distance too, which still feels strange given they're at a party.

"Welcome and thanks for coming, those from our network and those of our friends from other stations too. This is our unofficial New Year's Eve party that didn't happen. Feel free to celebrate that or Australia Day, either way, it's a party ..."

He continues but Molly stops listening. She is sensing that Emma has stiffened since Richard has turned up and goes to get more drinks. She hands Emma another champagne, Richard a beer and she is holding her gin and tonic. Emma tips the whole glass into her mouth in two gulps. She is definitely uptight, but the alcohol will help with that.

The speech wraps up with enthusiastic applause, and in no time, the room hums with energy as everyone dives back into the party. Colleagues who've known each other for years are laughing and exchanging stories, the vibe electric with old friends reunited at a long-overdue celebration. Music pulses in the background, fuelling the growing excitement as glasses clink and voices rise in cheerful chatter. There's a buzz of anticipation, a sense this night will be one to remember, with dancing, drinks, and stories to keep the fun rolling well into the night.

Molly heads to one of the bathrooms, there are two on this floor, where the smell of dope is ubiquitous. Before she can enter the bathroom, Jonathan, Emma's floor manager, asks if she wants a drag. Taking it from him, she takes a long, slow intake and feels her nerves settle quickly, Emma's behaviour is bothering her. Walking into the bathroom, three girls are enjoying themselves the white lines on the bench and holding their noses afterwards. They're giggling and obviously stoned because they don't even notice her. As with many of these parties, there is always something to take so she decides to go and find Jonathan again, Emma's behaviour is annoying her and she wants to enjoy this party.

When Molly returns looking for Emma and Richard, she sees Emma walking towards the balcony.

Molly follows her. "Everything alright?"

"Oh, umm, sure. I needed some air, that's all."

"Don't lie Emma, I can see straight through you."

Emma turns to look at her, "You know Molly, you really are a good friend but right now I'm not up to talking about my feelings."

Molly is puzzled by Emma's sudden mood change; she wasn't this rude when they had talked earlier. "Hey, don't take this out on me. Look, why don't you go and see Jonathan, he has stuff that will help you to calm down." After saying this, Molly decides to leave her alone on the balcony. Molly is here to have a good time not to hold Emma's hand. She heads back to Richard and the others.

"... I'm telling you, it's the truth," laughs Richard. "Oh, hi Molly, where's Emma?"

"On the balcony, said she needed some air."

"Oh, ok," says Richard craning his neck towards the balcony then turning back to the conversation he was having with Harold and Sophia. Molly tunes into their chatter and forgets about Emma, she's an adult and can look after herself.

THE GLOW of fireworks emblazons the harbour as the official Australia Day fireworks start. This balcony and the ones upstairs are now packed as everyone watches on. The party is in full swing, everyone is in a great mood, either drunk or stoned or both. What isn't on offer here isn't worth offering. The smell of various drugs permeates the mansion. A few people had hooked up and found themselves in the bedrooms, and Richard is whispering in Molly's ear that they should move upstairs. With bleary eyes, she smiles at him and then Emma says, "What? Richard, what did you say to Molly?" Emma's speech is slurred, she is high and holding onto the railing. Richard whispers the same thing in her ear loud enough for Molly to hear. Emma is intrigued, "Ooh, that sounds like fun. Let's go." Emma takes his hand and leads the way. Molly is dragged along by Richard not really sure Emma knows she's tagging along.

MOLLY WAKES to the sun peeking through the space under the curtains, a thin sliver of light. It takes her a minute to get her bearings. When her eyes adjust to the semi-darkness, she sees Emma lying next to her face down and naked. Richard is on the other side of the bed, his head at the base. His taut butt is in full view. She admonishes herself for reacting to this sight, she should be horrified. Noticing she has her knickers on, she wonders where the rest of her clothes are. She also thinks of how she had fantasied about Richard, were those dreams a premonition?

Her phone pings. A message from David saying he's going out with Bono in case she comes home in the next hour. Her heart skips a beat as she realises what has happened is a betrayal of their relationship. She notices the time, 10am. She also notices her furry tongue and that she is hungry. Did she eat anything last night?

Creeping out of bed trying not to disturb Emma and Richard, she steps onto a shoe. "Ow," she cries under her breath. She crouches onto her knees and uses the torch on her phone to look for her clothes. Finding them, she dresses, and leaves the bedroom looking for a bathroom.

Walking past the other five bedrooms on this floor, there is an array of bodies either in the beds or on the floor. Picking her way through bodies once she's on the main living area, the smell of stale alcohol and leftover food hits her nose. Shouldn't this place have been cleaned up by now? She stifles the feeling to vomit and finds a cleanish glass in the kitchen. Filling it and gulping down water, she refills the glass twice more.

"Good morning."

Molly turns to see Sophia. "Morning."

"We're the only two up so far. I have a craving for some junk food, want some?"

"That would be great, thanks. It's the best thing for a hangover."

"Sure is," says Sophia and starts tapping at her phone.

When the food arrives, they place it on the kitchen bench where they had cleared a space and start eating. Molly stares out the window to the glistening harbour as she shoves fries into her mouth.

"These parties are good value; I had some good shit last night," says Sophia, "but damn I'm feeling like crap now."

Really? How can Sophia say that she looks so together after the night they've had. Come to think of it, Sophia always looks immaculate, Molly had never seen her look otherwise.

"Yeah." This is all Molly manages to say. She is trying to remember what happened last night. Did ... did she have a threesome with her best friend and Richard? Richard isn't her type even though she does harbour fantasies about him, which obviously came to fruition last night. And for that matter, Emma isn't her type either. Stunning as she is, Molly wants Emma as a friend, not one with benefits. She cringes and keeps shovelling food into her mouth. "Umm, thanks for the food, Sophia. I might head home."

"Ok, I'll see you at work later. We can tape the two interviews, one with that theatre actor whose name escapes me right now, and the celebrity chef."

"You're thinking of Matthew Bing. Yes, see you later."

"That's him, thanks."

Molly heads for the front door and takes in the morning heat as she flags down a taxi. The last thing on her mind is work.

SHE IS in the carpark heading home after taping the interviews when her phone rings. Richard's number comes up. "Hello."

"Molly, hi. You left without saying goodbye. Are you ok?"

"I'm fine, why do you ask?"

"I wanted to say thanks for an amazing night."

"Right. You're welcome." She couldn't think of what else to say, this is a weird situation to be discussing with her best friend's lover.

"I don't remember whose idea it was, but both you and Emma were in your element. I am one lucky guy. Molly, you are very flexible."

She vaguely remembers being on top of him and bending backwards with Emma arousing her by doing something rather pleasant. Richard was moaning with pleasure too.

What the hell? Whatever they took last night certainly allowed them to let their inhibitions go. She shakes her head dismissing this vision even though her body is reacting. Molly is open to different sexual experiences and she and David enjoy experimenting, but she had never harboured thoughts of her, Emma and Richard together.

"Listen, Molly, do you know how I can talk to Emma? She wouldn't talk to me when we woke up and left in a foul mood."

"Richard, she's still processing what's happened. You, Trevor, the paps ..."

"I know, we discussed how she was feeling before the party. She told me she wasn't coming."

"Me too, I was surprised to see her there."

"Will you have a coffee with me tomorrow. I need some strategies, and you being her good friend ... please?"

This was the last thing Molly wanted but Richard's voice had the tone of a wounded lover. "Umm ok, I can meet you in the mall after work."

"Thanks, Molly, I appreciate it. I want Emma to be herself again, I miss the old Emma." Molly doesn't answer him but agrees that the old Emma was more fun.

TWENTY-FOUR

Richard

HE'S FLICKING stations not really interested in what's on. In a fit of fury, he throws the remote at the television. It clatters to the floor and the batteries fall out.

"That was smart. What's eating you?" Scott had walked into the apartment the minute Richard had thrown the remote.

"Women. I don't understand them. Emma has changed since Trevor died and I can't seem to reach her."

"Uh Dad, I'm the last person who can help you. I don't understand women either."

Richard smirks, "You and Bronte are having issues?"

"No, we're good. But there are times when she becomes unreasonable and emotional. This is when I give her a wide berth."

Richard doesn't answer knowing exactly what he means. And he's impressed with Scott's attitude, it's great for a young man to protect himself emotionally. Maybe the divorce has made him wary.

Emma's emotions have taken over and this is why she needs time, which he is giving her. But his patience is now wearing thin. He's hoping Molly will be able to shed some light and give him ideas on how to deal with this current version of Emma.

HE'S WAITING for Molly in Pitt St Mall where she had asked that they meet. Looking at his watch yet again, she is half an hour late. He texts her again. His phone pings this time.

On my way. Be there is 5mins.

No apology? Richard is not impressed and gives her an annoyed look when she finally turns up.

"Richard, Hi. I'm sorry, I had to re-record a segment."

"These things happen," he replies softening but still not impressed.

"Now, I need more than a coffee, how about we go to a bar?"

Richard looks at his watch, "Sure, but I need to be back at the studio in an hour."

"Yes, I know, just one drink."

He nods and they make their way to the nearest bar. Walking into the dimness, they head to the main bar that is adorned in fake black leather, dark timber with burgundy and black swirled carpet finishing the cheap effect. "Elegant," scoffs Richard.

"We won't be here for long. If you had more time, we could go somewhere more appealing."

"This will do. What are you having?"

"Gin and tonic, thanks. I'll go over to that table." Molly indicates to one at the side of the room.

As Richard walks over with Molly's drink and his beer, sitting down he says, "Thanks for meeting me. I'm worried about Emma and ..."

Molly puts her hand up and interrupts, "I am too. Look Richard, I was the one who suggested she speak to you about how she was feeling. I thought you two had worked things out?"

Richard swigs the beer and doesn't answer right away. He waits for the three office workers to walk past. One nods and says "Hey." Richard acknowledges him, he's used to being recognised and hopes they won't be bothered. "We talked for hours one night and then I was texting her for a few days ... you know, checking up on her. Then she turns up at the party, we have a good time and now she isn't speaking to me again. What is going on?"

"Apart from what we did, which I'm still trying to get my own head around, her still processing Trevor's death and those horrible pap photos ... that's a lot to unpack. Maybe take her somewhere nice for dinner and spoil her, let her see what she is missing?"

"I had thought of that. Ok, I'll give that a go."

They sit quietly for a minute. Richard can see the boys at the bar are talking about them. He's glad he has to leave soon, he isn't in the mood to deal with fans, especially ones who look like they are getting drunk. "Hey Molly, do you remember much about the three of us ..."

"Not much. And it's not something I want to repeat," she interrupts him before he can keep talking. "We were not in a state to make decisions, at least I know I wasn't."

Richard places his hand on Molly's knee. "I wouldn't mind a repeat, but only with you this time."

Molly's face shows surprise and a bit of disgust. "Are you fucking kidding? Ahh, thanks, but no. Richard, you and Emma are my friends. Let's not ruin what we have." She moves her knee causing Richard's hand to drop.

"That's a pity, I would like to know what other tricks you have. Your flexibility is a real turn-on. I'm asking you to help me, that's all. I'd like to enhance mine and Emma's lovemaking."

"Didn't you ask me here to talk about Emma and how she's coping? Stop making me uncomfortable. You can be such a dick sometimes."

"Ouch. I was paying you a compliment."

Molly stands up, "It's time to go or you're going to be late." Her voice is clipped, and Richard knows she is annoyed.

"Sure. Thanks again for your advice," he says following her out of the bar now feeling really pissed off. He will concentrate on organising a nice dinner for he and Emma, that will diffuse his anger at Molly.

HE OPENS the door and allows Emma to enter the restaurant. He took Molly's advice and is spoiling Emma to a dinner at Sydney's top Italian spot, asking for a table with a view of the harbour. He had asked her to dress for a special occasion and she looked elegant in her red off-the-shoulder number. His feelings stir, he has missed her and hopes the effort he's making is worth it. They are ushered to a quiet table away from other diners, he had requested this too. The water dances with the city lights, this harbour view every Sydney-sider loves.

Emma has been quiet all the way to the restaurant, and he is now nervous. Taking a deep breath he says, "You look gorgeous, Emma."

She looks up at him, "You asked me to dress for an occasion, so, what's the occasion?"

Richard clears his throat and takes her hand, "To woo you back to me. I'm trying to prove to you how much I love you." He sits down still holding her hand. Emma looks at her hand in his. The candle on the table flickers showing the tears in her eyes.

"Please don't cry. I want this to be a happy night."

She sniffs and moves her hand away. "This is so hard, Richard. The guilt I'm feeling is intense, I failed Trevor."

"Don't say that. He would have had a heart attack even if you were with him 24-7. It's not your fault." A waiter comes over to ask whether they are ready to order. "Another few minutes please, thanks." Richard turns his attention back to Emma. "But can we talk about us tonight. Nothing is going to bring Trevor back."

"I know," she whimpers. Taking a deep breath, she continues. "Ok, you've gone to a lot of effort, let's talk about us. But I'm warning you, any mention of the party and what we did ..."

"Understood."

The rest of the night goes well with Emma agreeing to start seeing Richard again, slowly at first. This will have to be enough for now.

"As long as I see you once a week, then we can work up to where we were. Please don't leave me waiting for weeks on end, I've missed you too much."

"I've missed you too, Richard, but I needed to process some things. There is something I want to clear up though, the thing with Molly. That was a one-off, it is never to happen again."

So much for it not being mentioned. Richard wishes both Molly and Emma didn't see that night as a negative. He found that it cemented their friendships. "If that's the way you feel, then fine. I must say it was very enjoyable for me and I will cherish the time we had together."

"Molly and I have spoken about it. We are both *not* going to talk about it again and we want you to do the same." She emphasises the 'not' to make sure he understands.

Richard indicates to the waiter to bring the bill then takes hold of Emma's hand again, "You have my word."

TWENTY-FIVE

Molly

SNAPPING shut her laptop after the video-chat with her manager in India, Molly sighs. Tulip Treasures Orphanage has survived unscathed during the pandemic. Some of the children and staff contracted the disease, but with careful isolation and vaccinations, things had settled. The government had allowed the more vulnerable to receive free vaccinations, something Molly was grateful for. She was pleased to hear of the progress and promised to visit when travel restrictions were eased.

Heading into the kitchen, her phone pings. Richard has messaged again. This was his third message saying 'call me' but up till now she had ignored him.

"Hi, what's up that you had to text me three times?"

"I wanted to say hello, that's all. Can't a friend send another friend messages?"

Molly's skin prickles, yes, they were friends, but now that is tinged with weirdness. He obviously doesn't feel the same way. She clears her throat, "Richard, I know what you're doing but I'm not interested, we're both in committed relationships. Go and make up with Emma."

"Did that already. We're taking things slow, but I'm interested in what you know, I want to learn ..."

"Let me stop you there ..." She waits as David walks into the kitchen and takes a beer from the fridge. He plods back to the lounge to keep watching the cricket. When Molly is sure he is out of earshot, she continues, "the other night was a mistake, I don't want to discuss it further."

"You and Emma are looking at this all wrong. It was beautiful, so spontaneous and rewarding for the three of us. I honestly feel closer to both of you now."

"You are kidding, right? We were all stoned and drunk, I don't remember much of what happened."

"Which is why we should do it again. You and I, the two of us. I want to learn more about Tantric Sex." Molly hears a distinct bit of sleaze in Richard's voice, her body shudders. He's kidding, right?

"Listen, this isn't going anywhere, just look it up on YouTube, there are many tutorials about it." She hears him laugh.

"And what's the fun in that? I want you to teach me. Come on Molly, I'm telling you we had a connection." Molly keeps listening as he continues saying how she must have felt it too. Her stomach flutters as she remembers more bits of the night when Richard was doing his best to please her, Emma's wet mouth on hers. *Why is her body betraying her?* It was different to anything she has done before, but Emma was right, it should not happen again.

Richard keeps talking as she walks to the bedroom with her tea and sits on the bed. He is flattering her and isn't talking about another threesome. He wants to feel her hands massaging his body again and if she does agree, he wants her to set the mood with candles and maybe light some incense.

Her body is reacting to his newsreader voice, deep and convincing, as she tries to remember the last time David and she had taken the time to enjoy themselves in this way. As Richard keeps talking, she decides to set up their bedroom ready to surprise David tonight. Deciding to let Richard keep begging she ends the call not committing to whether she will take up his offer. Why is her body now tingling after his pleading?

MOLLY WAKES up early the next morning, stretches and smiles. David has already left for work, but he had left a note – *Last night was great. You're so sexy when you're horny. xx*

Guilt rises in her as she walks to the bathroom thinking that speaking to Richard had put her in the mood and sparked a wonderful night of lovemaking for her and David. Shaking her head, she admonishes herself, she loves David and reminds herself Richard is a colleague. And her best friend's lover.

Walking into the hall, she finds the leash and calls Bono, "Come on, let's go for a walk. Or actually, I feel like a run today." Bono stretches as he pads off his bed and wags his tail. Molly bends to clip the leash onto his collar. As they walk out the front door, it's already warm even though it's 7am and the sky is blackening with angry clouds. "Let's go Bono, before this storm hits."

While she is running, Molly can feel her phone pinging with messages, but she concentrates on her run. Bono is enjoying himself running ahead of her as they reach the off-leash park. Other dogs, many of whom are Bono's doggie friends, are bouncing around playing and they welcome him. Molly walks towards the other dog owners and joins in on their conversations. They spend the time discussing what is happening in their lives. These catchups with her neighbours are a pick-me-up for Molly and she cherishes the time with her suburban friends and their dogs.

She doesn't look at the messages until after her shower. She answers the one from Emma about having lunch later with a yes, and the ones from Tim and Samantha, she'll answer in the car as she heads to work.

Driving, she answers Tim telling him to have a good trip. He had texted saying he was going to Melbourne for a few weeks for a conference. He is a GP with an interest in medical research and travels regularly. Ever since their parents passed away, he always lets Molly know if he is going away. They had become closer as it was just the two of them and closer still after his partner died. She finds it ironic that Tim and she are orphans, and she helps to run an orphanage. That wasn't in her plan when she built it.

Next, she answers Samantha's message telling her she will call her after work about Tim's birthday. It is only months away now. They had discussed a venue and booked it already. Samantha is organising invitations and all Molly has to worry about is making sure no one ruins the surprise.

WEEKS later she is at a café around the corner from the Ch33 studios. Emma comes to the table after going to the toilet. "Sorry, I was busting."

Molly nods, "It's ok. I've already ordered so you had better order too. I don't have much time today." She watches on as Emma goes to the counter. Their friendship has been a constant for years, a bond that has weathered highs and lows. It's not just the shared memories, it's the quiet understanding, the unwavering support that she's come to rely on. Molly often finds herself feeling grateful for it, for this kind of friendship is a rare gift, something that has shaped their lives.

When Emma returns from ordering and is settled again, Molly asks, "How are things with you and Richard?"

"Ok, I guess. He is making an effort; I should really appreciate that. But I'm not sure I feel the same way about him anymore."

Molly is almost pleased to hear this, given she has seen Richard again. Not that's she's too pleased with herself right now. He had worn her down with many more calls and texts and she was flattered by the chase, he chased her until she succumbed. She had to admit she was enjoying their sexual trysts, making her want it even more because it was taboo. This was the thrilling part, the scheming and hiding made the sex all the more tantalising. The fact she wasn't fond of Richard in a sexual way was perplexing though. He had somehow fooled her by his flattery and she had reacted in a primal way. Not that they had seen each other often, it was only twice more so far. But the guilt she felt about hurting Emma and David is making her have second thoughts. "I'm sorry to hear that. Look, why don't we do a girls' getaway? Maybe some time away will clear your thoughts."

"Good idea. Let's go somewhere fun, maybe Fiji? It will be like old times."

Molly wasn't thinking of going that far away, but then thought they could do with more than a weekend away. They both had things to think about. Molly especially wants to get Richard out of her system before Emma, or anyone else, finds out. With trusting Emma sitting in front of her, Molly needs to finish whatever this is with Richard.

TWENTY-SIX

Emma

SHE UPLOADS the photo onto her Instagram account and tags Molly. It's the second day of their holiday away from everyone. She looks towards the pacific as Molly comes out of the aquamarine water. Her friend is not glamorous, but she has a confident style, an air of being happy in her skin. Molly is an everyday person, relatable. Emma can't imagine her life without Molly in it.

Molly had booked them seven days in Fiji, and they planned to fill each day with sunning themselves, swimming, eating, drinking and lulling the days away.

"Oh look, the likes are coming in already."

Molly grabs the towel off the beach lounge and wraps it around herself. "Emma, we said no social posts, remember?"

"Calm down, it's the one from last night. We both look fabulous," she says showing Molly the post. She doesn't look impressed, so Emma says, "Ok, that's the only one I'll post, I promise."

"Thanks. We're here to chill and forget about home, so that

means no posting, it takes time away from us enjoying ourselves. Now, where's my drink?"

The waiter had taken both their drinks away as the ice had melted rendering them tasteless. "I ordered two more," says Emma explaining.

"Ok, thanks. You should go in, the water is warm and the little fish nibble at your feet as you go in. The warm water kept me in there."

"Yuk, are you for real? Fish nibbling your feet, that sounds gross. No, I'm enjoying this sunshine for now." The waiter arrives with their drinks and the snacks Emma had ordered. "Thanks," she says to the waiter. "It's amazing how hungry you get lying around all day."

Molly laughs and keeps staring out to the water. Emma asks her if something is bothering her. "Me? No, what makes you think that?"

"You seem far away and not as chatty as usual."

"Am I? I guess I'm slowly relaxing into this holiday. It takes me a few days to come down from all the stress."

"Hmm, ok, but if you need to talk about it, I'm here." Molly doesn't answer and this piques Emma's interest. Molly always confides in her. She decides to let this slide for now, taking in the beautiful surroundings of this paradise they find themselves in.

DINNER IS NEARLY OVER, and Molly has left the table leaving her phone upside down on it. After a few minutes the phone chimes and Emma calls over to Molly as she returns from the toilet. "Your phone is ringing."

When Molly arrives, she picks up her phone. Her face drops, colour seeping out of it.

"What? Is everything ok?"

"Yes ... no. Sorry, I have to return this call. Meet you back at the room, ok?"

Emma can't believe this is her friend speaking to her with such fear in her voice. "Molly, are you in trouble? Let me help you."

Molly changes her tune suddenly, "What? No, of course not. It's Samantha wanting to discuss an issue with Tim's birthday, that's all. No need for you to hear her whinging about the organisation of it."

Not convinced, Emma agrees to meet Molly back in their room and watches on as Molly walks towards the bar with her phone at her ear.

Back in the room, Emma phones Richard but he's engaged. She doesn't bother leaving a message, he'll call her back when he's ready.

A few minutes later, Molly comes into the room with a smile on her face. "Well, that's all sorted. I have one happy niece now," chirps Molly as she flops onto the bed.

Before Emma can answer, her phone rings. "Hi, just a minute," she says into the phone. "It's Richard, I'll take this on the balcony." Walking out, she smells the damp sea air and looks over the water with the moon lighting it up in a diminishing line towards the horizon. Richard asks how the holiday is going so far, "It's nice to be away but Molly is worrying me."

"Oh really?" asks Richard with concern. Emma explains how quiet she is and doesn't seem like herself. "Well then, she's in the perfect place to contemplate whatever is going on."

"I'm worried Richard, she's unusually quiet."

They continue talking with Richard allaying Emma's mind. "Molly has been through some stuff lately, you know, with the abduction, maybe she just wants to chill."

"You're probably right, that abduction fiasco was harrowing. But then, it was a while ago" Emma listens as Richard continues to appease her worries telling her to enjoy the time with her friend.

Walking back into the room, Molly is flicking stations on the television. "How's Richard?"

"Uh, oh fine. He told us to enjoy ourselves, which we're doing right?"

Molly beams at Emma remaining quiet. Emma decides to take this as a positive.

. . .

EMMA WALKS towards the cabana at the adult's only pool to find Molly with her nose in a book. "Good morning, you were up early."

"Couldn't sleep so went for a run." Emma nods and proceeds to take off her sundress and starts applying more sunscreen. Molly's phone rings just as she's about to make conversation.

"I'll go for a walk so I'm not disturbing you. This is work."

"Sure," says Emma wondering why work is calling Molly when they know she's here for a well-earned break. Molly is back quickly and makes herself comfortable again.

"Why is work calling? Didn't you tell them to deal with stuff on their own?"

"It was Sophia confirming something, nothing major."

"Well, if it wasn't important, she should not have bothered you."

"Emma, what is up with you? Is there anything else you'd like to complain about? Sophia called me to check about an interview that has been rescheduled, why is that a problem?"

"Calm down, I'm looking out for you, that's all. We're supposed to be leaving work and everything behind us this week remember?"

Molly doesn't answer. Picking up her book again, she clears her throat and reads.

Emma is hurt but leaves her thoughts to herself. Standing up, she dives into the cool, aqua water. Coming up at the other end of the pool, she moves to the infinity waterfall placing her arms on the ledge and stares out to the calm sea. Silent tears well in her eyes but she breathes deeply and doesn't let them shed. Molly is bothered by something, and Emma knows it, but unless she wants to talk about it, there is nothing Emma can do. She moves to the other wall and does a few laps, letting out her frustration with each stroke.

Coming out of the pool, she pats herself down with the towel. Molly has gone leaving her book face down and her phone next to it. Emma sits on the lounger pondering whether she should say anything when Molly returns. This is not like her easy-going friend;

she isn't even interested in partying and that's what they came to Fiji to do. Who doesn't party on a girls' getaway?

After Emma has made herself comfortable, Molly returns with drinks and fruit. "That run made me hungry. Help yourself, the pineapple is so sweet."

"Thanks," says Emma taking a piece. The mood change is obvious, and this makes Emma feel better. "So, what shall we do this afternoon? Maybe a massage?"

"Oh, yes. Let's book it. We can ask the waiter when he comes to collect these," says Molly indicating the plates and glasses.

Emma smiles and breathes a sigh of relief. Molly is back to her usual self. She hopes.

TWENTY-SEVEN

Richard

HE'S WAITING at arrivals and spots Molly. "Over here," he calls. Molly pulls her suitcase towards where Richard is standing. He kisses her cheek. "Good holiday?"

"Yes, thanks. Emma should be here in a minute, she's collecting her duty free she bought before we left."

"Are you ok? Emma called me worried about you."

"All good. I was feeling a little guilty about what we did and being with Emma brought it all into focus."

Richard places his hand on Molly's arm saying, "Stop worrying, no one knows about that. Remember you're teaching me about Tantric, it's what I asked you to do."

Molly looks at him baffled, "Richard, it's still sex and we're cheating on our partners. It doesn't matter how you spin it, it's still wrong."

Richard is about to answer when Emma comes up behind him. "Hi."

He turns abruptly taking his hand off Molly's arm, "Hi, babe. Welcome home." He bends kissing her lightly on the lips, "Missed you."

Emma smiles at him then looks towards Molly, "What's up now, you look lost? And you two were deep in conversation."

"Were we? Richard was just welcoming me home."

"Well then, let's take you home, Molly. I'm sure David has missed you too."

EMMA HAS BEEN SURLY since arriving back yesterday morning and Richard is fed up. She isn't giving him a reason as to why. "What is up with you, didn't you have a good holiday?" Maybe something happened between her and Molly?

She turns to look at him from the armchair, her face dour and condescending. "Nothing, just tired." She proceeds to keep reading. This is what she has been doing since breakfast this morning. Richard had stayed with her overnight, they had enjoyed a lovely night together, albeit Emma having been quiet. That quiet has continued.

"Right then, I'm going out. You enjoy your own company." He is sick of trying to find out what is up with her. Richard leaves his phone and car keys on the arm of the lounge as he walks towards the bathroom. The phone pings as he walks away.

Emma looks over casually to see a text from Molly. See you soon xx

Stunned she picks up the phone and confronts Richard. "You bastard, are you seeing Molly?"

Richard turns from washing his hands in the bathroom sink and is about to answer when he is confronted with his phone and Molly's text. "Emma, it's not what you think, it's about us improving our relationship."

"No, you prick. It is what I think, and we agreed to never again discuss what happened at that Australia Day party. Get out!"

"I was leaving anyway, but let me tell you ..."

"Out!"

Emma's face is a fury of anger, so he decides to leave and let her cool down. They can discuss this later. Once outside her townhouse, he flags down a taxi and heads to his apartment to change.

MOLLY HAD ASKED him to meet in the city and he finds her in the back corner of a café in Pitt Street Mall. He bends to kiss her cheek, but she moves abruptly. "Oh, for fucks sake not you too."

She hands him a menu, "What would you like?"

"Uh, just a long black, thanks." He is mortified that the two women he likes to be with the most are both acting strange towards him. *What the hell happened in Fiji?*

Molly calls the waiter over and orders. Once he leaves, she clears her throat and stares into Richard's eyes, "I can't do this anymore. The guilt is eating me up."

Richard is perplexed. He says, "But we've only been together a few more times since that night, there is more I want to learn."

Frustration is showing on Molly's face as she shakes her head. "You can learn by watching YouTube videos, like I told you when you first asked. I'm not prepared to risk my friendship with Emma any longer. Nor my relationship with David."

He thinks about the text that Emma saw, the friendship may already be at risk. "You've made up your mind then?"

"Richard, be reasonable please. This will hurt Emma and David if they find out, I can't continue. We can go back to being friends and you need to repair your relationship with Emma."

He thought his relationship with Emma was going quite smoothly until they went away, but obviously Molly knows something he doesn't. "Did something happen in Fiji?"

"What do you mean?"

"Well, both you and Emma are treating me like shit right now. What the hell have I done wrong?"

Molly scoffs, "You're unbelievable. You've been having a thing with me, Emma's best friend. I'm not even sure what to call what we are doing. But what you ... what we're doing is wrong. And, nothing happened in Fiji, I was quieter than usual, and Emma picked up on that."

Richard knows not to argue because as much as he sees this thing with Molly as a learning exercise, they are cheating on their partners. He is about to answer when Molly's phone pings. She holds it up for him to see.

Leave Richard the fuck alone.

"Oh, for Christ's sake, Richard. How does she know? Did you tell Emma already?"

His face burns red in an unusual fit of embarrassment. Richard is tough and doesn't do embarrassment, but Emma seeing Molly's text earlier, well, it's embarrassing and stupid at the same time. "She ... well, um, she saw your text just before I left her apartment."

"You idiot, how could you let that happen?"

"It doesn't matter how it happened. She knows. I'd better go and try to appease her; she basically threw me out of her place. Hopefully, she has calmed down and will see reason."

Molly waits until he stands up. "She had better because I don't want to lose her friendship."

As he walks out of the café, he thinks that maybe she should have thought of that before she agreed to have sex with him.

HE STANDS at the front of her townhouse and hesitates before pressing the intercom. He hears the click, but Emma remains silent. "Please let me in." His voice is weak and full of remorse. Sweat drips from his brow as he waits. The door releases and he walks in.

He finds her in the kitchen preparing a cup of tea and asks, "Do you want to talk about this?"

"No, you screwed my best friend. Not much more to say is there?"

Richard tries to remain calm and decides not to let this escalate.

He will explain the reason behind what he and Molly did, and their relationship will be repaired. "Well ... I was just interested ... come on, you enjoyed that night as much as I did. That's why I asked Molly to teach me about Tantric sex. I wanted to know more so we could enjoy the practise together."

"How righteous of you. Please ... that is the weakest excuse for cheating I've ever heard."

"Emma, it's not an excuse, it's the truth. I'm not attracted to Molly like I ... look, I love you and I'm sorry I've hurt you. Please talk to me."

Richard hopes his grovelling helps but Emma is still furious and yells at him to go home and leave her alone. "I don't want to see your face around here anymore. I hate you, you cheating prick. Now get out."

He thinks about trying to reason with her and as she storms out of the kitchen, he follows her, but she slams her bedroom door in his face. He is shattered. He keeps his open palm on the door for a few minutes then whispers, "You win. Bye Emma."

TWENTY-EIGHT

Molly

SHE KEEPS SITTING in the café for some time after Richard leaves. His whole body was slack with remorse and Molly's heart was breaking for him. But ... she is sorry she had agreed to his request and sorry that Emma may never forgive her. She indicates to the waiter and when he arrives at her table she orders a double-shot espresso and a piece of cheesecake. Knowing she is eating out of emotional stress, she devours the cake and drinks the espresso in one go. Throwing some cash onto the table, she gives a generous tip. She leaves with anger surging through her veins and heads back home.

As she drives, she thinks about whether she should call Emma. She wants to apologise and explain her actions before this becomes too big an issue. She can hear her phone pinging but ignores it until she arrives home.

"That bitch!"

"Molly is that you?" asks David as he pops his head into the hallway. "Everything ok?"

Ignoring Emma's text for now, Molly walks towards him and gives him a tight hug. "Hi, no not really. Umm, I need to tell you something." She waits until he sits on the lounge, then she sits next to him and explains what she and Richard had done.

Tears pool in her eyes as she avoids David's shocked eyes. "I'm so sorry, I don't even know why I did it. I'm such an idiot and I know I've hurt you. And Emma too. Fuck." Molly eyes shed tears when she finishes speaking, her body goes limp with utter disgust.

David had held her hand since she sat next to him. He lets go of it and stands up, brushing his hand through his hair. Apprehensive, he asks, "I can't believe it, you don't even like the guy. What were you thinking?" His voice is strained, the hurt seeping through it.

"I don't have an excuse because it was a moment of bad judgement. I'm so very sorry."

"Bad judgement? Three times! Or was it more? I'm so disappointed in you Molly. Of all people ... Richard. Bloody. Penser."

Molly sits with her head hanging, tears are dripping onto her hands. "I'm not proud of what I've done, and the worst is I've hurt you."

"Yes, you bloody well have. And Emma too." David's voice is low and frustrated. He walks backwards and forwards in the few paces it takes in their tiny lounge room. He is about to say something again then stops. Molly can see the frustration and sheer hurt on his face, it's almost like he's aged in the time she has told him.

Molly's tears swell into aching sobs, "I'm so sorry, David. Please forgi ... forgive me."

"You're asking too much. Not now, I ... you need to leave me alone for a while." David's voice cracks as he walks out and grabs the dog leash from the hall stand. She hears the front door slam as he and Bono leave.

She stays on the lounge allowing her sobs to subside. She is spent and looks for her phone. Finding it, she rereads Emma's message – Don't even think about contacting me. Both you and Richard are not welcome in my life from now on.

Finding Emma's number, she thinks about texting her an apology, but then stops. It doesn't feel right to say sorry via text. Especially after the message Emma has sent.

Deciding to have a bath, Molly walks into the bathroom and runs the water. Finding a bath bomb, she adds it to the water. Fresh, aromatic scents begin to chase her nose as she breathes them in. The stress is overwhelming, and she hopes this bath will ease her emotions. She dips her toe in and adds more cold water. Stepping in, she sinks into the warm water tinged with flecks of gold from the melted bath bomb. She breathes in the fragrance and dips her head under the water. Gasping as she slides her head up the backside of the bath, she breathes out the breath she had held whilst under water.

IT'S 9pm and David still has not returned home with Bono. Molly checks her phone but there are no other messages. She starts typing a text to him, then deletes it. What's the point? He has to come home soon; Bono will be hungry.

Staring at her phone, she decides to call Emma. She waits, but it rings out. Not surprising, Emma meant what she said. But Molly lives in hope, so she texts her anyway; Emma please call me I want to explain why I did … why Richard and I did this. Although Molly doesn't expect a response, she flatly refuses to give up on their friendship, it's too special to throw away.

She is making a cup of tea when David returns. Bono bounds over to her and she pats him absentmindedly. She hears David walk down the hall to their bedroom. He won't be in the mood to talk tonight.

MOLLY HAS FINISHED FILMING another two shows and heads to her office for a break. It's been a week since the text from Emma and Molly has called and texted her every day. Richard had called because he received the same message. His attitude was that if that's how Emma felt, then he'd had enough of trying to deal with her, she's an emotional load he doesn't want to try and appease. This made Molly sad as Emma needed someone after Trevor's passing and she could do worse than have someone like Richard. Deep down he loved Emma. *Fuck, I should have known things would end this way.*

Sighing deeply, she checks her phone again, but Emma hasn't responded. Molly has to find another way to reach her.

TWENTY-NINE

Emma

SHE IS READING YET another text from Molly. A part of her wants to answer because she misses her friend, but Molly ruined it by shagging Richard. Emma can't forgive Molly and what she doesn't understand is that Molly doesn't even like Richard in that way. Sure, she had mentioned at times how attractive he was, but to go this far? Why do it and hurt the two people she loves the most? Or did she harbour a secret desire for him? He is a man who is suave and commands power, something many women find alluring. She wonders whether Molly has told David yet. Because he will find out soon enough.

Emma is not going to let this slide, she will ruin Molly and Richard.

Opening her laptop, she opens the photos app and begins adding photos of the three of them into a folder she has named, 'Demise of M & R'. Emma has a plan to devastate both of her ex-friends, and the fans will have their say.

. . .

THE NEXT MORNING, Emma wakes to three hundred notifications on both Instagram and Twitter. Before going to bed last night, she had posted a photo of the three of them to both platforms saying – *These two are no longer my friends.*

The photo is from an event they attended a few years ago. They are all smiles and the best of friends. Anger seeps through Emma again as she reads through the comments.

Richard – Emma, WTF. Really?

Molly – Oh no! Why did you do this, Emma?

Friends – Emma, no! What has happened? What is going on? Are you ok?

Fans – What is going on Emma?

Is your relationship with Richard over? What has Molly done? Emma, I'm your friend.

Noooo Emma, Molly and Richard have betrayed you?

Those fuckers, you're too good for them.

Emma, you're better than both of them, they are trash. Fuck them.

Most of the comments are positive towards Emma and hating on Molly and Richard. This allays her anger and is what she had hoped would happen. She knew fans had discussed whether she and Richard were an item, but neither she nor Richard ever confirmed or denied it. She throws the covers off and heads to the bathroom. Work is going to be interesting today.

THE MINUTE EMMA walks out of the lift the receptionists both ask her what has happened. "Keep watching the socials, all will be revealed," she says as she saunters up the stairs to her office. Richard is waiting for her there. "Get out."

"Emma don't do this. Don't drag this out for everyone to comment on. It's career suicide."

"For you and Molly. That's what I'm aiming for. Now get out."

She yells this more than she intends, and Richard is stunned into silence.

As he walks out, he says, "Emma, you have no idea who you're dealing with. If you keep posting like this, be prepared."

She laughs inwardly, he should have thought of that before screwing her best friend. Of course, she's prepared for a fight. And she is determined to win. Her phone rings and Molly's number appears. She flips her phone over and lets it ring out. She already knows what her next post is going to say.

SHE'S in bed with her laptop open picking another photo. She edits it, removing herself and leaving Molly laughing with Richard. This one is actually from the Australia Day party, which is fitting. She opens Instagram and sees a post from Richard. It was posted only two minutes ago and already the comments were up to fifty.

Richard had posted a photo of a wedding they had attended together captioned with – *To think I was thinking of doing this again. Your loss Emma.*

They were standing either side of the bride and groom. The comments were similar to the ones on her post, fans wanting to know what is going on. This time there is no comment from Molly. And she hadn't posted since before the Fiji holiday, not even anything about the orphanage. This wasn't like Molly, maybe her little lackey who looks after her social accounts is dropping the ball.

Emma pushes on with her own post and captions it – *These two betrayed me.*

She watches as the comments begin within seconds of her posting. Her fans are all praising her and offering to help. Many are saying they will stop following Molly and Richard. She is touched but doubts this will happen because they will want to know all the juicy gossip that this is going to generate. Everyone loves celebrity gossip and spats, and this one is already a doozy.

Over the next few days, Emma and Richard go head-to-head with scathing posts.

You bitch, she is your best friend.

Was my best friend. And you're no longer welcome in my life. Fuck off.

With pleasure. Molly and I don't deserve this shit.

The comments from fans urge Emma to post even more.

Fuck them both, Emma. You deserve better.

You go Emma.

That bitch, she is no friend of yours.

Emma you're doing the right thing.

THIRTY

Molly

SHE IS WATCHING the crisis unfold on Instagram and Twitter on a daily basis. Neither Emma nor Richard has actually come out and said that Molly and Richard had a thing. She refuses to call it *an affair*, but it's obvious to everyone following what has happened. Calling what they did an affair is a bit of a stretch. She was helping him with his knowledge of Tantric Sex so he and Emma could improve their own sex life. Even thinking this makes her feel shallow. Still, it wasn't an affair. Should she mention this when she eventually posts something? Maybe not, who will believe her.

Walking into the kitchen, David is finishing his breakfast before leaving for work. He nods but keeps quiet. Things have not improved between them, but at least he acknowledges her now. "David, I have to show you something."

"Not now, I'll be late for work."

"This will only take a minute," she says handing him her phone. "Scroll through Emma's posts."

David spends a few seconds looking through Emma's feed and then hands the phone back to Molly. "You're problem. You caused it. Both you and Richard."

"This affects you too, David." She may as well be talking to the wall as David leaves ignoring her. Bono jumps up and places his paws on the kitchen bench. Molly cups his face with both hands placing her forehead on his head. "Oh Bono, what have I done."

A FEW HOURS later Molly is deep in thought about this whole mess when Sophia walks into her office, "You need to deal with this before it gets out of hand."

"Good morning to you too."

Sophia pulls a chair closer to Molly's desk, "I'm serious, this is a scandal and fans are having a field day. There needs to be a 'Team Molly'."

"You are serious, aren't you? I was hoping it would all blow over soon if I kept out of it."

"Molly, fans are already talking shit about you, you need to tell your side of the story. Was it an affair you were having with Richard."

"No, I wouldn't call it that, but it doesn't matter now. I don't want to discuss it."

"Fair enough but you need to sort this out. It's a bad career move to let it slide."

Molly has seen the posts Sophia is referring to and Harold had told her the same thing. Fans will want to know more and she needs to deal with all the fallout.

Sophia continues, "I'm not judging but this is not like you Molly and it's something you need to fix if you value your career.

"Ok Sophia, I'll post something later. I'll have Evan come up with some ideas." As Sophia walks out of her office Molly knows she was being judgemental, but she is right, if Molly does nothing then this situation will only get worse.

Molly sighs, this is a mess she needs to clean up. She misses talking to and seeing Emma, but one good thing has come out of this, Richard is completely out of her system.

EVAN IS SITTING opposite her in her home office. They have been working on a strategy to combat what is happening with Emma and Richard's fight on social media. She asked him not to go overboard, she only wants a few posts to put her side of the story out there, this daily fight between Emma and Richard is depressing.

"So, I'll schedule these four posts for the next four weeks, one per week. You agree the apology one should go first."

Molly nods and rereads it again wanting to make sure is sounds sincere.

Photo: Molly and Emma on the beach at their recent holiday.

What is happening between Emma and myself (and Richard) was not meant to be played out on social media. I have attempted many times to apologise to Emma and do so again here. Please Emma, I miss you, let's put this behind us. Talk to me off these platforms. Remember all the good times we've had together.

"Evan, it's the best I can do under the circumstances. Place them up on the dates we've agreed to, and we'll see what happens."

"Sure. You know you did need to respond, this was not going away on its own. You're doing the right thing for *you* now." He stands and picks up his laptop, "I'll leave you to it. I'm catching up with Samantha later, I'll say hi for you."

"Oh, lovely, please do. And thanks, I know you have better things to do on a Saturday morning, your help is appreciated." She says this as she sees him out. Closing the front door, she leans against it and blows out a huge breath. *This had better work because I have no other ideas on how to fix this stupid situation.*

WAKING, she stretches and then picks up her phone. She sees David has already left, he doesn't bother to wake her, he is still hurt about what she has done. Even though she has apologised and told him she will never do anything so stupid again, he only speaks to her if necessary. They are living like two strangers; she feels like she is invisible to him. He might come around in time and time is all she can hope for when it comes to this relationship.

Sitting up, she looks at her phone. The notifications from Instagram and Twitter have gone ballistic, she and Emma are trending. She opens Instagram first and looks at her DMs.

Richard – I've tried apologising too.

Samantha – I'm sorry this has happened, hope it resolves soon.

Tim – Molly, call me whenever you need to.

Then she looks at comments from her fans and followers -

Molly she is not worth having as a friend. If she truly was your friend, she would talk to you.

Accept Molly's apology Emma.

People make mistakes, Emma grow up.

Fuck her and her petty issues, Molly.

You're better than her Molly.

A few were negative -

You did the wrong thing, what do you expect?

Accept you are in the wrong, Molly. If you and Richard expected anything different from Emma, you were wrong.

Then she opens Twitter, and the comments are similar. Reading as many as she can, and answering some of them, she feels some relief that most of the comments are positive towards her. There are fans who are being horrible and brutal to Emma with many calling Richard a tool along with other disparaging terms. Some people are calling Molly awful things as well. Sighing she hopes to convince both Emma and Richard to come off the socials and the three of them talk like sensible adults. The problem is getting them to agree, especially Emma.

Getting up she notices her phone battery is low and plugs it in. She might leave it there, so she won't see all this shit that is happening while at work. Heading to the bathroom, she screams out in frustration, her body shaking with rage. Bono runs in wondering what is going on. He barks and tilts his head to the side. "Oh, darling Bono, I'm fine," she says bending down to give him a cuddle. "At least you still love me."

Once ready, she collects her keys and heads out the door. Her phone is ringing on her bedside table, but it's too late, she is already in the car.

SITTING AT HER DESK, her desk phone is flashing, there are messages. Picking up the receiver she listens to them. Three are from Richard and two are fans. The person she wants desperately to hear from is still ignoring her. "Hi, you called?"

"Good morning, Molly. I did, I saw your post and wanted to know if you can meet me for lunch? We need to fix things and stop this ridiculous battle for everyone to comment on."

"I agree, Richard. Can we do tomorrow? I have a catchup interview to do so won't have time today. Do you think Emma will join us?"

"We can both send her a message, but I doubt she will turn up. Her posts are relentless, and people are enjoying her character assignations of us."

Molly doesn't answer right away as she tries to compose herself. Richard is right, Emma is being brutal to both of them and the gossip columnists are lapping this up. "She is angry, and I understand, but if she would just see reason. Yes, we did the wrong thing but it's over."

"I've told her, Molly. She refuses to believe that I was doing it to help our relationship. As much as I enjoyed being with you, my ultimate aim was to please Emma."

She smirks at how ridiculous that statement is. "We've betrayed her Richard, and this has hurt her as well as David. He's still not talking to me and that hurts as much as Emma not talking to me. We were stupid to think this wasn't going to hurt the people we love. I'll see you tomorrow at the pub and hopefully Emma will show up."

"Yes, ok. See you at one?"

"Aha, meet you there."

She places the phone down after saying goodbye and heads to the studio to start her day. But she feels more like walking the other way, exiting the building then going to find a more peaceful life out of the limelight.

THIRTY-ONE

Molly

SHE WALKS BACK into the hall after having driven home to change ready for Tim's party. She and Samantha had been setting up Tim's birthday bash. David had declined to come, and although she understands why, she still wishes he would put what she did aside for the sake of Tim. Samantha is also disappointed he isn't coming because they are best pals. "It won't be the same without David," she had said. Well, this is how things are right now and Molly must live with the fact that of the two people she loves most won't be there tonight. David and Emma are MIA from her life, something she hopes will change in future.

The band is playing some chilled tunes as the hall fills with family and friends. Many of Tim's friends came from Bali, the USA and Europe to celebrate his 40th birthday. There is laughter and much drinking going on with Molly looking forward to chatting with many of them, they had been away for years and there will be a lot to catch up on.

· · ·

BY 10.30PM EVERYONE is happily drunk or stoned, the cake had been cut and Tim had worn most of it courtesy of his friends. A cake and food fight had started much to everyone's delight. Tim was still wiping his face and laughing. Samantha was pleased to see her father having a great time.

"Thanks for all your help with this, Aunt Molly. Wasn't Dad surprised?" Samantha is wiping cake off her face too.

"Yes, he had no idea, did he? It was my pleasure to help, and in the end, it wasn't too difficult to keep it away from your dad, everyone played their part and didn't say a word."

"I know. That's what has made it such a special night." Samantha sways and holds onto the wall to steady herself.

Molly had already propped herself up on the wall, she had drunk way more than she needed too. But she was drowning her sorrows so she wouldn't spoil Tim's night. He had hugged her more than once tonight saying she was the best sister and how much he *loooved* her.

The band is playing INXS songs and there are a few people on the dance floor. Evan comes over and asks Samantha to dance leaving Molly on her own. She slinks down onto the floor and pulls her phone out of her bag that she had slung over her shoulder. Opening Instagram there are more posts from Emma, but one catches her eye more than the others.

The photo is an old one from when they met all those years ago.

I miss my friend.

But I want the one that I trusted, not the bitch who had it off with Richard who was supposed to be mine.

Molly is horrified. Emma has put it out there, the thing Richard and she did. The fact she and Richard had been together. This made it all the more real. Mentioning the reason for this fight is the last straw. This is war and Emma is going to regret pushing Molly to the limit.

. . .

THE NEXT DAY she is in her kitchen and has no idea where David is. Deciding not to worry about him for now, she opens her phone. Evan has emailed her more ideas to post. She picks two of them and posts one on each platform. Two other ideas he sent are too scathing for her to post, but she will keep them in case they are required. She is amazed at how the younger generation can feel comfortable saying the most awful things online. Would they say the same things to the person's face?

Photo: Angry dog

Who won't let go of a petty fight? You say you miss me but then you announce to the world what Richard and I did? It wasn't a full-blown affair and you know why we did what we did. Richard explained it to you many times. You bitch, this is war.

#teammolly #mollywins #bitchfest

Photo: Molly with a sad face emoji gif.

Emma, this is how you're making me feel. I'm sad you won't speak to me or accept my apology. But if you keep going with this fight, I'll crush you.

#teammolly #mollywins #bitchfest

When she finishes posting, she checks Emma's posts. The anger spilling from them takes Molly by surprise, but she knows it is she and Richard who are at fault. Still, it betrays belief that Emma has forgotten all the good things about their friendship because of one stupid mistake. How long is this going on for? It has been three months now and there seems to be no stopping Emma and her tirade.

One good thing is that Richard has given up posting. He texted Molly last month saying this was a fight between two people, he was just the third wheel. Besides, he doesn't think Emma will ever want to see him again and things are awkward at the station. He has started looking for other work. When Richard had sent that text, Molly called him.

"You're looking at changing stations? I guess things are too much there, are they?"

"It's impossible, Molly. We see each other every day and we're fighting on social media like enemies. I can't take it anymore. I'm looking at moving interstate, I don't care where I work as long as I don't have to see Emma on a daily basis."

"Richard, I'm sorry it has come to this. Were you really thinking of marrying Emma?"

"I was going to ask her on my birthday. Well, that has passed and there is no chance of it ever happening now. Look, I know she didn't come that day we met at the pub but at least you and I are trying to be in a better place. I appreciate you being there even if we did get heckled."

"It was awkward, but I'm with you, you and I are back to being friends and that's how I like it. Now all I want is to be friends with Emma again."

"Good luck with that, she doesn't seem to want to stop this, and you've upped the ante now."

"I know. I'm losing both David and Emma ..." She stops as tears begin to flow.

"Let it out, Molly. And I'm #teammolly all the way."

Molly sniffs, "Thanks. Somehow, I thought you'd be #teamemma, but she has blasted you as much as me."

"Yes, which is why I'm leaving. As soon as a job comes up, I'm out of here. Scott can stay in my apartment, and I'll visit. Maybe catch up with you when I'm in town?"

Molly is shocked he is basically running away but then again, she feels like doing that too. "That will be nice, Richard. Good luck with looking for the job you want." She had clicked off the call and checked her socials before making herself dinner. The #teammolly hashtag is trending.

A FEW DAYS later David is sitting on the lounge watching the football. He has a beer in his hand and looks up when she walks in.

"We need to talk."

"Fine. Talk."

Well, at least he answered her, this is a plus. "I'm thinking of going to India, travel has opened up again now. There are things I need to do over there, and I haven't seen the orphans for three years."

He doesn't answer immediately, and she can sense he is thinking about what she has said. "So, you're leaving me. And Bono."

"I haven't decided when I will return, but no, I'm not leaving you. I love you, David. That hasn't changed. But things at work have deteriorated, the show is losing viewers and guests are refusing to come. It's heartbreaking and I need a break from all of this. You're welcome to come and visit if you like."

"Me come to India? I don't think so. Besides I have Bono to consider."

She hadn't expected that he say yes, but the invitation stood in case he changed his mind. "I understand, you know where I'll be and are welcome if time permits." That sounded so formal, but lately she had felt David was a stranger, their relationship was hanging on by a thread.

"So, what's happening with the show?"

"I was hauled into the CEO's office and told they will place *Daytime* on hiatus pending what happens with this fight Emma and I are having. Apparently, the same thing is happening with Emma's show. We're both losing out."

"I'm sorry to hear that, Molly, but what did you expect?"

"Yeah, well, the gossip columnists are still having fun with it and the station's Board is not pleased. The trip to India will help clear my head and I hope you'll be here when I return."

David looks at her, his eyes filling with tears. "I can't promise that right now."

Molly stifles a gasp and walks out. By the time she reaches her bedroom, her face is wet with big fat tears.

THIRTY-TWO

The Fallout Explodes

THE WEEKLY EXAMINER, The Heraldist, The Sydney Cove News ... all these media outlets' gossip columnists are having a field day reacting to the #teammolly and #teamemma debacle. Online and in print, the fight between Molly and Emma is escalating. Richard is now out of the picture, conveniently for him.

Molly had been asked by each paper to comment but she flatly refused to be interviewed. This meant some gossip columnists had taken Molly's posts out of context and embellished their stories to the point of them being *click bait*. Emma, on the other hand had accepted to be interviewed and made more scathing comments about her ex-friends. It all added fuel to the fire in the explosion that was their dying friendship.

As she walks into the lounge after arriving from work, she sees David on his iPad ignoring the TV news ...

... host of *Daytime* on Shine TV and her friend, now ex-friend, Emma Beers Jones of *Evening with Emma* fame, are having a very public fight over the social media platforms Instagram and Twitter. As the fight goes on with #teammolly and #teamemma hashtags trending for months now, both hosts have had their shows cancelled.

Molly turns the television off slamming the remote onto the coffee table and storms into the kitchen. David remains quiet, which is expected, but she is craving his support, especially as she is leaving for India soon. She texts Richard about the news story and he quickly answers saying every news show is featuring it except Shine TV. It's obvious to Molly why they're staying away from it. Richard is glad he stopped posting when he did, Emma was determined to ruin his reputation and Molly's. She stares at her phone screen; Emma has ruined their careers already. Richard has run away to a second-rate station in Queensland and now Molly will be running away to India. Emma has won.

THE NEXT MORNING, Molly wakes to more messages and posts on her socials. Many are from fans, which she appreciates because they are keeping #teammolly trending. But it is Emma's posts that hurt her the most. This hurt seeps through every muscle in her body, the exhaustion caused by this is affecting her daily life.

Evan has kept Molly's posts up, but these are more apologetic than scathing. Emma is attacking Molly personally but has let up on attacking Richard. Looking up from her phone she sees David has left and it's only six. He seems to leave earlier every morning now. The sadness grips her body with a ferocious thump, tears flow easily. She has cried every morning since Emma's first post.

Molly hasn't stopped trying to contact Emma to talk face to face. She had also tried before Richard left wanting the three of them to talk as adults. It had been futile because Emma didn't return any messages or calls. Sighing and wiping her eyes, she walks to the bath-room and wets her face with cold water. Bono is watching on waiting for his breakfast. "It's still early, Bono. Come on we can go for a walk before we both eat. That will cheer us up."

Placing her pods into her ears, Molly decides to listen to a podcast, something funny to take her mind off everything. This morning she is walking the opposite way from the dog park because she isn't in the mood to socialise with whoever might be there this early. She is only half listening to the podcast, her mind going over the things she still has left to do before going to India. This is happening in two weeks.

She is stopped in her tracks when an advertisement for her local paper hits her ears. They are promoting their top stories and one of them is about #teammolly and #teamemma. *For fuck's sake, I can't even escape the crap that is happening while listening to a podcast.* Deciding to return home, she rips the pods out of her ears not wanting to hear anything more. "Come on Bono, time for breakfast I guess." They had walked for all of fifteen minutes.

AN HOUR LATER, Molly is on her computer in her home office. She is talking to Tim and Samantha about her plans for India. They are videoing and Molly can see that Tim is not pleased with her decision.

"Honestly, Sis, you're risking a lot by leaving like this. David won't wait around you know, what if your stay is extended? I know what you're like when you're over there, you lose track of time."

"Thanks for your support too, Tim. Honestly, it's bad enough David is ignoring me, I was expecting more from you."

They continue arguing when Samantha butts in. "Will you two stop. You sound like teenagers placing blame on each other. Dad, Molly has to do this, and I think it will do her good. If she and David are meant to be together, they will be."

"Thanks, Samantha, at least you're on my side."

"I'm sorry your life has played out on social media, Aunt Molly. It really is the worst when everyone knows your business in this way. Go to India and do what needs to be done then come home with your wounds healed."

Molly thinks how profound this is from someone so young. However, Samantha has had to grow up fast since losing her mum and she does look after Tim, not that he will admit that. "I appreciate that, Samantha, it's sweet of you to say."

"I have to go," says Tim, "but I'm happy to take you to the airport if you need me too, just let me know."

"I think David will take me, but thanks for the offer. If he changes his mind, I'll text you."

"Ok, take care, Molly. You know I love you."

"I do, thanks Tim. I love both of you. Talk soon." She clicks off the video app on her computer and walks out to the kitchen. Tim's attitude is still bothering her, she thought of all people he would have her back. Taking a wine glass from the cupboard, she fills it with the left-over merlot. Taking a sip, she moves to the lounge. Sitting down she guzzles the wine in two gulps. Placing the empty glass on the coffee table, she lies down and after fluffing the cushion, she starts to nap. All this kerfuffle is exhausting.

THIRTY-THREE

Emma

HARLEY IS SITTING with her with his head on her lap, his warmth warming her legs. She is rubbing his back distracted by her thoughts. Her hand is moving slowly and without effort. It is now two weeks since her show was cancelled and she is scouring through job ads but with little interest. With the sale of the farm and her apartment rented, she isn't in a hurry. It has been years since she's had a good long break.

She had fared the worst out of this #bitchfest with Molly. Her crew had heard that *Daytime* was only placed on hold, and they were angry with Emma that they had lost their jobs. Some of the crew was placed on other shows, but many more were looking now. She felt for them as some of the *Daytime* crew who were also looking for work, they couldn't wait around until the board decided on its future. It was likely *Daytime* would be shelved anyway. What a mess!

She looked at a Facebook memory again, it had popped up this morning. A photo of she and Richard at one of her charity functions.

They had gone as 'colleagues' and at this time absolutely no one knew about them seeing each other. It was a year later rumours started.

Missing Richard was something she had not counted on. Their relationship had been long-term, almost as long as she had been married to Trevor, give or take a few years. Yes, Richard had an ego and was brash at times, but he loved her, and she now knows she still loves him. But there is no way she is reaching out to him, not yet anyway. Besides, he has moved to Queensland and didn't leave his details. One day if she wants to contact him, she can call his son, Scott, who might provide them. For now, she is on her own, something she is slowly getting used to.

Her phone pings. There is a message from David.

Hi, I know I'm the last person you want to hear from, but I thought I'd let you know Molly left for India today. Maybe go slow on the social media, she needs to sort herself out. And it might be good for you to do that too.

She is affronted by his text at first, but then she realises David has Molly's best interest at heart, and hers as well, it seems. She actually appreciates that he took the time to let her know. So, Molly is heading to her spiritual home and Emma knows this will do her good. Maybe Emma should consider going somewhere? It will help clear her head as well.

She stops looking at job ads and checks her socials. Her latest post was last night on Twitter and Instagram. There are still many #teamemma comments, but she is sure this goes for any of Molly's posts too. Checking, she sees #teammolly is still trending, something #teamemma is not doing as much. She shuts down her phone and throws it on the lounge. Harley looks up startled. "Sorry, I didn't mean to scare you. Come on, let's go for a walk." Harley jumps down with his tail wagging and heads to the stand where his leash is kept. When Emma opens her front door, she breaths in a long sigh hoping the fresh air will give her mood a lift.

. . .

SHE IS SITTING outside the café near her home having wanted a coffee after their walk. Harley is obediently sitting by her side. A few people are staring, she tries to ignore them wanting to be left alone. Maybe David is right, it is time to put this feud behind her. Molly has fled to India, neither of them has their shows, Richard has left, and their friendship is in tatters. That's what hurts the most, Emma misses Molly and all her antics. Their last trip to Fiji wasn't the best holiday they have had together (and now Emma knows why), but they have had many good times, especially when it was just the two of them. The times they had spent together, just the girls, were the times Emma will cherish forever.

Emma remembers a time they were in Melbourne for the television awards, quite a few years ago, when they went on a three-day bender. They had fun, laughs and got into such mischief they both received warnings about not being invited back the following year. Emma is smiling as her coffee is placed on the table.

"Thanks," she says.

"I'm #teamemma," says the young waiter.

Emma looks up and smiles, "Oh, right, thanks." She isn't sure why, but this makes her feel uncomfortable. This is a stranger telling her he is on her side. All because of social media and a stupid fight that Emma is now becoming bored with. David is right, as of today she will stop posting anything, it's time to take a social media break. She gulps down the coffee, leaves money on the table and pulls on Harley's lead. They walk home and Emma is feeling the best she has since her show was cancelled.

When they walk into her home, Emma's phone, which she had placed on silent, shows five messages. Four were from crew members wanting to catch up and talk business ideas, but one is from Richard.

Hi, not sure whether you want to hear from me, but in case you're ever on the Gold Coast, look me up, here's my details ...

He is the last person she had expected to hear from, but her heartbeat quickens as she thinks there may be a chance, but then she sees reason. No, she and Richard are in the past, she has to look to a different future.

JACK BRITEN, Emma's ex-producer from *Evening with Emma*, is sitting opposite her at the same café she had a coffee at yesterday. This time she had left Harley at home as Jack was here to discuss a work proposal. She listens as he explains his idea, and she is pleased he has come to her first. Jack joined her show only one year after Emma began hosting and he had turned the show into an award-winning news program helping Emma to become a respected news presenter. Jack is five years her junior and for the first time she notices his green eyes are flecked with brown and he has a scar under his right eye.

As he finishes talking about his idea, she asks, "It sounds great, a new show would be good for me, not that I like the early morning though. We can discuss this in more detail when you have a firm offer from a studio, I can wait for now. By the way, that scar?"

"Oh," he says placing his finger to it, "I was attacked by a dog when I was ten. Luckily it missed my eye. It has faded somewhat since then."

"Oh, now I know why you're not a dog lover."

"Hmm, well I'm ok around smaller dogs, like Harley for instance, but bigger dogs make me nervous."

They chat about animals in general as they eat, with Emma feeling particularly happy to be in the presence of someone she is comfortable with and doesn't have to try to impress. For the first time in years she has been able to relax and be herself. This is a foreign feeling and she will enjoy it as long as this hiatus lasts. Will she take on the job of hosting a morning show? If nothing better comes up, yes. And working with Jack again will be a plus.

THIRTY-FOUR

Molly

AS SHE SITS in her Mumbai office, the fan overhead whirrs. The sweat on her body is cooled by it as well as by the peach iced tea she has gulped down. She and her executive team – Sharma, Uma and Eeshan had returned from a meeting at the embassy where they had discussed more funding. The meeting had been mildly successful with the ambassador agreeing to look at their proposal, but no assurances were given.

Having been in Mumbai for a week now, Molly can feel her stress levels being released. Her mind is clearer and she is enjoying the regular yoga and meditation sessions. She had not kept up her practise back home. Sitting deep into her chair, she wonders how David and Bono are doing. She had sent messages when she arrived letting David know all was well, and apart from a quick message of 'great' from him, things had been quiet between them. She tries not to focus on the negatives as she has only just arrived here and David hasn't had time to miss her yet. She hopes.

Emma has been quiet on the socials and Molly had already stopped posting the day she left for India. This was a great relief and she hoped there may be a chance she and Emma can repair their friendship. She had thought of sending Emma messages as there was no one here to talk about her feelings, no one to discuss things like she used to with Emma. Their girlie chats were like therapy, usually hilarious and silly, but *oh so welcome.*

This is what she misses the most, having her best friend to talk to whenever she needed. Her anger about some of the things Emma said and posted still bubbles under the surface so she doesn't think their friendship will ever fully recover. And she had been swept up by it all and had joined Emma with her own scathing words.

Standing up, she turns the fan up higher as the humidity increases with the rain beginning to beat against the windows once again. The menacing greyness outside suits her mood. But she needs to focus on the work that needs doing here at the orphanage, she has enough to deal with and must put her personal issues aside.

She presses the intercom on her desk phone and asks Sharma to come in.

"Hi, is there a problem?"

"No, not at all. I'd like to buy some gifts for the children, will you join me in some shopping? I could do with your help."

"That would be lovely," she answers, "let me finish up with things in my office. Meet you at the car in say, half an hour?"

"Brilliant. See you then."

Molly enjoys spoiling the children because they have very little. To see their faces light up when she gives them even the smallest of gifts is precious, these are memories she will treasure throughout her life. She pays for the gifts from her own funds, it is her way of feeling a part of their journey. She will buy special gifts for the eighteen-year-olds who will leave soon, something she always finds heartbreaking. Once the children reach that age, they must leave and join the workforce. With the skills they have learned during their time at the orphanage, they manage to find work and a place to live. Uma and

Eeshan help them to navigate this process. Eeshan is particularly good with this as he is only twenty-two and relates to the young adults.

SHARMA DRIVES, she is good at negotiating the insane traffic conditions, but even so they are almost in an accident. Sharma swerved to miss a collision with a garbage dumper that was casually parked in the middle of the road. Molly is glad to have Sharma's help because one thing she had never become accustomed to is driving in Mumbai.

"Let's stop at the market first, I'd like to buy the younger children some shoes. They grow out of them so fast."

"Yes, they do," agrees Sharma with a smile. Molly smiles back knowing she has stated the obvious. Within minutes they arrive at their destination and Sharma manages to manoeuvre the car into a tight spot. After they get out of the car, they walk to the stall where they know the owner quite well and greet him.

"Welcome back, Miss Molly. Good to see you have survived these past three years." He acknowledges Sharma as well who bows slightly.

"Thank you, Rajesh, I'm happy to be back and see you are all well." She takes out her phone and clicks on notes where she has a list of shoe sizes, asking Rajesh to find her eight pairs of shoes in various sizes and colours. He goes towards the back and soon comes back with suitable shoes for children five to eight years.

"Lovely," says Molly paying for the eight pairs and indicates to Sharma they move onto the children's clothes area. Here Molly buys jumpers, shirts, shorts and skirts. Also, a few dresses for the girls who are leaving. "That should do us here, Sharma. You know where the superstore is, right?"

"Oh yes, and they have expanded it since you were here last. So many more shops." Molly isn't sure whether she is pleased about this because more shops mean more people. But she gives Sharma a smile anyway.

Two hours later and holding many bags, Molly and Sharma pack everything into the boot and head back to the orphanage.

"You are good to the children, Molly, no other orphanage buys for the children, most live with hand-me-downs."

"I know, Sharma, but I have the means to spoil the children occasionally. And, they have missed out for nearly three years. Now, let's get back, I need a long cool bath and some of cook's lovely food for dinner." Molly sees Sharma nod and knows she too looks forward to nightly dinners at the orphanage. Sharma lives in one of the staff homes Molly had built, there are six altogether. Like Uma and Eeshan, Sharma is an orphan herself and some, like her, come back to work at the orphanages because it is all they have ever known. Molly is lucky to have Sharma, she manages the orphanage as well if not better than herself.

THE NEXT DAY, Molly gathers the younger children into a classroom at the end of the school day. "Good afternoon children."

They all reply in unison, "Good afternoon, Miss Molly."

"I know it has been a scary few years but now we are looking forward to a brighter future. Miss Sharma has told me of your progress in your schoolwork and I am proud of each of you. Well done."

The children squirm and fidget with some giving Molly weak smiles. She feels humbled by being able to give these children a safe place to grow up. "So, as a reward for your hard work, I have a surprise for each of you." She bends down into a large bag and begins calling their names one by one. The children come up one at a time and take their gift, some having the courage to say thank you, others simply bowing towards her.

Sharma waits until the children all sit again and announces, "Children, what do we say to Miss Molly?"

They all thank Molly with beaming smiles, both in English then Hindi. She places her hands together in prayer and bows her head towards them. "Dhanyavaad," she says in gratitude and thanks. "You are dismissed and please take care of your gifts." She can't help but smile as they all scamper out of the classroom excitedly talking to each other.

MONTHS TURN into years and Molly is surprised to find she has been living in Mumbai for three years and the angst she had when she arrived had dissipated. There had been a lot to do after her absence and because of being busy, the time had passed quickly. She and David are talking but David has found someone else, which Molly understands but it's hard to accept because she still loves him. David had said he would look after Bono until Molly's return because he still lives in their house. They may have to sell it when Molly is back home, something she is dreading. She does have the means to buy him out and may consider this option.

Her ticket is booked and in two weeks she will be home. This is when all the hard conversations will happen. Both Tim and Samantha had kept in touch with her during her time here and they were looking forward to having her home. Emma and Richard had both become her past, neither doing anything to keep in touch. She had streamed Emma's new morning show, *Wake UP*. It was good and Emma was ever the professional with the following she had from *Evening with Emma* increasing the viewership of this new show. This show is on Rust Television, a smaller streaming station that specialises in news and current affairs. The fit is perfect for Emma.

#teammolly and #teamemma were also a thing of the past, Molly had left everything to do with social media to Evan and only checked in with him if needed. The controversy of the fight between the two of them died down once they both stopped posting. All the gossip mongers moved onto other celebrities and bitchfests.

Leaving Mumbai will feel bittersweet as this city has a special place in her heart, but it is not her home. She needs to return to Sydney and deal with the fallout of her's and David's relationship.

TORRENTIAL RAIN HAS BEEN BEATING down all day, the Tulip Treasures lawn and garden soggy with mud. Her flight is booked for 8pm and Molly is waiting in the orphanage's foyer for her driver. Sharma is waiting with her; Uma and Eeshan having said their goodbyes earlier.

"It's good your flight has not been cancelled as the weather seems to be clearing a little."

"Hmm," says Molly only half listening, she is scrolling through her socials catching up with what Evan has been posting about the Orphanage. Looking up from her phone she says, "Sorry. Yes, it does look like it's letting up. I do hope the driver isn't late." As soon as she finishes speaking, a car pulls up outside. The driver, complete with a rain trench and umbrella, runs into the foyer and smiles, "Are you ready, Miss Molly?"

"I am," she says turning to Sharma and giving her a hug while the driver takes her luggage. Molly is going home with less luggage than she came with because the other suitcase she had brought with her had been full of gifts for the staff. They had been in her duffle and it's now folded up in her suitcase ready to be filled again when she visits next.

Sharma smiles weakly at Molly as she leaves, "Take care of your-self and come back soon."

"I will, Sharma. Thank you for everything." She walks to the car knowing she will miss this place.

When Molly is comfortably in the car she looks towards the orphanage as the car pulls out onto the road. This is her proudest achievement.

The driver navigates the road, traffic, potholes, and the rain with ease. Molly feels sad to be leaving but knows she must face David and her home life in Sydney at some stage. She still loves him hoping he may still have feelings for her as he has kept in touch. They have remained friends even though he has moved on and Molly is not sure how she is going to react once she sees him in person. Or how she will feel once she meets Naomi, his new partner, in person. Will she be able to keep things platonic between her and David?

She is thinking about this when she is suddenly jerked against her seatbelt. Pain seers through her shoulder and her eyes blur. Tyres screech, glass shatters ... then they are hurtling down an embankment.

THIRTY-FIVE

David

DAVID'S PHONE bursts into life, the shrill shattering the peaceful silence of his sleep. Groggy, he fumbles to find his phone. Squinting at the screen he sees it's an unfamiliar number, some random overseas call. Exasperated, he smacks the silence button and places his head back on the pillow. Probably a scam call.

What feels like only minutes later, Bono is panting loudly at the side of his bed. "Umm, morning Bono. I guess you want breakfast?" says David giving Bono's head a loving pat. Picking up his phone he sees there are three calls and a voice message from the same number, he promptly deletes them. Why would someone be calling from India at that ungodly hour? Molly is the only person he knows there and that was definitely not her number.

He heads to the kitchen and starts making coffee then places a full bowl of food for Bono on the floor. Bono proceeds to slurp the contents before David has finished making coffee. David gives him a pat, "You were hungry, huh?" With breakfast made he sits at the bench as Naomi walks in. Pouring herself a coffee, she asks, "Did I hear your phone last night?"

"Yeah, some stupid scam calls from overseas. Annoying as hell."

"Oh, they are. Funny though, I thought I was dreaming, so I guess I didn't fully wake up. Hey, are you coming to the salon later, you need a haircut?"

"Um sure, after work. I'll be there around four." She nods and kisses him before leaving to get ready. Naomi owns a string of salons throughout Sydney, her business sense is extraordinary and one of the things he loves about her. He has picked up a few tricks from her to use with his own business. His face cracks with a smile as he remembers how they had met at a bar after 'meeting' on a dating app soon after Molly left for India.

His phone pings as he thinks of Molly returning home and sees it's a message from Tim. **Call me urgently.**

David hasn't heard from Tim since he and Molly split, so what could be so urgent? He calls out of curiosity.

"What!"

David's face drains of colour and he wonders if he heard correctly, "she's in a coma. How ... what happened?"

Tim explains how she was being driven to the airport when a bus veered in front of the car. Heavy rain had made the roads dangerous. They were thrown down an embankment. The driver died but Molly survived, however, her injuries are serious. Head trauma, leg and shoulder injuries, broken ribs ...

David's mind whirls with disbelief. "Umm, then the calls I had last night were from the hospital. They weren't scam calls."

"Yes, the hospital in Mumbai. When you didn't answer them, they called me. I've been in touch with the doctors and they say they had to place her in an induced coma. The head trauma is the worst of her injuries." Tim's voice trembles.

"I'm going over to Mumbai; she needs someone with her."

"David, we don't know how long she will be like this ..."

"I'm going and I'll organise to have her brought back here. Our medical system is more reliable, and I want her home." David interrupts Tim, his words falling over each other as his mind whirrs with what he needs to do.

"I know of the Indian medical system, she is in good hands, but it may be best if she's home. Not sure if she can be moved though? And wouldn't it make sense that I go, although I'd have to shuffle my patients around."

"Leave it to me, my team can look after things for me here. I'll talk to the doctors when I arrive. Thanks for calling, Tim. I'll keep in touch." David stares at his phone as Tim clicks off then hangs his head. All he thinks about now is having Molly brought home, what Naomi will think of him rushing to save his ex-girlfriend is not his problem.

The next two days are a flurry of buying tickets, sorting out staff to cover his upcoming jobs and dealing with Naomi, who has not stopped him from going but is quieter than usual. She drops him at the airport with a quick peck asking him to call as soon as he lands. He watches as she drives off wondering whether she will still be his partner when he returns. The last thing he needs now is to lose her.

DAVID IS SITTING on a lounge chair staring at Molly willing her to wake up. She has her mouth agape with a tube inserted, her face swollen with blue, grey and red bruises, along with several cuts, there are tubes in her nose, a catheter on her wrist ... machines are keeping her alive. He is distraught and exhausted. He arrived to find Molly almost unrecognisable, her face swollen, her leg in a stirrup and her hair shaved at one side.

Having managed to find a flight to Mumbai two days after Tim had called, he had left in the evening. He has slept at the hospital since and is not bothering to book anywhere as he has organised for a mercy flight to bring Molly home. The air ambulance has all the necessary equipment to keep Molly safe, and although the care she has been given so far has been excellent, both David and Tim had agreed it was best to bring her home, no matter the cost. This is better for all of them, they can help with her care once she is back in Sydney.

He places his hand on Molly's arm and speaks to her again. He is hoping his voice may help her to heal. "Don't leave us Molly, please." Tears begin to slip down his face and he lets his emotions take over for the first time since he received the news. He is spent and drawn when a nurse comes in and checks Molly's vitals. She slips away without saying a word.

AFTER A FULL DAY since he arrived he is waiting for confirmation of the mercy flight, which he was told could take days. He had only brought one change of clothes and wasn't bothered about sleeping in the uncomfortable hospital chair. If this is what it means to save Molly, then it is the least he can do.

When David had arrived at Naomi's salon for his haircut, he told her what had happened. If she was upset about him leaving suddenly, she didn't show it. In fact, she had even encouraged him to go. Not that it would've mattered, David was determined to leave, no matter what. His feelings for Molly were still strong, and for a moment, he almost let himself think about what he'd choose if it ever came down to her or Naomi. But he quickly pushed that thought aside. Naomi had been there for him during a rough time, and she deserved better than that. At least Bono, his dog, was in good hands with her. This gave him some peace of mind because Bono was probably missing Molly too.

Standing up, he stretches then bends towards Molly's face giving her a gentle kiss on the cheek. "Bono wants you home. And he's not the only one."

IT'S three days before a flight is confirmed and Molly can be safely transported. David is holding her things, the items that survived the crash. With the rain and mud, much of her luggage had been ruined. Her phone had been in her pocket and it survived with just a cracked screen. A kindly nurse had placed it in rice to soak up any moisture, so it was working. He is standing watching her being loaded into the plane as his body shakes with sobs. Sniffing, he composes himself before boarding checking his protective gear. To his surprise, the inside of the plane is a mini operating theatre complete with the paramedics in protective gear as well. David has never been religious, but he gives a quiet prayer out to the universe as the plane takes off, it's going to be a long flight.

THIRTY-SIX

Emma

HER MORNING SHOW is doing well with Emma happy to be out of the main spotlight. Rust Television is relatively new and still finding its feet. With the latest equipment and even some AI robot cameras, it's a whole new way of producing. The crew is good to work with, most of them young and in their first jobs, but they seem happy to learn from the *ancients* as Emma and anyone over thirty is called. They say this with respect and no one takes offence. She walks off the set heading to her office when Jack calls after her.

"Don't forget we have an extra production meeting this afternoon."

She had forgotten but lies anyway. "Yes, I know. See you there." She waves her hand as she keeps walking. She was looking forward to going home a little earlier to walk Harley ... well that's not happening, is it? When she arrives in her office, she picks up her phone. There are five messages from Tim, Molly's brother. Why would he be calling her? She dials his number wondering why so many calls.

"Emma, thanks for calling me back. I'm sorry to bother you but I have a favour to ask." Tim continues and asks why she hasn't been in contact about Molly, he is surprised she hasn't heard about the accident.

"What accident? I'm off the socials and have been for years, is Molly in danger?" She listens as Tim explains that for the past week Molly has been in a coma and he thinks that if Emma visits maybe her voice will trigger something.

"Tim, oh my, I'm so sorry. Why hasn't anyone contacted me before now? Oh, poor Molly. And you, how are you coping?"

"We're all distraught, it's been a huge shock. We are really clutching at straws now. David, Samantha and I have been tearing our hair out wondering what else we can do. Samantha suggested we contact you."

"And I'm glad you did. All that stuff that happened is in the past now, of course I will help. Give me the details, where is she?" Emma picks up a pen and scribbles in her notepad. "Tim, I'll go tonight, and I'll do whatever is needed."

"Emma, thank you for being decent. We weren't sure how you would feel, so, well, thanks."

She hears Tim's voice cracking and assures him she won't let them down.

WHEN EMMA ENTERS Molly's room, the sight of her is a shock. Emma's hand is on her mouth stifling a scream. Molly is pale with most of her face covered in bandages, especially over her right eye and cheekbone. Her hair is cropped short and there are patches missing. He left foot is in a stirrup and covered.

"Oh, what the hell have you done to yourself?" she asks half expecting Molly to answer. Although how she would even answer if she wasn't in a coma Emma doesn't know because she is hooked up to machines with tubes in her mouth and nose, which Tim had warned her about. This is the first time Emma has seen anyone in a coma, and it is more than concerning.

She places her bag down on the lounge chair moving slowly and apprehensively, closer to Molly. She tells her how sorry she is about what happened between them, how if she could, she would go back and change things. They should not have played out their feud for all to see and hear. They, especially Emma, had acted like children. Emma catches a glimpse of what she thinks is a twitch in Molly's eyes but is not sure.

"Seeing you like this, oh Molly, I am so sorry." Tears fill her eyes then silently tickle her cheeks. She keeps talking to Molly in between sobs until a nurse comes in. Emma wipes her face then asks her a few questions. The nurse gives her a kind smile but says that she should speak to the doctor. She tells Emma she will let one of the doctors know she wants to see him.

She sits and waits, keeping her hand on Molly's arm, which is warm but horribly skinny. She cringes at how skeletal it feels.

JACK IS SITTING at her desk with an impish look on his face. "Emma, how did you not hear about the accident? Everyone was talking about it at the time. I assumed you knew but you didn't want to talk about it."

Emma sits in her chair appalled by his attitude. She takes a few deep breaths before answering, "Next time, don't assume. We had a spat, well that's what it feels like now, how could you think I wouldn't want to know?"

Jack looks at her without answering, she guesses he has nothing else to say. The accident happened more than a week ago and he, along with everyone else, had assumed she was ignoring the situation. Did they really think she was that much of a monster? She and Molly had been friends for years before their falling out. Emma is flabbergasted. She is also surprised no gossip columnists had asked her take on the accident. "What about the gossip journos, they weren't inter-ested in my opinion? Am I that much out of the limelight now?"

"That was a decision made by the PR Department. Yes, there were enquiries at the time, but the department shut them down, saying you were privately grieving and wanted to be left alone."

Feeling miffed the PR team had not consulted her, Emma thinks about this a bit and decides she is grateful that had happened. Who knows what would have been taken out of context had she been asked about Molly's accident? "Fair call. I can now deal with my grief privately. Molly is a mess, Jack. Do you know she had her left foot amputated because it was so badly crushed?"

Shock takes over Jack's face, "No! How awful."

Emma proceeds to tell him about all of Molly's injuries and how the doctors have no idea of when or *if* she will come out of the coma. Emma shudders at this thought but finds relief that David and Tim are both covering the hospital costs. The doctor who had spoken to Emma on that first night was optimistic in his manner but cautious not to build everyone's hopes up. "The head trauma is significant, and even though they operated in India, until she wakes up no one knows the extent of the damage." Emma's voice is low as she stifles a sob.

"You're doing the right thing by visiting her, I'm sure David and Tim appreciate it. Look, I'll leave you to it, take care of yourself. I'm here whenever you need me."

Emma's eyes fill with tears as Jack leaves. How the hell did things become so complicated?

THIRTY-SEVEN

David

HE IS SITTING by her bed as he has done twice weekly since bringing Molly home. He, Tim and Emma take it in turns to be here, they don't want her to be alone. Emma had offered to help with the hospital costs, but David had said they would ask only if they needed to. He had appreciated her offer.

Naomi had been upset when David left for India without much warning, and now she was frustrated with him as he spent even more time with Molly at the hospital. She didn't hide it either, her surliness was impossible to ignore. At one point, she had threatened to leave him, giving him a harsh ultimatum: Molly or her. This had stung.

He had explained that he had a responsibility to help, to be there when Molly finally woke up from this nightmare. After a tense conversation, Naomi had softened, though he knew her resentment still simmered beneath the surface.

"You're the one I love," he'd reassured her, "Molly is a good friend. She always will be."

Naomi had reluctantly accepted his words, but with hesitation. David felt their relationship was still fragile, like it could crack at any moment. For now, it was holding on by a thread.

A doctor walks in taking David out of his reverie. "Hello, my name is Dr Hamilton, I've been brought in to assess Molly's condition."

David stands up and extends his hand, "Nice to meet you, I'm David. The other doctor is still seeing her right?"

"Yes, I've been asked to join the team. There have been some positive signs, small but significant. When I asked Molly to squeeze my hand earlier this morning, I felt movement. I believe she can hear us now."

David is in disbelief, is he really hearing this? "She could ... does this mean there is a chance she will wake up?"

"There is always a chance, but what long-term damage has happened to the brain, unfortunately, that we don't know. There are such things as nervous twitches, we don't know whether this is all we are noticing."

David walks back to the lounge chair and sits. "I'm overwhelmed. We have waited for some positive news, this is great. Thanks Dr Hamilton." He sits back and breathes deeply grateful he is the one to hear this little bit of good news.

"Please remember, it may mean nothing, but I mentioned it because the team looking after Molly has seen how you and your two friends have diligently been coming to see her. There are many who would have taken her off the machines by now."

David looks towards the doctor with his eyes shimmering with tears, which are about to flow, "That was never an option. Molly and I had a great relationship, there is no way I want to lose her."

Dr Hamilton smiles, "She's lucky to have good friends who care. Do you have any questions you would like to ask?"

David has so many but right now his emotions are scrambled, and he can't think of what to ask first. "Many, but I'm in shock, so may I get my thoughts together and ask later?"

"Sure, the two of us doctors and two nurses are on shift rotation, ask when you're ready."

"Actually, I did think of one, umm, this may not be allowed ... I was thinking of bringing Bono, Molly's dog, to see her?"

"There have been circumstances where the hospital board has allowed pets, yes. I'll have to check for you, but I do think Molly's case is a good fit. I'm sure her dog would love to see her."

David nods and looks over towards Molly as tears flow. He is sure Molly would love to see Bono too.

TWO DAYS later David is given the go ahead to bring Bono and both Tim and Emma had loved the idea. Walking into Molly's room with Bono feels surreal. Bono stops and tilts his head staring at her. He whimpers and as David takes him closer to her bed, recognition hits Bono and he jumps up placing his paws on her bed. He barks, not loudly, but a bark that David thinks says *hello*.

He allows Bono to stay looking at Molly for a few minutes then asks him to sit. "Come sit with me, Bono. We can stay here for a while and keep Molly company." Bono, obedient as ever, sits next to David and he doesn't take his eyes off Molly other than occasionally looking up at David. The feeling David has now is one of mild contentment, with what Dr Hamilton had told him and Bono's presence, he knows Molly will wake up soon. For the first time in weeks, he is hopeful.

Tim calls David as he and Bono are leaving the hospital. They are chatting about David's thoughts on Molly's recovery and Tim tells David he also feels positive. He asks Tim to hold for a moment while he sits Bono in the car. "Ok, he's safely buckled in now," David tells Tim. "I'll keep bringing Bono in for a few hours every time I visit. The look on his face when he recognised her was priceless."

"I have heard of patients recovering faster when pets are around, but with coma patients, I'm not too sure."

"It can't hurt Tim. It's certainly good for Bono to see her, he didn't take his eyes off her." They continue talking as David drives home with Bono in the back, his head out of the open window, his tongue hanging out loving the cool breeze.

THIRTY-EIGHT

Emma

EVEN THOUGH DAVID and Tim didn't want Emma's financial help, she felt she needed to help in some way. So, she had renewed her relationship with social media after three years without any accounts. The only reason for this was to raise funds for Molly because the hospital stint is only the beginning of the bills, once she wakes there will be the recovery time. Who knows how much rehabilitation she will need? Those bills will pile up.

So, she started a fundraising page on Instagram with reposts to Molly's orphanage account. The money had started coming in almost immediately as Molly's fans had not forgotten about her. Many followed her orphanage account and knew of her philanthropic work. Emma had set a goal of one million dollars and already the total was almost halfway. If Molly didn't need all of this money, the orphanage would benefit.

David and Tim had agreed to Emma doing this and with all her contacts from the charities she had worked with, the total would easily be reached. When many of Sydney's richest families found out about the cause, they donated without hesitation.

As Emma arrived at the hospital after setting up the posts, Molly's team of carers praised her efforts. She was a good friend they told her. This brought tears with Emma being grateful and hoping Molly felt the same way when she finally awoke from this coma.

Heading down the ward to Molly's room, she remembers how close they had been. The parties were the best, this is when they opened up to each other in ways they wouldn't when they were sober. One such party stands out more than others, details are sketchy, but Emma recalls a poignant conversation ...

They were at Harold's place again, one of the many times he looked after his parents' home. Harold was known for throwing the best parties and his parents' sprawling house was the perfect setting. It was end-November and shows were mostly in the can, this is when everyone started to let go of the working year. Emma was sitting with Molly and Harold on the upstairs balcony. Harold was passed out on the banana-lounge. She smiles because it was a blow-up lounge in the shape of a banana. He looked hilarious with his mouth agape, dressed only in board-shorts and his head lolling to the side away from them. She's not sure, but she thinks she remembers him snoring.

"Poor Harold, he ... hic. Oops, sorry," says Molly who begins laughing out loud. "He's a tired host."

"Sure is," slurs Emma, "and he knows how to throw a, ah, umm, a party. That's the word I'm looking for."

This makes Molly laugh even more. "You forgot that word?" Molly slaps Emma's leg, "How funny."

Emma looks at Molly and joins in with her laughter. "I'm so pissed. My brain knew it, but I couldn't get it to form in my mouth." Molly is now in fits, and this is contagious. The two of them enjoy their hilarity for a few minutes until they tire and wonder what they were laughing at in the first place.

"You know I love you, sis."

"What? Are we si ... sisters now?" Molly hiccoughs and stumbles with her words again in her drunken state.

"Nah, not like blood relative. But you know what? I'm closer to you than anyone else I know. I consid ... you're like a sister to me."

"Ah shit, Emma, that's bloody sweet. I love you too."

Emma watches as Molly hangs her head. Both of them are coming down from the alcohol and drugs they have taken through the afternoon. "Tanks, it is sweet that we would do anything for each other, right?"

"Yeah." Molly says this as she places her head onto the back of the chair and slumps down further. "I need to slee ..."

Emma tries to stand up but falls out of the chair onto the balcony instead. This brings on another fit of laughter from her as she lays there making herself comfortable. Putting her head on her hands she remains there and joins Harold and Molly falling asleep.

Smiling at her memory, she puts thoughts of how she and Molly felt about each other aside but keeps the fuzzy feeling the memory has given her.

She looks towards Molly, "Hello lovely, how are we doing today?" Emma greets Molly with this chirpy line at each visit hoping against hope that she will answer one day. "How good is it that Bono can visit now?" She continues chatting as if Molly can hear, telling her about the fundraising efforts and what is happening in her own life. All the research Emma had done about coma patients had mentioned that talking to the patient as if they could hear had been proven to work with their recovery in many cases. Hopefully, Molly is one of those cases.

LATER, Emma is out walking with Harley. She had had a busy day beginning with visiting Molly, then recording two segments for her show, and another production meeting that ran overtime. Even though it is late, Emma decides to still go for a walk. She needs to clear her head and with Harley cooped up at home all day, he appreciates it too.

She had hired a dog walker due to having limited time to walk Harley, but she did walk him at times too. The dog walker was reliable, and Harley enjoyed being walked with the other dogs, this was a decision Emma was glad she had made.

They walk for an hour before returning home with her head cleared somewhat after a long day. Emma goes through the freezer to no avail so calls her local Thai restaurant who delivers a hot, spicy laksa that will go down well on this wintry night.

Settled in watching television, the discarded laksa bowl sitting on the coffee table, Emma is watching a documentary when her phone rings. Picking it up, she sees David's number, "Hi," she answers.

"Emma, I have good news, Molly is awake. Come to the hospital, Tim is on his way too."

"David, that's ... wow, how incredible. I'll be there as soon as I can." She goes into the hall grabbing her coat again, which is still cold from the walk, and grabs her keys as well. She can't wait to be at the hospital. "Harley, be good, I'll be home soon."

THIRTY-NINE

David

THE DOCTORS HAVE LEFT LEAVING him alone with Molly. David is waiting for Tim and Emma to arrive. He had received the call that Molly is now in a *minimally conscious state*, her eyes are open, but they are unfocused. The doctors had given her simple commands, like asking her to move her fingers, which she did. David is elated that she might be able to hear.

"Molly, oh you have no idea how good it is to see those beautiful eyes open. Can you hear me?" There is no response. He was warned to expect this. Molly's condition might improve over the next coming days, something he is looking forward to.

Tim rushes into the room, "I, uh, sorry. I came as soon as I could." He is breathless taking a few minutes before he speaks again. "Molly, hi." No reaction. David explains how this will happen as she recovers and tells Tim about the state she is in now.

"A minimally conscious state? Holy hell, that means she will get better."

"This only happened a few hours ago, it's too early to tell. The doctors told me her condition should improve in the coming days, but not to expect too much."

"David, this is better news than we've had so far. The little I know about coma patients means this is a good thing." Tim takes Molly's hand in his as he sits in the lounge chair. "You gave us a bloody scare. Please let me know you can hear me." When she doesn't respond, her eyes staring into a vacuum, Tim is deflated.

"Don't be upset, we need to give her time."

"It's been the longest four weeks of my life, David. I have a right to be angry. I want her to be Molly again."

Emma walks in smiling and oozing happiness. A little over-zealous but David understands why she is thinking positive. "David, Tim, hi. Isn't this wonderful?"

David explains the situation to her, just as he had done with Tim. The three of them talk amongst themselves not noticing that Molly's eyes are wide open, she is focusing on the three of them. As David looks towards Molly, he notices and places his hand over hers. "Molly, can you see us?" Her hand twitches under his. Tim and Emma are at the end of the bed, both noticing too. "She moved, I felt it. Her hand moved."

"It did, I saw it too," says Tim with Emma acknowledging this. The three of them gasp in unison.

"Molly, can you hear me?" asks Emma looking towards David as Molly's hand twitches again. "Oh, it happened again. Her hand ..." David notices that Emma is beyond happy, even more than when she walked in. If that is even possible.

"Calm down, Emma, this may not mean anything. It could be a nerve twitching."

"A nerve twitch means she's alive. That's positive right? Anyway, I choose to believe this is Molly communicating she will be ok."

Both David and Tim nod with David looking towards Molly waiting for more signs.

. . .

BONO IS behind the front door, his tail wagging like chopper blades. David has arrived home from the hospital having left early that morning. Naomi was still asleep when he had left. "Hey, fella. Have you been a good boy?" asks David stroking Bono's back as he walks in. "Naomi, are you home?"

"Where else would I be at six on a Saturday night?"

She is not pleased. David knew this would be the case, he had been gone all day and hadn't let her know. Even though she knew where he was, he did make a point of calling her at least once. With everything that happened today, he had forgotten to call. "Ok, sorry. I should have called. There was good news and we spoke to the whole medical team, so the time flew by."

"Good news?" She waits as David explains what is happening with Molly. "That is good news. How are you feeling about it?"

"I'm quietly positive. How much she will recover depends on her attitude once she comes out of this stage. She has lost her foot and along with her other injuries, she will have to learn to manage all of it." David looks at Naomi who gives him a slight smile and hopes she forgives him yet again for spending time with his ex-girlfriend.

FORTY

Molly

WHAT THE HELL has that bitch Emma been doing visiting her? Even though she can't focus her eyes, Molly assumes she is in a hospital because she remembers the accident. She has flashbacks, they are sporadic, but she knows for certain she is in a hospital bed. She can sense machines beeping and she feels tubes in her mouth and nose. There is no pain, something she is grateful for, but why is her left leg up in a stirrup?

Her mind comes back to Emma. After they haven't spoken for years, she has the hide to come and see her. And in this state where Molly can't tell her to leave. *"What the fuck is she doing here?"* This is what Molly had yelled when she focused on who was in the room. But they didn't hear her. They kept asking if she could hear them, and she could. Frustration was beginning to eat at her, not even the doctors could hear her.

She remembers Bono visiting, this had lifted her spirits. After noticing David sitting in the chair, she had sensed Bono was also in the room. She could hear him breathing. When David was leaving, he allowed Bono to place his paws onto her bed. Oh, how she wished she could have patted him.

Molly has no sense of time, so it felt like ages since Emma had visited. Maybe she wouldn't visit again? Although somehow Molly knew this wasn't going to be the case. Their exchanges on social media three years ago had been a total bitchfest. Emma had been especially brutal attacking Molly for being a slut, a bitch and a cheater. These slurs had fired up #teammolly to the point where #teamemma had had to back down. Both hashtags had been trending, and it was during this time that they had both been taken off air. Their feud went on for more than six months, with their fans and gossip columnists fuelling it even after she and Emma stopped posting. Why Emma was visiting her now is weighing on Molly's mind. Did she really want to mend their friendship now when Molly can't even communicate?

SHE CAN HEAR the doctors discussing her progress as they tried to predict when she would be out of this state. The weird thing is she feels fine. She can focus her mind, her words are fully forming, and although she can't move, she can see who is in front of her occasionally. Moving her eyes sideways does give her more depth of field. The problem is, no one is noticing her eyes moving or that she is trying to speak. She closes her eyes in frustration.

A little later, opening her eyes she sees Emma is at the end of her bed. She is mumbling something about the donations coming in, but Molly has no idea what she is talking about. She is willing her hands to move but obviously nothing is happening because Emma keeps talking. She tries again asking her to leave, *"get the hell out."* Molly can hear herself clearly. The frustration is growing along with her anger. How long has she been in this hospital bed? When will she be able to let everyone know she is getting better?

David and Tim walk in and the three of them exchange greetings. Emma tells them about donations reaching a million and they are all smiles. Has Emma taken over the fundraising for her orphanage? Rage burns in Molly's soul. How dare she! Molly wills herself to fully recover so she can stop her. The orphanage is her baby and no one is going to take it from her, especially not Emma.

They continue talking with David discussing rehabilitation and mentions how Molly has to learn to walk again. She will have to get used to not having her foot.

This is why her foot is in a stirrup, she has lost it. This disturbs her, she is an invalid now. How many other injuries does she have? David doesn't mention anything else; he is now talking about a roster of rehab that the doctors have approved. So, does this mean they know she is better? But how? She still can't communicate or move.

Emma is the first to leave with Tim following her soon after. It is just Molly and David. Alone. She can see him from the corner of her eye. He is sitting and his face is intense, it is more wrinkled than she remembers, and he is rubbing his chin deep in contemplation. *"David, hold my hand, let me show you that I know you're here."* She knows it's futile trying to talk because he can't hear her, but maybe he can sense it. Then, he looks towards her touching her arm. Her middle finger moves.

"Molly, hello. I know you can hear me because the doctors say you are improving every day. It's slow progress but we're all hopeful."

"I'm fine, David." This is all she can say as she moves her finger again willing him to notice. *"But I have lost a foot. What else am I missing?"*

He is holding her hand now. "I can feel you moving, Molly. This is wonderful, please show me you can feel my hand on yours."

She wills her hand to move again but nothing happens this time. Damn! This really is slow progress. She sees his face drop as he takes his hand away. Brushing it through his hair, he mumbles about having to leave, Naomi is waiting for him at home. And Bono needs a walk.

Molly wonders whether she will be able to take Bono for a walk soon too. She feels tears drip slowly down her cheeks as she watches David leave.

FORTY-ONE

David

HE IS WALKING out the front door with Bono and can still hear Naomi talking loudly and swearing to herself. They had another fight about Molly. Naomi is fed up with David spending so much time with his ex-girlfriend despite assurances from him that he loves her not Molly. Technically, this isn't quite true because he hasn't stopped loving Molly, but it is now a close friendship. David hopes that Molly will want to keep in touch once she recovers.

Bono barks and David realises he is standing on the porch listening to Naomi. She is talking about him in unpleasant terms, this time she is angry to the point of manic. He can hear her throwing things around as something smashes. He hopes that isn't anything that belongs to Molly. Bono barks with more intensity and David looks down at him, "You have no idea what is going on, do you? It's probably better you don't. Come on, let's go."

The August winds have kicked in and David pulls the zip on his parka up to his neck. He enjoys walking in winter because it is invigorating, his body feeling alive. He needs this chill to wake him up and stop thinking about Molly and her condition. The doctors say she is improving but David hasn't seen anything different other than the twitches. These twitches could be nothing. Are they saying this to keep the three of them from feeling utter despair?

Despair has been a part of his life ever since Molly's accident. The thought of losing her had frightened him to the core. He felt guilty of the way they left things when she left for India, he wasn't exactly the caring boyfriend. The way he shunned her and didn't support her during that disgusting fight with Emma now feels so childish. Her life being dragged through social media was devastating and he had made it about himself. Was he jealous of all the attention she was giving the fight, the attention she should have been giving to him?

When they reach the dog park, he unleashes Bono who runs towards the other dogs. David greets the others and joins in on their conversations. These people are neighbours and they welcomed David and Molly warmly when they first moved into the area. Especially Carter and Jacob, their next-door neighbours, who they befriended the first day they moved in. All of these people know about Molly's accident but don't intrude or ask David questions unless he instigates the conversation. Everyone keeps their distance, which is the way he likes it.

People begin to say their goodbyes leaving only he and Carter. Carter has looked after Bono whenever David and Molly were away. He is a caring person and looks towards David asking, "How are you doing?"

David kicks his foot into the grass then looks down at Carter, a man of small stature with a big heart. "I'm ah ... ok, I think. Molly is improving, that's what the doctors are saying."

Carter stands up after placing a leash on his dog, a Pekinese who thinks she's a much bigger dog. "I'm glad to hear that. When we heard what happened we wanted to reach out to you but ..."

David interrupts him, "I know, thanks. I would have asked if I had needed your help. With Tim and Emma taking some of the slack from me, I'm managing. Naomi, well she's coping I guess." He doesn't go into the fact Naomi is struggling with David spending so much time at the hospital.

Carter looks down towards his feet, "Look, I have to go but if you need anything, even just to talk, you know where I am. The offer stands. And we're always happy to look after Bono."

There was no need for Carter to clarify that, David knows he and Jacob are available for Bono. "Thanks, I appreciate it. Enjoy your night."

He watches as Carter walks away. Of all their neighbours, he and his partner Jacob have been the most helpful. And David knows he can rely on them when and if needed. A tear falls onto his nose. He wipes it and sniffs hoping that Molly knows how many people are waiting for her to fully wake up.

HE TOSSES and turns for an hour then gives up trying to go back to sleep. He walks into the kitchen and puts the kettle on. Bono wakes up and looks at him. "Go back to sleep buddy, I just need some time on my own." Bono places his head down and stares towards David. "I'm fine, go back to sleep."

David takes his hot tea to the lounge placing it on the table. He flops into the lounge chair and fishes around for the blanket. The house is chilled at 3am and he can't be bothered with the heater. He thinks about Carter and his offer to help as tears spill down his cheeks. David has never cried so much as in the past weeks since bringing Molly home. When he first heard the news, he felt numb not knowing what to feel. Now tears flow easily because the thought of losing Molly ... well, he doesn't want to contemplate his life without her.

Naomi walks in. "I'm sorry."

He looks up at her. She is beautiful in a classic Australian way. Blonde, blue-eyed and skin that tans easily. Born on the northern beaches, Naomi went to a private school, has two athletic brothers and was used to an outdoor lifestyle. Since running her salons, this lifestyle has taken a back step, but she still manages to look fit. Yoga is part of her routine. She has this in common with Molly.

"This is hard on both of us. Here, come and sit." He pats his leg indicating she sits on his lap, which she does while placing her arms around his neck. "There is no need for me to be a bitch, though. I'm putting pressure on you that you don't need."

"I love you and appreciate the fact you're still here. Anyone else would have left by now. Molly will come through this and you two will get along because I love both of you."

"Maybe. We'll have to wait and see. It's you I'm worried about, and I will try not to let my jealousy get the better of me again."

David kisses her lips. He realises they haven't made love for some time and kisses her with a passion he thought he had lost. Holding her by the waist he pushes her up off his lap then he stands and takes her hand. They walk towards the bedroom and David throws her onto the bed as he removes his pyjama pants. All the frustration that has built up over these weeks is forcing its way out of his body. He makes love to Naomi with a ferocity she seems to devour.

"Where the hell has all this been? I've missed being with you David."

"I'm sorry, Naomi." He let's go and they both lie together spent. David knows Naomi is the woman he wants, and he will show her how much he need her from now on.

FORTY-TWO

Molly

SHE CAN HEAR the murmurs of the hospital staff, the machines beeping and now there is a sweet smell in her room. Not sure what it is she opens her eyes and tries to focus them to the dim light. Next to her on the side table are flowers. There are more on the moveable table.

A nurse walks in. "Good morning lovely. You are one lucky patient, one of these bunches is all the way from India." The nurse continues to check Molly's vitals humming a tune that Molly knows but can't quite remember. After raising her bed slightly, the nurse leaves. The song remains in her head as she hums it too. U2, it's one of their songs. But which one?

Light begins to filter through the window. The nurse had pulled the blinds back. Molly can see the city, some lights still flickering. She looks forward to the day when she will be out there again, living her life. Without a foot. Looking directly at the stirrup she can still feel her foot. How she's not sure? But there is a slight pain coming from there. How she wishes she could make everyone hear her, she has so many questions.

Another nurse walks in with two more bunches. Leaving them on the table, she walks out again. Molly assumes she has gone looking for vases. She also assumes the news of her slowly recovering has been circling around and these flowers are from family and friends. She is wondering which ones are from India when the nurse returns with two vases. The smell in the room intensifies and she sneezes. The nurse looks up, "Bless you." She proceeds to write something on the clipboard hanging at the end of Molly's bed. They must be monitoring everything that happens, but all Molly wants to be able to do is *TALK* to them!

DAVID IS SITTING on the chair. Molly doesn't know how long he's been there, but senses he is on his own. She wonders why Bono isn't with him. Suddenly, a large breath escapes her lips. She is breathing on her own.

"Molly? Can you hear me?"

"Yes."

David stands and places his hands on her face. "You're breathing on your own." She can see the disbelief on his face and even though she speaks again, this time he doesn't hear her. He presses the buzzer above her bed and a nurse comes in a few minutes later. "She's breathing on her own," David blurts out.

"What? Oh my. Umm, I'll be back in a minute ..." she says walking out. "With a doctor."

David is texting on his phone now. Molly assumes he's contacting Tim and Emma. Then Dr Hamilton appears.

He looks at David who nods confirming what the nurse had told him. "Molly, I'm checking your vitals. I can see you're breathing on your own, so that's one machine that can go."

David's face is beaming and Molly now knows how much David still has feelings for her. How she wishes she could let him know she feels the same. This is her hope anyway because she needs him now more than ever.

A heavy blackness takes over, suddenly she feels extremely sad. Her whole body feels a weight, like someone has added a lead blanket on top of her. She wants to scream because she feels like she is suffocating.

"Molly, can you say something?" asks Dr Hamilton.

"Yes."

David explains to the doctor this is the only word she has said to him as well.

"The fact she is breathing on her own now is positive. What we don't know is how much her brain has been spared. This will also determine how long she will be in rehabilitation." The doctor continues explaining to David what to expect from now on. This is not going to be an easy time for Molly let alone anyone who loves her.

Dr Hamilton has finished talking to David when Tim and Emma arrive. He leaves them asking David to explain what he had been told.

Molly isn't happy to hear the doctor's opinion. Hadn't she been through enough already?

A WEEK later Molly is transferred to Hunter's Hall Rehabilitation hospital. Her vocabulary has improved to more than one word, but she still isn't able to communicate everything she is trying to verbalise. Mostly she has questions about her foot, like how long before she will be able to walk again?

The room at this hospital is larger than the one she has left. The walls are not stark white, instead they are painted in bright, breezy colours. There are more flowers already in the room, many from fans. She looks forward to reading all their cards. The flowers from the other hospital had been thrown out after they smelled rank and were drooped.

David is guiding her towards the bed in a wheelchair. She can see

206 MARIA P FRINO

her stump, which is covered by a woollen sock. It is now six weeks since her accident. An accident that has changed her life forever. The heavy sadness begins to take over, this has happened often since she began breathing on her own.

"I'll wait for the nurses to come and help you into bed. Do you want anything? A drink?"

"No. Thanks for every ..." She is trying to tell him how much she appreciates what he has done, but again some words don't want to form.

"Molly, I am always here for you. No need to thank me. By the way, Tim is coming later and bringing Samantha. She has been asking to see you."

Molly had seen all the messages on her phone from Samantha, at least one a day since her return from India. She had sent messages of love, inspirational quotes and her own heartfelt words to help Molly recover. She desperately wanted to see both Tim and her niece and have a conversation with them too. Or at least try.

There had been many other messages too, from India and on the socials from fans as well. She tires of trying to talk and has been using her iPad to communicate her needs at times.

"Tim has warned Samantha what to expect. But you are looking much better than when I first saw you."

Molly had seen the scars above her eye and on her cheek. The stitches will be taken out in the next few days. Her ribs are feeling better, although she only felt the pain these past few days. The doctors told her they had given her heavy pain killers to help her body heal the whole time she was in the coma.

Six weeks of her life has disappeared. She vaguely remembers the torrential rain, the car rolling but nothing after that. This past week is the only time she remembers, ever since that first breath she took. David was so pleased he had been there to see that happen and she thought it appropriate that he was. It was the beginning of her recovery, something he had been wishing for her this whole time. She had heard more of his conversations that he thought.

Two nurses walk in and assist Molly in moving onto the bed. They ask if she needs anything else before they walk out. She was happy to be comfortable and have David here, this was all she needed for now.

"I'll go and let you have some rest before Tim and Samantha arrive. By the way, I saw Carter at the dog park yesterday. He sends his wishes and offered us help if we need it."

Molly smiles, David said '*us*'. Could this be ... she stops herself remembering he has Naomi. But, she looks forward to seeing Carter and all their neighbours soon. She is lucky to have friends and family who support her, and she now knows she will need a lot of support in the coming months.

David leaves after another short conversation via her iPad. Her loneliness is overwhelming as she watches him walking out of her room.

FORTY-THREE

Emma

SHE IS EXCITED about seeing Molly at the rehab hospital as she hadn't seen her since the days before she began breathing on her own. After paying the taxi driver, she heads into reception and is surprised at this modern facility. It is brighter and more colourful than the much older hospital in the city. Furnished in an upmarket style, it feels more like a hotel than a hospital.

Walking into Molly's room she sees Tim and Samantha. "Oh, hello, how is everyone? Sorry, I didn't realise you would both be here. Hi Tim. Hi Samantha."

"We're just leaving, we've been here for some time."

Samantha moves towards Molly and holds her hand. "I'm so happy to see you, Aunt Molly. I've been waiting for this day." Molly looks up at her niece as tears drip down her cheeks. Emma's body twinges with sadness, she knows how close Molly is to her niece.

"Things will become easier, the doctors told Dad and David you will make good progress if you work at it. I'll help with whatever you need." Samantha's tears flow too as Tim guides her from the room.

"Bye Molly, see you in a few days," says Tim as he reaches the door.

Emma moves closer to Molly who glares at her making Emma feel uncomfortable. "Molly, what's wrong?"

"Get ..."

"Do you need something? Will I call a doctor?"

Molly closes her eyes and gives an emphatic wave towards the door for Emma to leave. This startles Emma as she had only arrived. "Oh, I guess you're tired. I'll come back another time. If you need anything, text me. I'm here for you Molly, remember we are leaving the past behind us. Please don't shut me out." Molly's eyes remain closed, and Emma assumes she does want to rest. She walks out of the room feeling hurt and confused. Why is Molly treating her this way?

EMMA IS on set and Jack is listening to her speaking about Molly. How things between them are strained and Emma feels like Molly is still holding a grudge about their stupid fight.

"What do you expect? She is probably in a confused state and is still processing what has happened to her. I know it has been three years since your social media spat, but it was still ugly and played out in front of everyone."

"Ugh, I know. I should never have posted those awful things. I was fuming at the time and wasn't thinking straight. When I think about what transpired between us, it saddens me because we said things no friends should ever say to each other."

"How about we go for a drink after work? It sounds like you need to let off some steam."

"That would be great. Thanks for giving me your shoulder to cry on."

Jack smiles and calls everyone to their places. "Come on, it's time to start another informative show."

· · ·

SHE AND JACK are at a pub in her local area. She has offered he stay over as she plans to drink herself stupid and wants someone to be with her later. "Purely a platonic offer, Jack. I like you but not in that way."

"Fine by me. You and I getting together would be complicated right now, especially as I'm seeing someone."

"Jack, how wonderful. Who? Come on, spill."

Jack sits back on the chair. They are seated at the back of the room wanting somewhere quiet to talk, away from the crowd at the bar. The dim light is perfect to be incognito and this suits Emma's mood. "You don't know him, he's not in the industry. He's a chef and a good one. You'll meet him soon. But look, we're not here to talk about me, tell me more about you and Molly."

Emma knows about Jack's sexual prowess with both sexes and how he has managed multiple partners at one time. She is in awe of how he did it all, but from how he has talked about this chef, his face lit as he speaks of him, this seems more serious than usual. "I wish you well with this relationship, you deserve to be happy."

He laughs, "Ha, I thought I was happy. But thanks, he is quite special."

She knew she had caught the right vibe from him, Jack's face had glowed when he mentioned his new love. But she brings the conversation back to her issues, they can discuss his love life another time. "So, back to me and Molly. Things don't feel right and I'm not sure what to do given her limited capacity to communicate. I want to tell her about the donations and my plans of how to distribute the funds after covering her medical costs. I don't want to do this unless she is open to speaking to me amicably."

Jack is quiet for a bit taking a sip of his cocktail. She plays with her scotch swishing and swirling it around the ice cubes. Then she gulps it down. "I'm going to get another, want another cocktail?"

"Sure, ask for a tall glass this time. I had better take it easy if I need to look after you."

She walks towards the bar, which is now quiet. The after-work crowd has left and the night revellers haven't arrived yet. "A double scotch on the rocks and a Tom Collins, thanks. In a tall glass for the cocktail please."

Back at the table with their drinks, Jack speaks once she sits down. "I've been thinking about how you can communicate with Molly. You told me she uses an iPad to speak for her, well, send her text messages about your ideas."

"I had thought of that but it's a bit impersonal, don't you think?"

"Keep it in mind, it may be the only way to get through to her while she is mad at you."

Emma gulps down the scotch and this time Jack goes to buy the drinks. Emma's sadness is all consuming and she will obliterate it by drinking. Jack is the ideal person to be with because she knows she can rely on him. His presence brings her comfort, and she feels secure he won't relay what they discuss to anyone else. There's a deep sense of trust between them that makes her appreciate him even more.

They talk for hours about their lives, about the show, about Molly. Every time the conversation turns to Molly, Emma drinks more. She is close to Jack's face with her elbows on the table, she blurts out, "She was my best frrr-iend. We were each other's besties, has she fer ... umm, forgotten all the good times? I made one bloody mistake, can't she forgive that?" She drops her head with a thud.

"I think it's time I got you home. Come on, up you get." Jack stands and places his hand under her elbow. "That's it, take it slow."

"You're a good frr-iend, Jack." Jack comes out as 'Yack'. Her words are slurred into a whisper as she allows him to lead her out of the pub.

FORTY-FOUR

Molly

IT WAS Samantha who had suggested Molly communicate through her iPad, and this is what she had been doing for the past weeks. Sitting up in bed, she is furiously typing as David looks over her shoulder.

David reads.

I don't want that bitch to visit anymore. Emma is not welcome. I want nothing to do with her.

He looks down at her determined face. "Molly, she helped with getting you to this stage. And what about all of those donations? That was all Emma's idea." David had told Molly he thought she was being unreasonable, Emma had apologised many times and asked that Molly put all that angst behind them. He keeps reading as she rants about what a bad friend Emma had turned out to be. Molly was using every expletive she knew. He was surprised at the fervour behind her words, when did Molly starting using the 'C' word?

Stop her coming, David. I never want to see that bitch again. Molly turns off the iPad signalling she has had enough and wants to rest. Placing her head on the pillow and closing her eyes, she whispers "Thanks," placing her hand on David's arm. She is due for another physio session this afternoon, so he leaves and allows her to rest. Molly opens her eyes and watches him leave hoping he will do as she asks.

THE PHYSIO SESSION IS GRUELLING, except for the massage at the beginning. Molly enjoyed that part. But it was the precursor to what was to come. The physiotherapist made her do exercises that her muscles screamed against, all her muscle memory had stayed in the coma, her body is weak and broken. She rallies herself to fight all this negativity, channelling her anger coming from how she feels about the bitch she once called her friend. But thinking about Emma deflates her as she tires. "I need a rest. Please. I need time to refocus." She is begging because they have been going for an hour.

Her physio acknowledges her hard work up to now and says she can have a ten-minute break. Molly appreciates this as she listens to him telling her about the prosthetic foot she will be trying on in a few days. This will help her recovery and once she has mastered walking on it, her recovery (and her life in general) will be better for it. Molly smiles not really feeling that her recovery is coming along as well as everyone thinks. Her body aches after every physio session and the pain isn't easing. Will this pain be with her for the rest of her life? For her, recovering from the accident is happening too slowly, she just wants her old life back.

A FEW HOURS LATER, she is back in her bed. She is going through the messages on the iPad and sees a few from Emma. She deletes them without reading. Looking around her room, she notices there are more flowers. The nurse had left some cards on the bedside drawer, Molly picks them up and reads. They are from fans mostly and one is from Sharma with a letter included. How quaint, who writes letters anymore? Also enclosed are drawings from the children, which make Molly's heart fill with joy. Reading Sharma's words brings tears to her eyes. Sniffing loudly, she laughs in places when Sharma talks of the antics the children are up to. Sharma sends their love and from all the staff as well, they are missing Miss Molly and want her to return soon. Molly closes the letter along with the drawings and uses the paperclip to pin the pages to the card, which is a handmade one from the children making it even more special. *I will return, I just don't know when, Sharma.* She mouths these words but isn't sure any sound comes out of her mouth.

The darkness descends through her body again. The demon thoughts are taking over and have been since she opened her eyes and began breathing on her own. As much as everyone tells her to think positive, these dark thoughts take over. Why didn't she die in the accident like the driver did? Why was she spared? All this work to recover, learning to walk again, dealing with Emma. Is it all worth it? Right now, Molly doesn't think so. Out of sheer frustration, she thumps both hands onto the bed many times until her hands hurt. When will this nightmare end!

She tries shaking the darkness by thinking of Bono and how she is looking forward to walking with him again. Bono isn't allowed to visit her in this rehab hospital, which she isn't happy about. Her dark moods have become worse since not being able to see her beloved dog. She is sure Bono misses her too. Having him with her is a reason to thwart these dark thoughts. Thumping her hands on the bed again she yells, *"No, you're not making me a victim, I will recover. Just watch me."*

FORTY-FIVE

David

HE WALKS out of the rehab hospital knowing Molly is being stubborn about Emma. But he needs to tread carefully not wanting to cause any further issues with Molly's recovery. She is emotional enough already. Walking to his car he decides he and Naomi will go out tonight, maybe even go dancing. He isn't keen on dancing, but Naomi enjoys it and he enjoys watching her dance. Yes, that's what they will do tonight because he needs to let off some steam, Molly is doing his head in.

Twenty minutes later, he walks in the front door greeted by Bono. "Hey buddy, how's things?" he asks ruffling his fingers on Bono's head. "Naomi, hi. Would you like to go dancing tonight?"

Naomi greets him wearing a towel as he enters the bedroom. She has just stepped out of the shower. "Of course, I'd love to. What brings this on? You don't like dancing?"

"Molly is being unreasonable, I need to do something physical before I do something to her I'll regret."

"Woah, that sounds serious. Then we should go dancing," agrees Naomi laughing as she gives him a cuddle.

He kisses her passionately pleased with himself to have made her happy. He is trying not to neglect her while he is helping Molly, and she seems to appreciate these thoughtful things he does for her. David doesn't want to lose Naomi and will keep being the attentive partner to make sure this doesn't happen.

THEY ARE ABOUT to walk out the door when David's mobile rings. Glancing down, he sees its Emma. "I'll take this, won't be long Naomi. Meet you in the car." Naomi nods but is angered as she walks to the car. He will deal with that later. "Hi, Emma."

"David, I need to talk about Molly. She's not answering any of my texts nor my emails. I emailed her a few times about my ideas for the money donated but haven't heard a word."

David let's out a frustrated sigh, this is the last thing he wants to talk about right now. "Emma, she's angry and frustrated that her recovery is so slow. Give her time. I have spoken to her about you, but she won't budge. Look, let me call you on Monday, I'm on my way out."

"Ok, sure. Speak to you then."

He opens the car door to Naomi staring out, not acknowledging him. This is not a good way to start a night out.

Arriving at the club, Naomi hasn't thawed. Pushing her way through the crowd, she is determined to be where she wants to be, at the back of the room away from the loud music. She turns abruptly and faces him. "You can't even give me your full attention when we're going out." She blasts this at David as he reels back.

"What? I told Emma I'd call her back on Monday. It was a short call."

"Did you have to take it in the first place? You could have just called her back on Monday. Honestly David, I don't know how much more of this I can take. I don't want to be the third wheel anymore."

David rubs his hand over his face, not this again. "You are my first wheel. It's you and me, you're the most important person in my life. Can we not do this again? Not here, come on, let's dance." Naomi sniffs holding back tears. "Don't do this to yourself, I love you, and once Molly recovers, I won't be spending so much time with her. She is doing well; it won't be long now."

Naomi clears her throat, "You promise." He isn't sure he can promise anything until Molly is more independent but promises her anyway. Naomi softens her stance taking his hand as he leads her to the dance floor.

DAVID IS onsite when Emma calls. "I'm taking a break," he yells to his fellow tradies. "Emma, hello."

"Hi David, do you have time? Sorry to bother you." When David acknowledges, she continues. "Molly is shutting me out and I'm devastated. I went to visit her and even before I made it to her bed, she threw me out."

"I'm sorry but I don't know what else to do. She is suffering both mentally and physically. We need to give her more time."

Emma keeps talking about what to do with the money she has raised, how to make Molly understand she should acknowledge these donations and how to distribute them. "How will she pay all her rehab bills, aren't they piling up? And I'm sure all the donors want to see their money put to good use."

"Her bills are being managed by Tim and me. We haven't spoken to Molly about bills yet. Again, we need to give her time. Look, let me see how she is going with rehab this week and maybe both Tim and I can talk to her."

"Please do, David. I'd like to mend our friendship, but more importantly, make sure Molly takes the money and pays her medical bills. Then the rest can go to the orphanage or wherever she wants it to be distributed."

David tells Emma he will do his best and hopefully with Tim's help, Molly may change her mind. "Goodbye Emma, enjoy your week." Ending the call with Emma, he sends a text to Tim hoping he will be available. Tim answers him within five minutes. Sure, let me know which day. Although, I think we still have an uphill battle.

FORTY-SIX

Molly

THE PHYSIOTHERAPIST IS SPRUIKING to her and her rehab team how much Molly is improving.

Liar.

This is all Molly can whisper as he's lying through his teeth. Yes, she is beginning to master the prosthetic foot, but it still needs some tweaking to be more comfortable. Yes, her vocabulary is strengthening and even her appetite is improving. Physically, she is getting around better. But mentally ... well that's another story.

After a gruelling day of rehab yesterday she has asked for a break today. The only thing she wants to do is walk outside for a short time to get used to using her new foot. The team had agreed as long as today is her only break, with another week left before she is discharged they want her to be at her best before she goes home.

Fear struck her when she was told of her discharge date, exactly three months to the day since the accident. She may be physically ready, or so they say, but the dark demons are still circling with her mind finding it difficult to dispel them. The fear has increased the power of these dark thoughts and the weight of them cripples her with dread. She closes her eyes trying to shut out the suicidal thoughts along with her rehab team who are still discussing her progress.

"Get out of my room."

She is even too tired to yell at them, the words come out as a whisper. She closes her eyes even harder to shut them out even more.

After what seems like an age, the team finally leaves as her physio gives her the rundown for tomorrow's routine. She opened her eyes momentarily to hear what he was saying. Her eyes are shut again when he leaves. Images of the studio and her old crew splash through her mind. She preferred the rundowns given to her by her PA on her old show. How long since she's thought about *Daytime*? What is the crew up to and where are they all scattered now? The public fight she and Emma had had affected so many more people than expected and the guilt Molly feels about this drives her demons. Both #teammolly and #teamemma became bigger than their own celebrity status, it was months of constant taunts on the socials. Even after Molly and Emma stopped, their fans kept the fight going for at least a year. She wonders what would have happened to ratings had both of their shows not been cancelled.

What is ahead of her now? Being a television show host was her life. Will her vocabulary recover enough for her to restart her career? The thought of not being able to do what she loves is something she doesn't want to contemplate.

She had drifted off into a dream of the filming of her show. Such good times with people she adored and now missed so much. Opening her eyes, she sees it is almost midday with the sun peeking through the window. She allows the rays to warm her, giving her hope. Her physio will be back after lunch to take her outside, something that lighten her mood. Maybe more of these walks will help her to mentally move on, to feel up to walking Bono again, to regain her life. Tears drip down her nose as she thinks about being in the real world again. Will the demons follow her?

SHE IS SITTING up in bed with her iPad open when David and Tim arrive. Placing it on the table in front of her, she greets them. "Hello. You're here together, what a lovely surprise." The walk she had taken earlier had changed her mood slightly, so she emphasised sounding happy.

"Hello you. How nice to see you smiling," says David placing a light kiss on her cheek.

"Hi Sis," says Tim, "you are looking better."

"Thanks. Baby steps but yes, I'm feeling better."

The boys pull up a chair each and listen as Molly tells them about being outside earlier. How good it was to feel the sun on her skin and the freedom of being out of bed without a wheelchair.

"Fantastic. Oh Molly, you have come a long way." Tim holds her hand as he says this, his eyes awash with unshed tears.

"Tim, are you actually crying?" She holds his hand tighter as she tilts her head towards her brother.

He sniffs. "Samantha and I have been looking forward to hearing of the day you'll be out of here. It's amazing, I'm so proud of you."

She gives him a weak smile because if he knew what she was really feeling, he would not be so proud. Pushing down these thoughts, she listens to both of them talk about what is happening in their lives. "Really? You went dancing, David."

"What is so surprising? I don't hate it that much. Naomi and I had fun."

"You were never one to go to a club, that's all. But good on you for making Naomi happy." Molly feels a pang of jealously as she says this, she had harboured a thought that she and David would reunite. Obviously, she can forget about this ever happening. It seems David and Naomi are destined to stay together.

Tim tells her that Samantha is dating again after her disastrous split with the mad hippy she had dated for two years. Molly had liked him, but Tim saw him as a no-hoper and didn't like what the future might hold for his daughter. Although, Molly had only met him once before leaving for India, so who is she to judge?

"I'm happy for her, but what about you? Isn't it time you found someone?"

"Me? No, I'm ok being on my own." Tim says this looking down with his shoulders drooping.

Molly knows he still misses Amanda, his partner who died fifteen years ago in a car accident. She shivers as she realises she has been wishing she had died in her accident. How would this have affected everyone who loves her? Seeing Tim still grieving after all these years touches Molly making her decide to review her dark thoughts, this is more about the people who love her than about herself.

"Listen Molly." David interrupts her thoughts. "Emma called me and I think you need to reconsider how you're treating her, she wants to discuss the donations and what to do with them. And repair your friendship."

Molly looks at both David and Tim, sighs heavily and begins a rant, "Fuck you, David. This is why you are here with Tim. You … you think having him for moral support will change my mind." She has to stop to regroup, her words getting stuck before they come out. "Well forget it, I don't want that woman in my life again." Closing her eyes she breathes and continues … "Yes, I did sleep with Richard and I regret that, but she went public with it, that's what I can't forgive. We've both lost so much out of this. Look where I am now."

David and Tim both have sheepish looks. They let her keep ranting allowing her to let off steam.

"What is my life going to look like now? Will I ever be able to resurrect my career? Remember that being a host was more than just a job to me." She takes another deep breath giving her mind time to catch up and formulate the words again. "No, Emma's influence would be toxic and I'm not willing to allow that to happen, I have enough to deal with when I return home. All … all I want to do is be with Bono, so David you had better move out. Both you and Naomi need to be gone when I move back in." She surprises herself at being able to talk this long with only one break, maybe she can still have a career as a host?

"We are organising moving, that's already underway, we found a place and are moving in next week."

"Good."

"Molly," says Tim carefully not wanting to upset her further, "you need to calm down and treat David with more respect. He is the one who has been here for you the most, risking his own relationship to care for you. You're acting like a spoiled brat. Enough!"

She is stunned by Tim's attack, they rarely fight or disagree. Maybe she is being too self-focused as Tim is right about David being there for her all this time.

"And Emma, too," Tim continues. "She isn't holding onto the past like you are, and don't forget it was you who hurt her in the first place. You need to give her permission to donate that money to who will benefit most, after your expenses are cleared."

David looks towards Tim, his face full of gratitude. Molly doesn't miss this and more guilt piles on top of her existing guilt. She has a lot to consider as the dark thoughts descend once more.

FORTY-SEVEN

Molly

SHE IS HOME. Bono is sitting next to her right foot, his chin on it and looking up at her. "Yes, I'm happy to see you too." He hasn't left her side. She arrived home two days ago with David and Naomi moved out and leaving the place freshly painted and cleaned for her. David was too good for her, he did deserve more credit for everything he did, he put Molly first before anyone else for all this time and she had repaid him with disdain. Her anger had seeped through and tarnished everything she said. Well, this was going to change, she has had enough of wallowing in her sorrow. The new Molly has come out of the ashes of her coma.

Samantha and Tim had been here when she arrived home. More flowers adorned the house, Bono was bouncing around like Tigger, and the three of them had cried tears of joy. The hugs they gave each other warmed her soul, they had not wanted to let go.

"You came so close to not being here. I can't ... I don't want to think about it." Samantha, with tears streaming down her face, had said after they let go of each other.

Tim had just stood there. No words were needed to express how he felt, and Molly was grateful both he and Samantha were there to give her support.

Once she had settled in and they felt comfortable she would be ok, they left promising to check in on her often. She had told them she would manage, but this was a lie, she wanted them to check on her. Why she can't accept help with gratitude and allow people to help baffles her? She had an accident and was in a coma, has needed rehab that is still ongoing. She does need help.

"Come on, Bono, let's try a walk." Bono is at the hall stand in seconds. Clipping on his leash having adjusted her foot that she now calls *Pete the prosthetic*, she opens her front door for the first walk with her dog, something she had looked forward to for so long.

They arrive at the dog park with Molly having to stop and sit a few times along the way. She spots Carter and Jacob, her neighbours and heads towards them. Letting Bono off the leash, he bounds to play with the other dogs as Carter turns to see her.

"OMG, Molly. I thought I saw you return home. Jacob, look Molly is back." He doesn't wait for Jacob to respond, "You're up and about, a little skinnier but generally you look well." They both give her a hug.

"Thanks for the warm welcome home. I'm fine. Well, getting there at least."

Carter places his hand on his hip, his stance whenever he is about to say something profound. "You are a trooper and you're on your way to bigger and better things. Nothing is going to stop Molly Edwards."

She laughs, "As always, you are my biggest fan, Carter. And I love you for it, both of you." Carter continues to fill her in on the neighbourhood gossip, with Jacob adding the odd snippet here and there. Molly relishes listening to their animated words, both of them full of life. This is one of the things she took for granted before her accident, being able to chat and socialise, to relax with her friends. A feeling of calm descends on her, this is the sort of thing she will think of when those demon thoughts try to take over. Her mood had been better since moving back home. Having her things around her, Bono to keep her company, and interacting with her neighbours again was now precious time she will cherish.

"We're here if you need anything done. Shopping, washing, whatever. Even just a chat."

"I appreciate that Carter and I will take you up on some of those, especially the chats. I've missed you both." Her voice breaks and Carter pulls her towards him in an absorbing hug. She has missed these hugs as Carter stands on his toes to place his head on her shoulder bringing himself closer to her.

Walking back home with both of her neighbours, Bono and their Pekinese dog off-leash in front of them (she has momentarily forgotten their dog's name, she still has some gaps in her memory) Molly walks into her home after saying goodbye feeling blessed again. Has it taken a horrible accident for her to appreciate these little things in life?

A FEW DAYS later she is sitting at her kitchen bench with her laptop open scanning for ideas of what she might do for work. Samantha and Evan are on video helping her out. With money now tight, which makes her wonder about the money Emma has raised for a second, but she stops because her anger still won't let her pursue that avenue yet. She wants to work and pay her own way. She will not be indebted to Emma in any circumstance.

She is chatting with Samantha and Evan who are both throwing ideas at her. "Ok, slow down both of you. How about you both email me your lists of possible jobs so I can mull them over?"

"Sure, will do." Samantha answers. "But take it easy, don't rush into a job you're going to hate. Think of your health first."

Molly appreciates what Samantha is saying and will keep her health in mind, but she needs a job.

"Yep, me too, I'll send my list soon. Gotta go now, I have a tennis match to play. We're in the semi-finals." Evan is a good tennis player and is in his local league. He and his doubles partner have won many a tournament over the past few years.

"Go get 'em. Evan," she says before she shuts her laptop down. Molly realises it is late afternoon and she has skipped lunch. This job hunting has her totally engulfed, which isn't bad because it keeps her mind off her troubles. Jumping off the stool, she hops over to the kettle, turning it on. When she is home, she doesn't wear Pete, her prosthetic foot, she uses a crutch instead. For short distances, she hops, and she considers this a form of exercise. Her physio is keeping her fitness levels up too with the continuing rehab.

Placing two pieces of bread in the toaster, she hops around taking out a cup for her coffee and a plate for the toast. Once her snack is ready, she settles in front of her laptop again.

This time she messages Harold who immediately calls for a video chat.

"Well, hello. Nice to hear from you. How are you doing?"

"Hi Harold, I'm doing ok thanks. You?"

"All good here too. I'm working at Rust Television in case you hadn't heard."

She didn't know this and wonders whether he is working on Emma's show. She didn't have to wonder for long.

"I'm working on Emma's morning show. So, what are you up to?"

"Well, I'm still doing rehab three days per week and looking at ideas of what I should do. I need to find a job soon, apart from boredom setting in, I need the money."

"I'll put out some feelers. I don't suppose you want to work at Rust?"

"If I can help it, no. Emma isn't someone I want to associate with again."

"That's a pity, you two were friends a long time."

Harold seems about to continue but then stops. She figures the less said about Emma the better. "Thanks Harold, I appreciate any help, take care. Maybe a drink some time?"

"Sure, send me a text when you're ready to go out socialising, it will be good for you and possibly your career."

She hadn't thought of socialising as networking, but he's right, she needs to be seen again to have any chance of finding work she wants to do. Harold signs off the call and her screen goes blank. Her battery is on low, so grabbing her crutch, she hobbles to the office and places it on charge.

FORTY-EIGHT

Emma

IT'S 5.30am and she's on set chatting to Harold, there is still half an hour before the show starts.

"I'm devastated. She still won't talk to me. So, tell me more, did she actually said she won't work at Rust?"

"Yes, she is still mad at you. I did say how you had been friends for a long time and it is a pity to lose someone who was so close, but she seemed to ignore this."

"You know what, Harold? I've had enough of her pettiness, I have moved on from that part of my life. Richard has moved on too, to another state. Only Molly is holding onto the past. Well, let her. If she wants to resume our friendship, then she can come to me. Then I'll listen to her because that's what good friends do."

"Good on you, Emma. But I don't think Molly will be running to you any time soon."

She drops into sadness, her head down. "Probably not, but I will keep an open mind about all the shit we said to each other and hope she lets it go too. Thanks for letting me know she contacted you, Harold, I do hope she comes to her senses." Harold nods and calls to everyone to be ready in fifteen minutes, another morning show is about to start.

IT'S the end of the working day, and a Friday, so Emma is looking forward to the weekend. She is in Jack's office having discussed the shows for the coming weeks. There were only a few people left in the building, everyone had been keen to start their weekends too.

"Molly is job hunting and not keen to come to work here," says Emma.

"I heard she went home from that rehab hospital. Glad to hear she is recovering well. And would you expect her to want to work here?"

"No, but she needs to let go of what happened between us, it's so far in the past now I hardly remember what we said." This is not true, but she is trying to make a point.

Jack laughs, "Yeah, right. You're never going to forget unless something happens like your friendship being repaired."

"I'm hopeful we'll be friends again someday. For now, I wish her well in finding a job she wants. You know, all that money that was donated, I have no idea what to do with it?"

"Maybe talk to Tim and David, let them help you work out a way to do something with it. Talk to a charity expert, or financial person who might suggest putting it in a trust. I'm sure Molly's orphanage will need it one day."

"Thanks, Jack. That's a good idea. Now, let's go and join the others at the pub."

"Definitely. And I think you need a drink more than me."

HARLEY IS WAITING like the obedient dog that he is as she stumbles in the door. He barks and she knows he is not happy having been left alone for so long. She left home at four this morning to finish off some things with Jack before the show. "Shh, I know it's late," she places her finger to her mouth, "and you're upset." Throwing off her shoes, she wobbles into her kitchen with Harley following. She pulls out a bottle of water from the fridge and guzzles it down. Having walked home from the train station, she is parched. She had drowned her sorrows at the pub, something she does regularly on Friday nights. *Fuck Molly. Fuck you and your stupid attitude.*

She flops herself down on the lounge and turns on the television. She's not interested in what's on, she just wants it on for background noise. Harley jumps onto her lap. She strokes his back then lets him cuddle into her. She isn't lonely with him around because he is such great company, she knows having Harley around helps her to forget her troubles.

But it's her anger at Molly, this is the reason she drinks more now. As much as she tries to forget and move on, which she delights in telling anyone who is interested, she hasn't let go of their friendship. Molly was essentially her sister, the sister she never had. Emma can't imagine her life without Molly in it, like right now, Molly not speaking to her for the rest of her life is inconceivable. Picking up her phone she sends Molly a text, she is drunk enough to say what she feels.

Molly, it's Emma. But you already know that. Listen, I'm drunk and you're going to have to listen to this, err … I mean read it. We are friends, you and I, so please don't forget that. We had a glitch that we both fuelled into a huge deal. And it's over. Nearly four years over. I love you Molly and I miss you. Please put this behind us, I need you to be my friend again. Harley misses Bono too, do you really want to keep them apart?

Emma decides this is a good ploy, pulling on the doggie strings will help.

Our dogs only just got to know each other with the last walk Harley had with Bono being over a year ago. David, Naomi and I would meet at the dog park near your place often so they could run around together. They had so much fun, do you really want them to miss out on this? And what about us? Our future can be full of more fun than we ever had. Molly, please answer me, I miss you more than you know.

Emma sends the text and realises she is crying. Harley sits up and tilts his head then places his paw on her hand. This makes Emma cry even harder. She lets herself cry, lets it all out because she hasn't allowed herself to grieve the loss of her friend enough. Molly may not have died, but their friendship has, and this is the consuming sadness that is now coming out. Emma cries until she falls asleep on the lounge with her head lolling over the side of her couch.

FORTY-NINE

Molly

SHE WAKES up to two things – one good, one bad.

She has text messages on her phone. The good one is that a radio station is asking her to come in for an interview for a new drive time show. She hadn't expected to hear from them as she had sent her resume on the off chance something was going. Well, what do you know? They have something that might suit her. A job in radio is perfect for her right now because she won't have to worry about covering the scars on her face. Although they are fading, she is still conscious of them. Especially the one above her eye that tugs her eye down. She scoffed at Tim when he had told her she now looked like she was constantly winking at people with that eye. Well that made her even more self-conscious of it and hopes people don't think she is winking at them.

Then there is Emma's text message. Her feelings towards Emma haven't changed yet, but the more she thinks about how much she misses Emma's friendship, the more she is beginning to keep an open mind. Especially now she has read her drunken message. Molly is the one who caused the fight in the first place and now Emma is the one doing the forgiving. Doesn't that show how good a friend she is?

Stumbling out of bed she falls to the floor. She still forgets she doesn't have a left foot. Sliding along the floor she finds her crutch, it had fallen onto the floor during the night. Placing her hand on the end of the bed, she lifts herself up. Her arms are now buff and strong because she falls more often than she'd like. Having stronger arms is a benefit, she tries to think of this as a positive.

Bono is still in his bed when she hobbles into the kitchen. "Hey, buddy. Are you ok?" He lifts his eyes then proceeds to lick his paw. This is unusual because he is usually in her bedroom the minute he hears her waking up. He hadn't moved even with the thump of her falling. "Is there something wrong with your paw again?" It's the same paw that was injured when Molly's stalker kicked him. *Wow, that seems like a lifetime ago.*

Taking care, Molly makes her way onto the floor and cringes at how cold the tiles are. "Let me take a look," says Molly taking his paw in her hand. Bono whimpers. "Oh, Bono, it's red raw. I guess this means a visit to the vet." Placing his paw back down, she pushes herself up slowly, hops toward the coffee machine and makes a coffee, grabs a biscuit and then heads to the shower. She needs to find out what Bono has done to his paw before she can deal with the two text messages.

THREE HOURS later they are home again with medicine and ointment for Bono, a new bootie for him to wear and a treat for Molly. She bought herself a chicken burger and chips for lunch, the smell as she places it on the bench is making her stomach grumble. Her appetite had certainly returned, she was going to enjoy this meal before tackling her messages and emails.

Placing the medicine for Bono on the bench, it turns out he has Pododermatitis, which is an inflammation of the paw. She then places her lunch in the oven to stay warm. The medicine for Bono is to relieve the pain, with the bootie to stop him licking his paw and removing the ointment. The vet showed her how to fasten the bootie to Bono's paw so he can't take it off.

After medicating Bono and placing the bootie on, as well as finishing off her lunch, Molly walks into her office and calls the radio station first. This is easier to deal with than Emma, and at this stage, slightly more important. She is placed through to the HR manager and given a date and time for the following week. She is also told to bring in a demo tape and any references.

References? Does she have any? Molly had worked at Ch33 since returning from India the very first time, she hadn't needed a reference until now. After finishing the call, she messages Sophia and Harold. Both come back saying they'll send something when they can.

With that done, she rereads Emma's message again. The mixed emotions of sadness and despair come up, same as the first time she read it. Did she expect anything different?

Molly sighs and looks around for Bono. He isn't in the office with her. "Bono," she calls. Nothing happens so she grabs her crutch and hobbles into the kitchen to see he has made a mess of his bootie. "Oh, Bono, what have you done?" asks Molly as she looks around at what is left of the bootie. "You've chewed it completely off. You naughty dog, how is your paw supposed to heal now?" There is fluff on the tiles, but it looks like Bono may have eaten most of the bootie. She hopes this won't mean another trip to the vet.

Bono looks at her with his huge brown eyes. How can Molly stay mad at him when he gives her that look? "You are a silly sausage, aren't you? I'm going to find something bigger and stronger to put on your paw. I suppose you've licked off all the ointment as well." Bono drops his head down then looks up at her with his huge brown eyes again. Her heart melts as she smiles and goes to find an old sock of hers, or maybe two. By doubling them up, she hopes Bono will take longer to remove them.

A week later, Bono's paw has healed enough for him to walk again. He hadn't touched the two socks Molly had covered his paw with, and she assumed him eating the bootie had given him a stomach issue. Well, isn't he a smart dog for not trying it a second time?

"I'm here," Carter calls out. Molly had left the front door ajar for him.

"Thanks for this, I'm sure he'll be ok on his own but he's still moaning a little."

"Not a problem, I love being with Bono." Carter bends down and ruffles the fur on Bono's back, "You're happy for Uncle Carter to look after you, aren't you mate?" Bono barks and licks Carter's hand. "Well, there's your answer Molly, now go and get that job."

THE OFFICES of Radio Lab 101 FM are in the city. Molly had taken a cab and arrived fifteen minutes early. Giving her name to the receptionist, she is told to take a seat. The small reception area is tidy with some quirky artwork on the walls. There is also a cast of a face in a brown resin on the table next to where she is sitting, it makes Molly feel strange as it looks like the beady eyes are staring at her. She decides to focus on her phone instead, she certainly didn't want anything to distract her from this interview. She needs this job.

It is half an hour later before Molly is ushered into what they call the boardroom. It is not much bigger than her old office with only four chairs around a glass table. Maybe they don't have a lot of staff or entertain many people? She sits and says no to a coffee or drink. Smoothing down her dress, she waits.

Eventually, two people walk in. One, a female, is about Molly's age with a shock of red curls and deep green eyes. Such an incredible combination, it takes Molly's breath away. She introduces herself as Isabelle, the station manager. Her colleague introduces himself as Rowan, the program director. He stands a foot taller than Isabelle, who is not short and both make Molly feel insignificant. They are both stunning and stylish and seem to be at odds with their surroundings. Isn't this station too small for them? They look like two ambitious people who belong at one of the larger top rating stations.

"We were impressed with your resume, thanks for sending that in and coming in to see us."

"I appreciate you taking the time to see me, Isabelle."

She listens as they talk about the drive time show that they are planning. As with other drive time shows, it's based on light-hearted banter between the hosts along with songs that are charting. She had listened to the station and found it pleasant enough, it had the same feeling as her old show – light entertainment with minimal news and popular songs. She begins to feel comfortable as the interview continues and thinks she might fit in here.

"I'M BACK." She places her bag on the hall stand and finds Carter and Bono both asleep on the lounge. Bono is the first to look up. "Look at you two, aren't you a sight? You both look so comfortable."

Carter wakes saying, "We were having a lovely kip until you rudely interrupted us."

Molly laughs, "Sorry, boys." Carter joins in the laughter and Bono woofs as he jumps off the lounge to greet Molly. "You're jumping so easily Bono, your paw must be feeling better. Thanks Carter, you being here made it easier for me to go out."

"Anytime, you know where I am when you need me," says Carter, "how did you go?"

"Uh fine, I think. They seemed happy with what I had to say. But who knows? Am I what they are looking for?"

"That's the million-dollar question," says Carter as he waves goodbye. "Let me know when you receive the offer."

She smiles as he walks out looking back towards her with his cheeky smile and hand waving in the air. Molly wishes she could be as positive as Carter.

FIFTY

Molly

HER MOOD IS as black as coal and she is moaning under her breath. Bono looks at her with a whimper. "I'm not in a good mood, Bono. You had better be good today." She bends down and holds his face in her hands kissing him with love.

She hasn't heard from the radio station yet and it is this that is annoying her. It's been ten days since the interview and she has heard nothing, absolutely nothing. She is browsing job ads because she is going stir-crazy being at home day after day. Boredom has led her to depress herself even further by scanning these ads. There is one ad she answered yesterday for a host of a late-night show, which she is mildly wanting and will take if it is offered. The only issue is her scars. Being self-conscious of them, she feels older because of her droopy eye. Although, if this TV station has a decent make-up department, this may not be a problem.

She stands up and shuts the lid of her laptop. Picking up her phone she rereads Emma's message yet again. Reaching the lounge, she plonks herself down dropping her crutch. Bono jumps up and sits with her and she looks at him through bleary eyes. Wet, soggy tears drip down her face whenever she reads the message. She has missed Emma, this she now knows because with all this time on her hands, it is Emma who comes to her mind when she needs company.

Samantha and Tim have been great with visiting and taking her out, but she can't say the things she wants to them. She needs Emma for these types of conversations, the ones where only a good girlfriend will do.

Opening the notes section of her phone she writes down the pros and cons of mending their friendship. Looking at them when she is finished, it seems this was a positive exercise. But does she have the courage to action the result?

Finally, later that afternoon, an email comes from the radio station. They want her to come in for another interview. What? What the hell happened to the days when you were offered the job soon after the first interview? She answers the email agreeing to meet them in two days. Well, hopefully, this is something to look forward to.

YET AGAIN SHE is waiting in the reception of Radio Lab 101 FM. This time forty minutes have passed, and she is tetchy. It's another twenty minutes before she is taken into the boardroom again. How can they be so lax with time?

She sits placing her crutch on the floor. There is someone else sitting there besides the two people who had interviewed her the first time. He is introduced to her as her co-host on the drive time show. *My co-host? I have the job.*

"Hi," Brendan says smiling towards her. His warm, deep voice easily belongs on the radio. He may not be the most striking person in the room, but he has a friendly, approachable look. She already feels comfortable and knows right away she'll like him.

"Nice to meet you, Brendan." He offers her his hand and the shake confirms her comfortable feeling.

Isabelle explains they have decided to give both of them a three-month trial starting in two weeks. Both she and Rowan want to see how they perform together, whether their banter will bring more listeners. She continues explaining their contracts will be emailed to them and if they have any questions to contact either herself or Rowan. With this, Isabelle and Rowan leave Molly and Brendan in the room to chat allowing them to have the room for another half an hour.

"Well, that was unexpected. The email I received said this was a second interview."

"Same here. But here we are, we're a partnership in a drive time show."

Molly laughs, "Yes, we are. G'day, partner."

Brendan laughs and stretches out his hand for a fist pump, "Let's make this official. I'm Brendan Schutter and I can be funny at times."

Molly balls her hand up and touches his, "We're officially drive-time partners now we have touched. I'm Molly Edwards and up until I had an accident that placed me in a coma, I was a host of a light-entertainment show."

"I know who you are, my mother loved watching your show and was devastated when it was cancelled. Wait till I tell her I'm working with you." Brendan feigns surprise and awe.

She already likes him and laughs at his mocking of his mother. "We'll have to discuss ideas before we go to air, are you up for maybe meeting up or zooming a few times?"

"Yes, we should get to know each other better, I'm up for either," he says picking up his phone. "I think our styles will complement each other going by this short chat."

She agrees with him and stands holding onto her crutch after they exchange phone numbers and email addresses. "This is going to be interesting, I haven't worked in radio before. I hope we can make it work. With the break I've had from working, I have a lot to learn."

"All we can do is give it our best shot," he says as they walk out.

WHEN SHE ARRIVES HOME, Molly begins a video chat with Tim and Samantha. They are both ecstatic for her, especially Samantha.

"I was worried about you lolling around your house. You're not the type to do nothing. How are you feeling?"

"Really good now. I know it's too early to call, but Brendan and I have agreed to give this our best shot. And with radio, I won't be worried about my appearance."

"We know how much this has bothered you," says Tim, "but honestly, the scars are looking better every day."

Molly knows Tim is trying to keep her spirits up and neither he nor Samantha talk about her scars or lack of a left foot unless she mentions it. Pete the prosthetic is comfortable now and with her tendency to wear maxi dresses, long skirts or pants, she feels better when it's covered. She is still seeing her physiotherapist once a week and knows she has come a long way. This is something she must remember when the black moods takeover.

"Any thoughts on talking to Emma yet?" Tim asks her this often and she usually ignores him.

"Funny you should ask, yet again," she scoffs. "Emma sent me a text a few weeks ago. She was drunk ... and well, her words moved me. Once I settle into this job, I might call her."

"Wonderful." Both Tim and Samantha say this in unison with Samantha clapping.

"I'm still thinking about it, don't get ahead of yourselves."

"It will be the best thing for both of you, Aunt Molly. You had so many good times together, don't you want more?"

Molly smiles and understands their concern. "I guess I do. Let me start this job and then I'll tackle repairing my friendship with Emma. Love you both, mwah." She clicks off the chat calling Bono, it's time for his walk.

FIFTY-ONE

Emma

SHE IS DRIVING down the coast highway to Bowral. Emma hadn't been back down since selling the farm. Trevor's brother, Barry had asked her to come down and stay with them on their farm as she is attending Clark's wedding. Clark, their cousin, had allowed Barry to stay with him at his apartment in Wollongong after Trevor's passing. Barry is his best man, which is appropriate. Barry owes a lot of his recovery to Clark, who watched over him when he was at his worst. Trevor's family is a close bunch, a real country family who look after their own. She is pleased to be still considered a part of this family, it makes her feel closer to Trevor, who she misses every day.

She is listening to Molly's drive time radio program and had felt a pang of love from the moment she heard Molly's voice. The music is popular pop and rock and is easy enough to listen to on a long drive. Molly's partner on the show is a well-known comedian and DJ who tells some droll dad jokes at times. Molly gives him grief for these and the banter between the two of them seems to be working. Emma is happy that Molly has found a job, which she is sure she needed after all her time off, but she still wants to talk to her about the money she raised. It is sitting in a trust that a friend of Tim's had set up for them. Molly is the main beneficiary and the three of them are signatories for the account.

Harley is sleeping in the back seat, snoring away blissfully. She is spending five days in Bowral, so he has come along for the ride. She takes in the scenery and because of all the recent rain, everything is lush and green. This is better than the bushfires that devastated much of Australia's east coast, although the floods were still wreaking havoc. It seems Australia's weather is one of extremes, it is either fires or floods. Today though is a resplendent day of vivid blue skies and she hopes the next five days are the same.

A SUNDAY WEDDING in Bowral is pretty and peaceful. The ceremony is held under a white tarpaulin with birds chirping in the summer sun. Everyone is in attendance at Barry's farmhouse and they have now moved into the bar area while the happy couple have photos taken. Many of the family members greet Emma warmly making her feel at home. She had worried that some of them would not want her here, but this isn't the case. At least, not in front of her anyway. "This is lovely, Barry. What a nice way to pay Clark back for everything he did for you."

"Yes, it is my way of saying thanks. Besides, you know he has struggled financially since his business failed during the pandemic."

"I do. Like so many other restaurants, they couldn't cope."

"But let's not talk about that today. This is a happy occasion. What do you think of his bride?"

"She seems nice, but I haven't said much to her other than 'hello, I'm Emma'."

"She is a few years younger than him and has her own stud farm, so he is set for life now."

"Clark a kept man? Wow, that's something for a chef who ran his own restaurants for twenty years."

"He'll find something smaller down here, sell up his apartment in Wollongong and things will be great for him, you'll see."

"I am sure it will be. How are you going?"

Barry explains how he fell into a slump after Trevor passed away and it was Clark who helped him survive. Death has a way of changing your perspective on life and at times it takes longer to accept how final it is. "In my case it took two years before I could wake up without crying and missing Trevor so much it hurt. I was physically unable to go on." Emma nods as she knows that feeling and at times, it does come back to haunt her.

"What about you? What are you doing these days?"

"I'm hosting a breakfast show on Rust Television. You probably don't get it down here, it's one of the smaller off-shoot TV stations. It's great but I still struggle as I'm not a morning person. Once I'm up and ready on set, it's fine. Getting to that point is the problem."

Barry laughs, "I remember how Trevor complained you were never up early enough to do the main chores, you left it all to him.

"Yeah, I know. He was the farmer, not me." They both continue laughing as the happy couple come into the bar.

THE DAY AFTER THE WEDDING, Jack sends a message asking how it all went. Emma answers saying it was great with a photo of her alongside the happy couple. She is walking Harley so tells him she will call him later with all the details. She isn't in the mood to talk right now because she is clearing her head after another drink fest. Her head throbs and she wonders whether she is bordering on becoming an alcoholic. She dismisses this immediately because she remembers everything that happened.

Jealously had reared its ugly head when she was watching the happy couple, both at the ceremony and the reception. Richard had popped into her head and she had contemplated contacting him. In her drunken state, she texted him. It was the first time she had looked up his details since he sent them to her after moving up north. This was last night at midnight and he had said he would call sometime today. It was three in the afternoon, she hadn't heard from him yet. Was she disappointed? Not really, it was the alcohol that had put her in a melancholy, reminiscing mood.

She and Harley are back at Barry's homestead an hour later. Emma has made herself a cup of tea and is on her laptop checking emails when Richard calls. "Hello, how are you?" she asks him.

"Well, thanks. Nice of you to contact me. Are you ok?"

"I'm well too. Down in Bowral, I came for a wedding. Do you remember Clark, Trevor's cousin? He remarried."

"Umm, can't say that I do, but congrats to him. How is Bowral treating you?"

"I've had a better reception than I anticipated, which is a nice surprise. I guess country folk don't hold grudges."

"Why would they hold a grudge against you. What did you do wrong?"

"Oh, you know ... leaving Trevor to run the farm on his own while I followed a career. Some folk down here didn't take kindly to that. A farmer's wife is meant to stay behind her husband and support him."

"That sounds awfully old-fashioned and not something I could ever see you doing."

They continue chatting as if they have not been apart. Both slip into the comfortable place that has always been between them. She and Richard had an affair but it didn't feel like one. With her living in Sydney, their relationship was just as real as the one she had with Trevor. They were two special men in her life and she misses them both, but it is Trevor who fills her thoughts more often now. Death has a way of bringing things into perspective.

"Well, it has been great chatting Richard. Thanks for calling, and if you're ever in Sydney, we should catch up."

"I'd love that, thanks Emma. Take care of yourself and I'll let you know if I'm down." He clicks off the call before she has a chance to say goodbye. Staring at her phone she wonders whether she will catch up with him if he is in Sydney? Does she really want to open up old wounds?

FIFTY-TWO

Molly

SHE IS HALF DOZING on the lounge when her phone trills. Picking it up without focusing on who is calling her, she says a weary "hello".

"Sorry, did I wake you?"

"Hi David, no, I'm lying on the lounge and very relaxed."

"I'm glad to hear that. How's the new job going? I've listened a few times, it's good."

"Thanks. Yeah, it's going well." She raises herself up into a sitting position, having felt like she was mumbling whilst lying down. "We are still formulating our concept and Brendan is full of ideas."

David mentions he enjoys Brendan's comedy and feels that Molly and he have chemistry. She smiles thinking of Brendan's easy-going nature and his jokes, which can be silly at times. Molly thinks it's too early to tell how the show is doing but she too has a good feeling about their partnership. They have been on-air for a month with two more months of the trial period to go.

They keep chatting for quite a while, David explaining Naomi is away for the weekend. Molly had wondered why he had called, he usually sends text messages to check on her. He continues saying they are planning a trip to Bali soon, he needs a break.

"That will be lovely for both of you. I haven't been to Bali in years."

"Me either. Remember we discussed it before the pandemic?"

"Yes, but that feels like an eon ago."

"You sound ok, how are things going? Are you still having physio?"

"Fortnightly now. I am used to my prosthetic, which I call Pete, by the way. Pete the prosthetic." She hears laughter and continues, "sometimes I misplace him and call out 'Pete, where are you?'"

David guffaws and doesn't answer until he calms down, "Oh, Molly, you crack me up. At least that hasn't changed, I've always loved your sense of humour. But what about Emma?"

Molly sighs ... not David too. Tim has been hassling her about repairing the friendship, she guesses the two of them have been talking. "Tim asks all the time. I'm thinking about it. I'll contact her when I'm ready."

"I hope you do, Molly. You two were good together and we need to organise that money, I'm sure you have more medical bills to pay?"

He is right about her bills but she is hoping this radio gig goes well and she won't need the money Emma managed to raise. "I'm ok, especially now I'm working. But look, I'm hearing both you and Tim and, like I said, I'm considering contacting her. As far as the money, you three can give it to the orphanage, they always need funds."

"We can discuss the money once you and Emma are talking again. The donors wanted to help you as well as the orphanage. Think about it but for now keep going with the radio show, I'm sure your fans have followed you to the station. Stay well, Molly."

She thanks him and clicks off the call. Patting Bono who is sleeping next to her, she contemplates what may have happened with their relationship had Naomi not come along. Would she have stayed with David? The tingling feeling in her body tells her she would have.

MOLLY HAD DECIDED to meet with Emma at home. She felt more comfortable confronting their issues in the safety of her own surroundings. Not wanting to air their issues in front of others, who knows what that might start again?

She had finally gathered the courage to contact Emma a week earlier, and today she is coming over for brunch. Molly had ordered food and it arrived at the same time as Emma. She grabs her order from the delivery guy and stands awkwardly propped up against her front door as Emma walks up the drive. Bono escapes from behind Molly and jumps up to greet Emma. She can hear Emma greeting Bono as she tickles his head. "You're happy to see me. Oh, how I've missed you." Molly smiles as Emma emphasises *you*. She looks up towards Molly, "And you too," she says as she greets her.

"Come in," says Molly still feeling awkward and lost for words. She limps slightly because Pete the prosthetic is giving her grief today. Maybe the stress of seeing Emma again is causing her to notice the pain more acutely. Molly leads Emma into the kitchen and prepares the food onto plates. She remains quiet as her body is tense, her nerves as tight as an over-stretched elastic. This is probably why Pete is bothering her.

"You're limping, are you ok?" Molly nods not wanting to go into the pain of her foot. Emma doesn't push the point obviously sensing Molly is feeling anxious about this meeting. "I'm glad you called, Molly," says Emma breaking the awkward silence. "I know this isn't easy for you, I feel the same. We're opening issues that neither of us wants to face."

Molly limps around to sit on the stool next to Emma and picks up her coffee, sipping it. "Woah, that's hot." She gulps down some water before speaking again. "Your words in the text you sent, the one where you were drunk, they hit home. That was when I started thinking we could repair this mess. But I apologised multiple times and that never hit home to you. You were stubborn and, in the end, I gave up."

"I was hurt, no devastated, actually. You and Richard? I still can't get my head around the whole thing. And don't give me the bullshit about him doing it to help our sex life."

Molly smirks at that, she had thought it a weak excuse at the time too. "Richard justified it to himself, it made him feel better. But what was my excuse? He won me over with his charm, I guess. Still, it should never have happened."

Emma acknowledges that Richard was good at winning women over, her included. However, this doesn't take away the fact that Richard and Molly hurt two other people they were close too. Molly's relationship, Emma's relationship with Richard, and their friendship suffered the consequences. A friendship that had weathered other fights and disagreements, many they had laughed about after the event, but this one broke them.

Molly has her head down, nodding. She agrees. "So, how do we move on from this? Are you ready to apologise to me?" Molly wants an apology from Emma for all the awful things she posted and for not accepting at least one of Molly's apologies. Emma might have been hurt in all of this, but Molly didn't come out of it unscathed.

"Me apologise to you. What for? I wasn't the one screwing your boyfriend."

"No, you're right. But you screwed both me and Richard very publicly on social media. The fallout of that was we lost our jobs and Richard moved interstate. And look at the state I'm in, was it all necessary?"

Emma plays around with the food, then looks up at Molly, "I'm sorry about your accident but I have nothing to apologise for. You and Richard started this and I reacted in the best way I knew given the circumstances. I wanted to hurt both of you as much as you hurt me."

Molly stands up taking both plates of food to the sink. They clatter loudly as she throws them in ignoring the food left on them.

Neither she nor Emma had eaten much. "I think you had better leave. We have nothing more to say to each other."

Emma is shocked, "Molly, be serious. We can discuss this ..."

"I said leave." Molly turns on her good heal, and limps into the hallway to open the front door. "Now!"

FIFTY-THREE

Molly

THE OFFICES of Radio Lab 101 FM are meagre compared to the ones at Ch33 where Molly worked previously. The studio she and Brendan record in is compact, they can't fit more than two guests at a time. But this isn't an issue as they haven't interviewed any invited guests yet. Still, she feels comfortable here, at home. The small team works well together, they all have mutual respect for each other. Isabelle and Rowan have created a culture of creativity and collaborative ideas. Employees are not just numbers here. Radio fits Molly like a glove, she is meant for this job.

Their contracts were renewed for another year with an option for two more if ratings keep going the way they are. Their show has made an impact and 'Arvos with Brendan & Molly' is rating better than expected as well as trending on social media. Molly and Brendan are popular. This is a surprise to Molly although Brendan had had a good feeling from the beginning.

"Come on, we make a good team. Have some faith in yourself."

She smiles at Brendan who has more confidence than Molly will ever have. She had it before the accident, her confidence was what kept her show lively and entertaining. But the accident had changed many things in her life, with her confidence taking a big hit. Every time Pete gives her pain, the demons take over. This is something she is working on and somehow she is regaining some of her previous self and feels comfortable working in radio, with this station being the perfect fit for her right now. "We do make a good team, Brendan. And we have the fans to prove it."

Things have improved in Molly's life since she began working again. Her spark is flickering again, she feels happier and overall, her life is good. Except for Emma. Ever since Emma came to her house and she threw her out, Molly has felt guilty. Did she give Emma a chance? Why had she expected an apology when it was she who hurt Emma? Molly is chastising herself now because if the situation had been reversed, she would probably have done exactly what Emma did. Social media is rampant with fights like they had, it's the perfect platform for these spats, especially amongst celebrities. With trolls spurting their vile opinions it is hard not to take things personally. But Molly doesn't have the courage to ask Emma for forgiveness, not again. She has to move on and find other friendships, Emma is in her past.

"Molly. Molly, are you ready?"

"Wha ... oh, yes, sorry Brendan. Let's go," she says as she prepares for another show. She can only look forward to a better future from here.

TIM, Samantha and Evan are over. They are playing Scrabble in Molly's lounge room. It's pouring outside and has been all weekend. Molly had been feeling lonely, her dark mood closing in on her, so she asked them to come over for a games' afternoon. They were all at a loose end and had welcomed her invitation.

Evan supplied some good quality weed, Molly supplied red wine and Tim had brought over his famous tacos. He added a secret ingredient that made them extra delicious. Molly had tried to coax this ingredient out of him many times, but he remains tight-lipped. "I will take this secret to my grave. You guys can suffer normal tacos after I'm gone," he had laughed. She concentrates on the game again thinking he will tell someone one day.

"That's not even a word," laughs Samantha. "What the hell is cotija?"

"Look it up. It's a Mexican cow's milk cheese," Evan slurs.

Samantha checks on her phone. "Ha, you're right. How did you know that?"

"Firstly, it's appropriate given we've eaten tacos and secondly, I have a brain that remembers trivial words. It's a gift." This makes the four of them fall about in fits of laughter. They have been playing for two hours with this happening more than once. Molly's dark mood has been replaced by a chilled-out, happy one. She is relaxed, which is a great feeling as she thought relaxation was a thing of the past for her.

Even though the show is doing well, personally her demons keep lashing out at her. The darkness descends when she least expects it, abducting her whole sense of worth. When Pete gives her pain, she has days of feeling so despondent, she worries about herself. She hasn't spoken to anyone about these feelings as she has been able to cover them up. Samantha had detected something was wrong when Molly had first come home, but since she had started working again, everyone now assumes she is fine.

"Hey Molly, we need chips. Do you have any? The saltier the better," Evan slurs again.

She staggers up from the floor, "Yep, I'll get some. Woah!" she exclaims as she falters, "I'm worse than I thought." Pete is behaving himself today. Or is the pain numbed by the drugs and alcohol? Bono comes up sitting in front of Molly, "Sorry mate, no walk today, it's pissing down outside. Besides, in this state, I don't think I'd be able to walk." She laughs as she stumbles towards the kitchen. She continues laughing as she looks for the chips.

"You're mad, Aunt Molly," slurs Samantha.

"Oh, come on isn't it better that I'm laughing?" she asks returning with two bowls full of chips. Evan grabs a handful of each and shoves them in his mouth.

"Take it easy, Evan, leave some for the rest of us," laughs Tim who had been quiet up until now.

"So, you are with us. What's up?" asks Molly.

"Me? Nothing, just enjoying the show you three are putting on. This is hilarious, I've never enjoyed Scrabble so much."

"I told ya it was good shit," says Evan.

"Yeah, you were right. But, I think the company has something to do with it too. Nothing better than spending time with my little sister and my daughter, who I love dearly. Oh, and you too Evan."

"Gee, thanks bro." Evan laughs and this starts them all off again. Their laughter is contagious and Bono joins in by barking with his tail whipped into action.

It's after midnight when they stumble out of her door to the waiting cabs. Molly is left on her own again. What a great time they had, she makes a mental note to do this again. She is pleasantly stoned and slowly works her way through clearing up. If only she could feel like this all the time, the euphoria that good weed and alcohol give her, she wants more of it.

As she is tidying, Tim messages her.

Thanks for a great afternoon. Really enjoyed myself.

You're welcome. Likewise. BTW, are you ok? You were quiet there for a while.

Yeah, I'm worried about you. I noticed you swigging the wine more than usual and Samantha says she has noticed you being moody again.

Here we go. As much as she appreciates Tim and Samantha caring about her, discussing her demons with them is not something she wants to do. She promises herself she will make an appointment with a psychologist and sort this out herself.

I was enjoying myself, and no, I'm not drinking more than usual. I'm fine. She knows this isn't going to convince Tim and hopes he doesn't push even more.

Ok, but you know we're here when you need us. Love you.

Love you more. xx

Thankfully, Tim didn't push the point. And she loves him even more for it. She will open up when she is ready.

She switches her phone off not wanting to be disturbed again. Pouring herself the last of the wine, she sits on the kitchen stool thinking about whether she *is* drinking too much. But more so, her thoughts go to ... *where to from here?* Generally, she is happy. Lonely at times, but mostly happy. David is still in her thoughts and so is Emma. As much as she tries to place them in her past, they are always there, wanting attention. She doesn't see a future with David, and even though she wants this to happen, she will have to let go because he has Naomi now. He keeps in touch often and they always have amicable chats. Emma ... well, she is another story. Molly will call her again, but this time not to ask for an apology, but ask for the two of them to be friends again, this is what she really wants. When she will do this is still an issue.

Forgiveness is better than this anger that engulfs her all the time. Deep down, this is what's bothering her. Emma was Molly's best friend and so far, nothing Molly has done, or thought, has been able to replace her. Emma is a friend like no other, she is the sister Molly always wanted.

She gulps the last of the wine and shuffles off to bed, crashing on it fully clothed. Emma is a problem for another time.

FIFTY-FOUR

Emma

SHE STARES AT HER PHONE. It's been three months since they spoke and now Molly is sending her a message. It's unbelievable because since she was thrown out by Molly after their last fateful meeting, Molly hasn't been in touch nor has Emma tried to contact her. Emma decided to let her stew on her anger and hoped she would see reason. Now it looks like she has. She wants to meet again.

Emma is wary. Does she want to go through this again? Her body is retaliating with flutters in her stomach and a mild headache begging. Having tried to forget Molly, the fact Emma has over a million dollars sitting in a trust account for her is stopping this from happening. Both David and Tim have said to hold off distributing the money until Molly comes around, they are sure she still needs to cover her rehabilitation costs. "She's being stubborn, Emma," Tim had told her. "Give her time. She deserves some of that money." So, the money stayed where it was, which drove Emma mad at times when she thought about it. That is a lot of money to have sitting doing nothing when both Molly and her orphanage could use it well.

Hovering her finger over her phone, she decides not to answer Molly yet. Let her stew a little more. Emma is still angry about Molly throwing her out, literally forcing Emma out of her house. To say she was hurt is an understatement. And all because she wouldn't apologise for her behaviour. Which Molly and Richard caused! Anger is searing through her body now. "Fuck you, Molly. I'm not ready yet." She yells this at her phone and throws it on the lounge startling Harley. "Harley, let's go for a walk."

Outside the sun warms her, summer is only a week away. Walking down to the reserve, her energy level is extreme, the anger spurring her on. An hour later, she and Harley are still sitting at Berry Island Reserve enjoying the view. Why hadn't she walked down here before? It's peaceful but this is probably due to it being a weekday, she is sure the children's equipment is well used during weekends.

Taking Harley's leash off, she lets him run around. She isn't sure this is an off-leash park, but let him be free for a bit, it won't hurt. She raises her face to the sun allowing it to warm her, calming her nerves. How did this get so difficult? Molly and she were the best of friends, why the hell did Molly have to sleep with Richard?

Her thoughts turn to Richard, he'd been in town a few times and asked her to catch up. She had declined each time because she knows if she sees him, she will want to sleep with him. Her feelings for him are still strong even after everything that has happened. She had gone on a few dates, guys she met on dating apps, but nothing came of them. Not that she put any effort into finding anyone. She is quite happy on her own for now.

"Hey, lady. Your dog should be on a leash."

She is startled by a man who is near Harley giving him a pat. "Nice dog, what's his name?"

Looking towards the man, she smiles because he seems harmless enough. "Harley." Standing up from the sandstone block she was sitting on, she walks over and clips on Harley's leash. "I wasn't sure if this was an off-leash park, but as no one was around, I let him free for a bit."

"Sure, but you will receive a fine if a ranger is around. Hi, I'm Lewis."

"Emma." She shakes the hand he has offered.

"Yes, I know. Emma Beers Jones. Used to watch your show on Friday nights."

"Oh, right ... err, thanks. So, what brings you to a park on a week-day?" She steers the conversation away from her previous show not wanting to get into a discussion about why it's not on air any longer.

He proceeds to tell her he works as a fireman and, as it's shift work, he has some weekdays off. He keeps talking about his work as she takes in his fit physique. His bright blue eyes are the focus of his face because being bald, they are the first thing you see. She guesses he is in his late thirties, a couple of years older than her. They begin to walk back up to where he has his bike, he rides down to this park often he tells her. They chat amicably for what seems like minutes but an hour has passed. Emma feels a comfort being around him she hasn't felt in ages. It's a good feeling.

"I don't suppose you're free tonight, there is a gig on at my local pub, would you like to join me?"

Wow, this guy is fast. Not that she minds, he has a certain look she finds attractive. "I am free actually, I don't usually do much on Thursday nights."

"Great. I can pick you up or meet there if you prefer? It's the Thistle and Thorn in Crows Nest, do you know it?"

She thinks about him picking her up for a milli-second but opts to meet him at the pub, in case of needing a quick getaway. "Yes, I know it. I'll meet you there."

"Ok then, see you tonight at eight?"

"Sounds good," she says as he hands her his phone asking her to add her contact details. She returns the favour. As she watches him ride off, she admires his butt. Everything about him is buff and taut.

Hmm, I've never fancied bald men, but there is something about Lewis that is giving me flutters in places I haven't thought about since Trevor passed and Richard left.

Emma gives Harley a pat. "What do you think, Harley, is Lewis to your liking? He looks up at her and cocks his head. "I'll take that as a *yes*."

FIFTY-FIVE

Molly

IT'S BEEN months and Emma never responded to her texts. Molly ended up sending three in total but to no avail. She is not sure what she expected because having thrown Emma out of her house after she wouldn't apologise, did she think Emma *would* respond? How she wished Emma had answered. Molly is seeing a therapist about her demons and, as much as this is helping her, she wants to speak to Emma. She wants her best friend back.

She had confided in Tim at times, well a little anyway. She didn't want to say too much to her brother because he already worries about her enough. He is caring and helped her a few times when she was feeling particularly low. He had told her the accident was a massive blow to her life and she needed to acknowledge it. She knows this but it is harder than it sounds. Molly has tried to focus on the radio show and move on from the accident, which has worked to a point. The demons are harder to shift, they seem to keep wanting to keep her down.

Throwing her arms up above her head, she stretches and then throws off the sheet heading for the shower. She is meeting Tim and Samantha tonight, this is something to look forward to while she is at work today.

SHE IS SITTING with them at the Thai restaurant near Tim's home. He had suggested this so they could go to see a band afterwards. The pub is near his house too, they can walk there from the restaurant. "You'll enjoy the band, it's your type of music, Molly. You know, a chilled-out style," he had said when he suggested they get together.

"This food was great, thanks Tim. It's always good to see both of you. Samantha, you look particularly lovely tonight, are you meeting someone after this?"

"Funny you should ask. And thanks, I made an effort because one of the guys in the band we're going to see, well ... he and I are seeing each other."

"That's great. I'm happy for you. I hope you'll introduce him tonight."

"It's the reason we're going, Aunt Molly, I want you to meet him. With him playing gigs most nights, it easier this way."

Molly is always happy to spend time with her brother and niece, and now this is an added surprise. Samantha hasn't had a boyfriend for some time, at least not one she was prepared to meet her family.

"Come on, let's go. I've fixed the bill and look forward to some good music and more drinking."

"Lead the way, Tim." Molly and Samantha follow him. They chat all the way to the pub, the Thistle and Thorn.

It's only a few minutes when they arrive and the music can be heard from outside. It's mellow and people waiting to enter are swaying to the rhythm. This is going to be fun, Molly is keen to get inside.

"Drinks?" asks Tim once they are inside.

"I'll stick with wine, a house red, thanks," answers Molly with Samantha opting for a spritzer.

When Tim returns to the table they had found, he says, "You're not going to believe who is here?" Both Molly and Samantha give him blank looks. "Emma. Look over there with that burly guy."

Molly sees them, they are sitting at the bar and looking into each other's eyes. There is probably no way Emma would have seen Molly but she is already feeling uncomfortable. Without thinking too much about it, she blurts, "Err, look ... I'm going to go home."

"What? Why?" Samantha is stunned.

"Don't be silly. Anyway, you haven't met Clayton yet. We know him as Clay," adds Tim.

It takes Molly a moment to realise who Clayton is. "I'll meet him another time, sorry, but I can't stay here. Emma never responded to those texts I sent her, so she obviously doesn't want to know me."

"Molly, please wait until Clay's band has done one set. Then he'll come over to meet you." Samantha's eyes are pleading and Molly's heart melts.

"Oh, Samantha. Alright, but one set only. After I've met him, I'll leave." Samantha gives her aunt a hug and Tim gives Molly a curt smile. She knows he isn't pleased and wants this stupid mess cleaned up as he and David are still in contact with Emma. But Molly has been frozen out of her life.

After a few minutes Clay and his band, *Incendiary Sets*, begins to play. With a mix of acoustic guitar, keyboard and drums, they play their own songs with a couple of covers. Molly finds herself swaying to the tunes as she tries not to think about Emma being a few metres away. The house lights are down and she can't see her right now, so the chances Emma will spot her are minimal. It's not long before the set finishes and Clay, tats, earrings and all, comes over to say hello.

"It's nice to finally meet you Molly, Samantha has told me lots about her famous aunt." Shaking his hand Molly thanks him. He then moves towards Samantha and kisses her lightly on the lips, "Hi, babe."

Cute. Molly likes him already. They chat for a few more minutes with Samantha telling Molly how they met. With her event management business she had organised a function at a hotel and Incendiary Sets was booked as the entertainment. This was three months ago and Molly can see there are sparks between them. Clay is softly spoken, which is a surprise given his appearance and how he can belt out a song, his voice can boom when needed. He is wearing a leather vest and his tats are visible, he has a sleeve of colourful ones on his left arm. Samantha has her arm through that arm, her other hand on his shoulder. Samantha's style of designer jeans, heels and silk shirt are at odds with Clay's look, but this doesn't mean anything, he seems besotted with her. He touches her hand resting on his shoulder and looks into her eyes as they talk. Molly looks towards Tim who seems pleased, but she does wonder what he thinks about the tats. She'll talk to him later about that.

"This has been great. Clay it's nice to meet you and I enjoyed your music, you have great style and talent. Tim, Samantha, thanks for a lovely evening." She thinks she sees Clay's face redden, but it's probably her imagination with the dimness around them in the pub.

"I'll see you out," offers Tim and she allows him to follow her as she avoids the bar area where Emma and her man are still seated.

"Tim, how do you feel about Clay?" she asks when they're outside.

"At first, I was wary of him. Those tats are a bit much. But once I got to know him, he's a good guy. Samantha is happy, so why should I get in the way of that happiness?"

"I saw how they looked at each other, you're right, she is happy. See you soon," she leans in kissing his cheek. "Enjoy the rest of the night."

"Molly, are you sure you don't want to talk to Emma?"

"Tim, she's with someone. Besides, if she wanted to see me, she would have answered my texts. Leave it, you and David can still be friends with her, but she has obviously let me go."

Tim hangs his head in defeat. Giving Molly a kiss on her cheek, he gives her that curt smile again as she leaves. Let him be mad at her, it's not as if she hadn't tried with Emma.

FIFTY-SIX

Emma

OUT OF THE corner of her eye, she sees Molly walking out with Tim. She thought that was him earlier at the bar. Then she sees him walking back inside without Molly and calls him over. When he reaches them, she introduces him to Lewis and then asks about Molly. "Why has she left so early? The music will pump for hours yet."

"She was tired and needed to go home. Her foot was bothering her."

Tim seems cagey, his head down and not looking at her but she decides not to comment, instead saying, "Poor thing. That accident will haunt her the rest of her life."

Tim nods and begins heading back to Samantha. "Well, it's good seeing you Emma, I'd better get back to Samantha. Nice meeting you, Lewis." Lewis nods giving Tim a smile.

"Of course, yes. Say hello to her," says Emma. Tim looks back and nods again as he walks towards the table.

Emma understands why Molly didn't come to say hello, but it still hurts. The anger she had felt when Molly threw her out has subsided, and she has thought about answering Molly's texts, she is still not sure why she hasn't yet. Having met Lewis was a distraction, but she received the texts weeks before meeting him. The anger is still lingering in the back of her mind and this is probably the reason she hadn't answered Molly.

Lewis is holding her hand and listening to the music, which Emma admits is great. The lead singer's voice is melodic and charming. She and Lewis had come to this pub twice since meeting two weeks before, he is a fan and knows the guitarist. She takes in his face as he enjoys the songs, he is humming as he turns to see she is watching him.

"What?"

"Nothing, I'm enjoying watching you enjoying the music."

"I told you these guys were good. We'll come and see them whenever they play here, right?"

"Sure." She smiles knowing he is pleased they have music in common. He had told her his ex-girlfriend didn't like music and never came to the pub with him. Any wonder they broke up, which is fine by her. Lewis is great company and since Richard left, and she lost Trevor, she hadn't seriously thought about dating again.

"By the way, how do you know Tim?" asks Lewis.

"He's an old friend, the brother of someone I once knew. But we can talk about that later, come on, let's go and dance." Their relationship is too new for her to want to talk to him about Molly.

SHE AND JACK are sitting in her dressing room after the show, she is taking off her make-up. Emma had told him about seeing Molly and how she had left the pub early.

"Honestly, you two. You were great friends, I can't believe this is so hard for you to work out. Say sorry and be friends again. Simple."

"When you put it that way, yes. But it's not that simple Jack, we said some horrible things to each other over social media. And don't forget, she was the one who threw me out after we had agreed to meet and fix things." Emma is looking into the mirror as she is saying this, noticing the bags under her eyes. She and Lewis have been burning the midnight oil, and this isn't the only thing keeping her awake. Lewis is an amazing lover, happy to please her often.

Jack notices the smile creep across her face, "What's so funny?"

"Oh, nothing. Thinking about Lewis, that's all."

Jack laughs, "Oh the hunk has taken over your life, hasn't he? Tell me more." He leans in towards her.

"I'm not discussing my sex life with my executive producer," she mocks him, "a girl has to have some secrets." Both fall about laughing, which is a welcome distraction from all the talk about Molly.

"I'll see you at the production meeting." Jack says this when he stops laughing, "time to be your boss again."

"Thanks Jack, I do appreciate your thoughts about this Molly thing." He smiles as he walks out the door leaving her alone. Her own thoughts stay on Molly, her best friend since she was eighteen and that was almost fifteen years ago. Yet for the last four years, they have hardly spoken, which is so wrong. There are times when Emma feels guilty about what happened to Molly. Would the accident had happened if she hadn't gone to India? Did Emma's actions force Molly to go?

Emma decides not to go down this well-trodden path again. These thoughts had wracked her since Molly's accident, and it is no use asking these questions because they will never know. Molly may have had a similar accident here in Sydney. Whatever the reason, Molly is now scarred for life and they both are living with the fallout.

Pulling the jar of moisturiser towards her, she lathers her face with it massaging it in well. Then, leaving her face in her hands, she cries. *Oh Molly, I'm so sorry.*

FIFTY-SEVEN

Molly

TIM IS PACING the lounge room, his anger forcing him to stamp rather than walk. "Molly, you don't need to go to India again. Have your meetings via video."

"What do you think we've been doing? But I miss the children, and they me. Sharma has told me. Seeing them via video isn't enough for me. Besides, health wise, I'm stronger now."

"Obviously your foot, err, Pete, doesn't bother you that much anymore. And I guess it doesn't matter what I say, you'll go anyway." He stops pacing standing directly in front of her. "What about Samantha and Clay's engagement, will you be back for that?"

Molly had thought about that and knew Tim would ask, "That's six weeks away, I'll go after. I wouldn't miss it, you know that. But I want to spend the new year with the children." She can see Tim is thinking about how long she would be away for.

"What about work? Your radio show."

"We can work something out. I've spoken to Brendan, Isabelle and Rowan, they are happy for me to work from Mumbai. We'll work out the time difference. It doesn't matter that I'm not in the studio with Brendan, we know how to work with each other now."

Tim sits on the edge of the lounge. Molly is sitting with her legs tucked under her, Pete abandoned on the rug, and Bono has his head resting on her. "You have it all worked out. What can I say? I wish you a safe trip."

"Tim, I love you and as a doctor you worry about me more than you should, but honestly, I've come to terms with my non-existent foot and the accident has taken a back step, my future is looking bright."

Tim places his hand on her arm, "I guess all that money spent on therapy is worth it?"

She laughs, "I guess so. Come on, Samantha and Clay will wonder where we are." They both stand after Molly fits Pete back on and asks Bono to jump off the lounge. They are going to dinner and should have been there fifteen minutes ago.

Molly had now known Clay for a month and her instincts were right, he was besotted with Samantha. After only knowing each other for four months, they are getting engaged. They have opted for a long engagement though as Incendiary Sets is going on tour after their engagement. Clay is telling them about the places they are playing after Molly and Tim had made themselves comfortable. They are at a local Italian restaurant not far from the Thistle and Thorn, and as is usual with Italian restaurants, it is loud with diners chatting and laughing. They are leaning in so they can hear Clay.

"Oh, by the way Molly, my guitarist has a connection to you. He knows Lewis quite well, the guy who's dating someone you know. Emma?" He thinks for a minute, "that's right, her name is Emma."

Samantha had filled him in on the whole debacle obviously. Molly doesn't answer, she just raises her eyebrows and takes a sip of her drink. Tim, thankfully, changes the subject back to the gigs Clay's band is playing. As she listens, she wonders whether this meant she would see Emma at more of Clay's gigs. Well, she will worry about that if and when it happens. Right now, she focuses back on the conversation, which has now turned to the engagement.

"We're having a few of our friends and close family," explains Samantha. "The wedding on the other hand, well, we want something grand."

"Really? That's the first I've heard of this."

"We only decided yesterday, Dad. As we're having a long engagement, we will save up. We both want everyone we love to be there. Clay has family overseas, he wants them to come."

"Yeah, my cousins in London, I have three. We've always been close. And my dad's brother, his wife and her sister. She lives with them as she has some special needs. These are people I keep in touch with often."

Tim seems to accept this as he has no choice. "Right, well you should have people you love at your wedding. We don't have any family other than the three of us."

"Dad, stop worrying, we have time to discuss things."

He looks at Samantha and agrees, "You're right. Look, it's your wedding but I think the money could be better spent, that's all."

Molly interjects looking towards her niece, "Leave it to Samantha and Clay. I'm sure you two will work it out." Tim looks at Molly and raises his glass in acknowledgement.

TIM OFFERED to drop Molly at the airport at 7.30am. She is waving goodbye to him knowing he will worry the whole time she is away. As usual, she has booked a one-way ticket because she always stays longer than intended. Being her first time back since the accident, Molly is a little hesitant of how the children will react to her scars and her having one less foot. Some of the older children had asked what that felt like when they had chatted. She didn't tell them about the pain, instead she told them she hardly noticed the prosthetic. The other thing she was worried about was will the metal detectors be set off by the prosthetic. Her physio had told her no, but this still worried her.

In the end, she breezed through the detectors.

Samantha and Clay's engagement went well. It was a small affair of their friends, Clay's parents, his two sisters as well as Tim and Molly. Samantha had also invited David and Naomi, but they were on yet another trip having enjoyed Bali. Molly had been happy about them not being there, she preferred to see David on his own. Not that she disliked Naomi, it was just that she found that a jealous streak always popped up whenever she saw them together. Luckily this had not been often and that's the way she liked it.

Her flight is not until 10.45am so she has time to browse the shops after going through customs. Deciding to travel light because she doesn't envisage being in India too long this time, her carry-on is not a burden for her to drag along. She buys herself some make-up and skincare taking some with her and leaving the rest, along with the alcohol she bought, to collect on her return. With all of this done, she heads to the gate even though she has time to keep browsing. She has opted to rest and will take Pete off to ease the pain, the heat plus all of this walking has caused her skin around the fitting to become red raw.

An hour later she fits Pete back on and begins to board. Finding her seat, she is happy that no one is sitting next to her, the flight attendant had told her this. Room to spread out, all to herself, what a luxury in cattle class.

Molly sleeps for most of the flight and wakes only an hour before landing. She is looking forward to seeing the children again. Her heart is always renewed when she visits her spiritual home.

Collected at the airport by a new driver, she is saddened momentarily remembering their last driver who had been with them since the opening of the orphanage. It's also ironic that rain is coming down steadily as she is driven to the orphanage. Thankfully, not torrential though.

"Molly, it's so good you are here," says Sharma giving her a hug that takes her breath away. "You look fabulous."

"Thank you, so do you." Molly wasn't saying this to be polite, Sharma did look well, her bump is only just showing. She had married a few months after Molly left last time, and even though she had sent Molly an invitation, she knew Molly would not have been able to attend. Molly had bought Sharma a wedding present and will give it to her once she is settled in. "I take it everything is going well with the pregnancy."

"Yes, although there are still five months to go. Here's hoping things don't change." Molly sees no reason why they should but makes no comment. She takes Sharma's elbow as they walk into the orphanage together.

"Miss Molly." "Welcome back, Miss Molly." She walks into the foyer to the cheers and voices of the older children, the younger ones are in school. "Oh, my darlings, it's so good to see you. My, Suresh, look how you've grown."

Suresh was fifteen when she left, now he is a strapping young man, almost twenty. His dark unruly curls have been tamed into a close cut, his beard fully matured too. He blushes as Molly gives him a hug.

Sharma speaks above the chatter, "Tell Molly how cricket is going." Suresh's blush grows deeper. "Oh, don't be so shy. Molly, he has been chosen for the Indian cricket team, he is a brilliant bowler."

"Pardon me, ma'am, but I am in line for selection. I may not be selected."

"Oh Suresh, I have every confidence in you."

Molly takes Suresh's hand congratulating him. "Either way we are proud of you, you obviously have a good future in cricket even if not for the Indian national team. Now, as lovely as it is to see you all, I am tired, I will see all of you at dinner."

"Yes, Miss Molly." "Bye." "See you later, Miss Molly."

Sharma helps Molly to her room asking if she needs anything. "No, I need to rest that's all. Thank you, I'll see you at dinner too."

Sharma leaves closing the door behind her as Molly plonks herself on the bed taking in the familiar smells of Mumbai and the orphanage, a mix of rich spices, heat and damp vegetation. She is utterly exhausted but happy to be here.

FIFTY-EIGHT

Molly

MONTHS AFTER ARRIVING IN INDIA, winter is being taken over by spring. The temperate days of winter are giving way to warmer and steamier days. Molly's wardrobe of summer clothes suits all of Mumbai's seasons. Still, she loves this city no matter the weather, it is the people who are important to her.

The first thing Molly had done at that first dinner with all the children and staff of the orphanage was thank them all for their wishes and gifts. She had been humbled by the children's handmade cards and posies of dried flowers. After dinner she had presented Sharma with the crock pot for the many curries she knows Sharma makes.

That night now seems so long ago as much has happened. Sharma had a baby girl and took time off. The baby has Molly's heart and she is obsessed with her, the more cuddles the better. Suresh made it into the Indian cricket team. "Not the national team," he had explained, this would come later. And, in early January, twelve new children, two of whom were twins of only six months old, were settled in. As always, her time at the orphanage was busy and the months scooted by.

She is sitting on the edge of her bed in the late afternoon with the fan whirring above, stripped down to only her knickers, allowing the fan to cool her. In her hand she holds an invitation and even though she knew this would happen someday, it's still a shock to see it in writing. David and Naomi are getting married. At the end of April, two months away. Will she go?

Weighing up whether she wants to put herself through seeing David marry Naomi, she flops down onto the bed. *Aargh, what do I do?* She hasn't been in Mumbai long enough to want to leave yet and seeing David walk down the aisle without her by his side ... she shakes her head wanting to displace the picture in her head of Naomi being in her place.

Deciding to speak with Tim before making a decision, she throws on a shift and settles back on her pillows with her laptop on her knees. Tim face appears within seconds. "Hi, that was quick."

"Hello you. I was online already. How's things?"

"Can't complain, you know I love being here. How's everything back home?" She asks this question every time they talk and usually everything is fine.

"All good. I do have some news about Clay's band, they are set to play with Jack Foster on his tour of Australia."

"Wow, Jack Foster, I love his music. How fantastic, when is he coming to Australia?" Jack Foster is an English singer of some note, this is a great opportunity for Clay's band. She starts humming one of Jack's hits, he has had many in England, America and Australia.

"He'll be here in November for festival season. Clay is organising tickets for all of us, including you."

"Well, that is the reason I'm contacting you. Are you going to David's wedding?"

"Yes, he told me he was sending you the invite."

"Do you think he expects me to come? Because if I do then I'll stay for festival season. But it means this trip will be cut short."

"Of course he'll expect you to be there, David still loves you as a friend."

Yes, she does know this. But she loves him more than a friend, she will always have feelings for him. What happened with Richard was a stupid mistake, something she can't take back. "I'll have to think about it Tim."

"Ok, but I think you should be here for the wedding. Love you Sis, take care. Oh, by the way, give Sharma's daughter a cuddle from me."

"Will do. Love you more, bye."

She stretches to where she left the invitation, picking it up. She looks at the RSVP date, she still has a few weeks before she has to give them an answer.

SHARMA IS in her office with the baby. Molly is surprised how clucky she is, little Aashvi has stolen her heart.

"I'll drop Aashvi off home and come back in an hour. We must go through the financials."

Molly groans, this is her least favourite thing about running the orphanage. Sharma has a live-in maid, who helps looks after the baby when Sharma and her husband are at work. She had taken Aashvi to the doctors, which is why the baby is with Sharma now.

"I'll be here," Molly says blowing the baby a kiss. At two-months old, Aashvi is growing well according to her parents, Molly has no idea with newborns. And she is adorable, much to her delight, Molly has had many cuddles. The youngest children Molly has had to deal with are the twins who arrived in January. How sad that they lost their parents to the virus and their grandparents are too unwell to look after them. Their grandfather suffered polio as a child and was left with one leg, their grandmother was older than him and quite frail.

Caring for her husband over all these years had left her with severe arthritis. Molly is thankful that children in these circumstances have a place like Tulip Treasures to grow up, somewhere clean and safe.

Sharma is back within the hour and they go through the financials. They could do with more funds and this makes Molly think about the money Emma raised. This is the first time she has given Emma more than a passing thought since arriving in Mumbai. She wonders if she is still seeing that guy she saw her with at the Thistle and Thorn.

"We will need to do some fundraising soon, Molly." This brings her back to the present and she nods. "Maybe we can do another open day?"

"Hmmm, maybe. We can sell the children's artwork, or maybe do a fete? We can sell more than artwork at a fete."

"That sounds good. I'll put it to Uma and Eeshan and together we can start organising it. What about a date? Sometime in early April?"

Molly is startled by hearing the word April, she had forgotten about the invitation. If the fete is in April it will have to be before she leaves. That is if she decides to go to the wedding. "Ok, set a date for the first Saturday in April. Keep me in the loop and let me know what I can do to help."

"Sure. Well, that was productive. I'll see you after tomorrow, remember I'm taking Aashvi to the paediatrician in Thana tomorrow."

"Yes, I remember. Good luck but I'm sure he'll be pleased with her progress." Sharma leaves with a smile as Molly envies her being a mother.

April. Now Molly can't think about anything else except the wedding. Thinking about what Tim had said during their video chat, and with his subsequent phone call a week later, Molly has no choice but to go. This leaves her feeling anticipation but with a dose of dread.

· · ·

THE DAY of the fete arrives with a bustle of workers setting up stalls, rides and play areas. The weather has been on and off raining all week, but thankfully, it is sunny this morning. A little damp underfoot, but not so bad as to spoil the day.

Molly is overseeing the information stall where she will spend most of her time. This is where she will woo potential philanthropists to part with their money. The last fete they had, more than five years ago, had been fruitful. They should hold a fete every two years at least to keep funds flowing. Hopefully nothing like the pandemic will stop this happening again.

Sharma, Uma and Eeshan come up as she is sorting the marketing material into piles. "We should have a good turnout given the weather," says Eeshan.

"I hope you're right," answers Molly, "it's been a while since we did any fundraising." Looking at her watch, they have an hour before everything starts. "Things are ready, we can allow the younger children to come out now."

"Ok, I'll go and get them. They are so excited, Molly." Sharma is smiling as she walks towards the front entrance. Uma and Eeshan remain with Molly helping her with putting up the banners and posters.

The grounds of the orphanage are perfect for a fete. With mature trees giving shade and the grass areas kept maintained, there is enough room for all the rides and stalls. Uma had even organised a stage where her local Bollywood dance troupe will be performing three shows. Molly is looking forward to seeing them, two of the girls in the troupe grew up at the orphanage. She is always happy to see the children who had left when they turned eighteen, they had a special place in her heart. She smiles as she thinks of everything she has achieved with this orphanage, the lives she has enriched, and all the blessings it has given her.

FIFTY-NINE

David

HIS NERVES ARE CALMED by the scotch, he had scoffed two shots down in succession. He and Naomi had opted to prepare themselves for the day in their home. They weren't too fussed about the bride not being seen by the groom and all those superstitions, and they had opted for Tim and Samantha as their witnesses. "None of that best man bullshit," he had said when they began organising the wedding. Also, the festivities were happening in their backyard with thirty people attending. Even though the yard was large, they had opted for an intimate ceremony.

Molly had said she was coming, but David wondered whether she would. The last time they spoke, she had sounded down about leaving India. "I don't want to miss your wedding, David, but it means leaving Mumbai earlier than planned. I wouldn't do this for anyone else." She had laughed but it was a tense and curt laugh.

But this day is for he and Naomi, and this is what he will focus on.

. . .

AT ELEVEN IN THE MORNING, the sun drenches their backyard in a warm glow. David and Naomi stand before the celebrant, their fingers intertwined, each holding on to the moment. Naomi's eyes shimmer with tears at the ready, her heart spilling into the vows she recites. Her voice quiet, timid with emotion.

When it's David's turn, he gazes at her, his own voice thick with emotion as he speaks the heartfelt words, each syllable a promise, a piece of their shared future.

When the vows are complete, Naomi's tears escape down her cheeks. Gently and with tenderness, David lifts his hand wiping them away. As their lips meet in a kiss, their souls feel their love. This first kiss as husband and wife lingers in the air, like a promise whispered in the breeze.

Their friends and family clap, whistle and whoop as Tim and Samantha walk up to sign the documents. David spots Molly as he walks to the table. He smiles towards her, she replies by blowing him a kiss. He feels this but focuses on what he is doing, this is his and Naomi's day.

As they walk towards their guests they hear, "Congratulations." "Well done you two." "To the happy couple." Glasses are raised and photos are taken by many. David is slapped on the back by his sparky mates as they hold up their beers. He can't keep the smile off his face as he holds Naomi close. Everyone joins in laughter and jokes about David come thick and fast. "Hey, easy on boys, you'll scare my wife." More fits of raucous laughter ensue as more banter puts everyone in a party mood.

He sees Molly standing with Tim and Samantha. "Let's go and say hello to Molly." He says this without waiting for a response from Naomi. She has no choice but to follow because he doesn't let go of her hand. He wants her by his side for support, this is the first time he has seen Molly in person since before she started her radio show. As much as David had tried to stop his feelings for Molly, deep down he still loved her. He shakes this thought from his mind, he has chosen Naomi and she is who he loves now. His vows had reflected that.

"Congratulations," says Molly kissing both David and Naomi on the cheek. "Naomi, you look stunning." She did, her sense of style was evident in the fitted ivory off-the-shoulder dress.

"Thanks for coming, Molly," said Naomi before saying she was going to chat with some of the other guests. Tim and Samantha followed Naomi much to David's horror. Did they really think he wanted to be alone with Molly?

"You look well. I have forgotten how you brush up well in a suit."

He feels Molly's eyes as she takes in his linen wedding suit. "Err, thanks. So do you. How was India?"

"Great, we had a fete before I left and raised some good money. The people of Mumbai can be very generous when they believe in a cause."

Before he could stop himself, he blurts out, "Well, if you would accept that money in trust for you, the orphanage would be looked after for a long time."

"You really want to discuss this on your wedding day?"

"No. I'm just frustrated with your attitude towards Emma, she did that fundraising out of the goodness of her heart. And your friendship. Actually, Emma was invited, unfortunately she had a prior engagement."

Molly sighs, "I know what Emma did was to help me out. But let's not get into an argument now. I want to enjoy the party."

David clears his throat, "Yes, of course. Let's go and join the others." She is right, his wedding is not the place to discuss the Emma issue, but that money needs to be discussed at a later date.

SIXTY

The Other Wedding

FESTIVAL SEASON IS over and Clay's band is taking a break before their next tour. Samantha and Clay are with Molly in her kitchen, they have come to visit because they have news.

"We have a surprise, and believe us, it was a surprise for us too. We're pregnant."

Molly shrieks, "Holy hell ... really? Wow, that's wonderful. I've been clucky ever since Aashvi was born and the orphaned twins have my heart as well. Now, I'll have another baby to take my heart." She sucks in a breath and moves round the bench to give them both a hug, "Congratulations." Her voice squeaks with joy.

"You're almost as excited as Dad. And we have more news, we're getting married in February. Dad is super happy about that because we won't be having the large wedding we had planned."

"You'll put the money you save to good use. I'm sure Tim said something like that, right?"

"You're right, Aunt Molly. He's pleased we're being practical."

The three of them laugh as Bono jumps up on Molly's legs putting her off balance. She holds onto the bench but smiles at him and pats his head as he gets down. Bono behaves now having received some attention and Molly turns her attention back to her guests.

"Well, tell me more, where is everything happening?"

Samantha and Clay fill Molly in on the details. "I had better organise myself then, we only have a few months to go."

After they leave, Molly can't keep the smile from her face. She feels elated to have another wedding to attend. Right, time to check what's available in her wardrobe, she has to wear something ultra-special being the aunt of the bride.

THE DAY ARRIVES in spectacular Sydney fashion – beaming sunshine, a slight breeze coming off the harbour and twenty-eight degrees. Samantha and Clay organised an outdoor wedding at a waterfront venue, the view and sparkle of Sydney Harbour is a breathtaking backdrop. The shimmering water, gulls soaring and ferries and boats passing by make for a magical spot. Two pelicans soar past as the vows are taken.

After their vows and being pronounced husband and wife, they walk amongst their guests, sixty close friends and family. Samantha had kept her promise to her father.

Molly is so proud of her niece, who looks fabulous in her glamorous silk dress with a short train. Her blonde locks have summer flowers on one side and she has taken off the veil, which was basically a pull-over that had covered her face during their vows. Molly has her head on Tim's shoulder, she had had a few tears during the ceremony. She perks up as the happy couple comes towards them. "Oh, congratulations you two. This is fabulous and you both look amazing. And this setting, well, it's divine," says Molly sweeping her hand around the grounds.

"Thanks, we're pleased the weather behaved too. You two shape up quite well, love that blue on you Aunt Molly. Come on, let's go, there are more photos to be taken." Samantha leads them to a spot where the photographer has set up so the glistening harbour is the backdrop. After fixing her make up, Molly feels so many emotions as the photos are taken.

"Great, now we're done with that, it's time for a drink," says Clay leading them towards the bar. "Champagne for everyone, I want to make a toast." Foregoing tradition and saying his speech before they settle to eat, Clay picks up a flute with bubbles fizzing and, holding it up says, "Attention everyone, come closer. I want to toast my beautiful bride. Thank you Samantha for agreeing to marry me ..." He stops as their guests' shout, woot and cheer. Clay brings Samantha closer to him kissing her cheek. "This gorgeous person has changed my life for the better and I look forward to us being together, along with many kids, for a long time."

Samantha laughs, "Let's see how this pregnancy goes first."

Clay continues, "Sure babe." He winks at her as his smile broadens. "To everyone here today, thanks for coming and for your gifts. To my parents, you guys are awesome." He raises his glass towards them. "And to Tim and Molly, you're amazing people too. Thanks for welcoming me into your family. To my mates, you're the best friends a bloke could want and to everyone who supports our band, you're the best fans too. Now, enough of this waffling, bet you're sick of my voice already. It's time to eat and then party." He downs the champagne with everyone following suit.

Molly and Tim find their table. They are sitting with Samantha's friends. She is about to settle in her chair but she spots Emma. When did she turn up? Why was she even invited? "Tim, Emma's here."

"Yes, didn't you know? She was invited because Lewis is good friends with the band's guitarist."

"No one told me." Now Molly is pissed off, what a way to ruin the day.

"Molly, don't do anything stupid like leave." Tim is staring at her from his seated position. "Sit down. You don't have to interact with her if you don't want to." Tim is right as Emma is seated well away from them at Clay's side of the family. So, she decides she will ignore the fact Emma is here because she doesn't want anything to ruin Samantha's big day. *Be an adult about this, Molly.*

The usual formalities happen like more speeches, a hilarious one from Clay's best man, cutting the cake and then the first dance. They opted for a DJ because Clay had wanted everyone to enjoy the day including himself. Soon, the portable dance floor is full. Molly is dancing with Tim then Emma and Lewis are next to them. Molly is horrified, her insides in knots, but she keeps it together as best she can.

Lewis is about to speak but before anything can happen, Clay makes another announcement. Calling over his guitarist, he asks for a chair so Samantha can sit. "This is a song that I'd like to dedicate to my new wife." He says this without taking his eyes off Samantha, "I wrote it especially for you." Samantha places her hand on her mouth and an inaudible gasp spills out.

Clay begins.
"You came into my life. This breath of air
My love, my beautiful partner, my life
As I stare into your loving face, I fill with your love
You're my breath, my life ..."

As he continues singing, everyone is entranced, watching the young couple who seem to be in their own world, just the two of them. There are sniffles and sobs, everyone wiping their eyes. Some are taking photos and others are videoing this touching scene. The tattooed Clay singing in dulcet tones to his wife, Samantha, who is tanned, her hair billowing down her shoulders, tears spilling down her cheeks.

Molly is holding onto Tim, tears smearing her mascara yet again, but she doesn't care. Clay's song is poignant and Samantha is swaying to the sound of her husband's beautiful voice. She mouths, "I love you." As Clay finishes, everyone erupts with applause with Samantha jumping up to kiss him.

What a fabulous moment. Molly is standing with Tim and clapping, tears still spilling down her face. Tim is watching her cry with tears in his eyes too.

As everyone goes back to whatever they were doing, Lewis continues his interrupted conversation. "Nice to see you again, Tim. Hello, it's Molly, right?" Lewis' hand is outstretched to Tim first, then Molly who is wiping her eyes and awkwardly gives Lewis her hand, missing his hand completely.

"Hi." This is all Molly can blurt out as she looks everywhere except at Emma.

"I know this is awkward, Molly, but hello." Emma smiles and Molly feels like throwing up. *Not here, not now.* Her mind is thinking of any other place they could be having this conversation.

"Why don't you and I sit? Leave the boys to get us more drinks." She nods to Lewis who asks Tim to follow him.

This is the last thing Molly wants to do, all she wants is to run. She forces herself to calm down and follows Emma, not wanting to make a scene. They sit at Emma's table. "Molly, it's time to fix things between us."

Molly takes a deep breath, "Are you sure you have forgiven me?"

"I did that a while ago. I think it might be time for you to forgive yourself." Emma stretches out her hand to touch Molly's hand, she unwittingly flinches. Emma gives her time to respond.

"I have had a hard time without you, all this was my fault. I should never have fallen for Richard's charm."

"I understand how Richard convinced you, I fell for his charm for a long time. Molly ..." Emma reaches both her hands out to clasp Molly's hands, "I forgive you, I miss you and I need us to be friends again."

More tears ebb their way down Molly's face, "Oh Emma ..." Molly places her forehead on Emma's shoulder and cries. She cries huge sobs letting out the frustration of the accident and of missing Emma. Both of them had let this go on for far too long.

Emma pulls Molly's head up with both hands on her face, "We

both need to heal now. I never want anything to come between us like this has ever again. I love you, Molly."

Molly snuffles and gives out a chuckle, "I love you too, Emma." She takes Emma's hands off her face and they both hug. Molly notices that Emma is crying now too. They pull apart both wiping their eyes. "We must look a right mess," says Molly. Emma laughs as Molly continues, "But who cares, as long as we've sorted ourselves out, then nothing else matters.

SIXTY-ONE

Molly

BACK AT WORK after the weekend, Brendan, Isabelle and Rowan are listening to her talk about the wedding. "... and when Clay sang a song he had written for Samantha, well, there wasn't a dry eye. I was an emotional mess."

"Sounds fabulous. These photos are fab, too. I can see you and Samantha are related," says Isabelle. "You all scrub up well, it was nice everyone made an effort. And the setting near the harbour made it all the more special."

"It was beautiful, I'm so proud of my niece." Molly is still feeling euphoric from the weekend when Rowan speaks.

"Right, well now we're done talking about our weekends, it's down to business. I'm happy to be giving you some good news."

Molly listens as Rowan rattles off numbers of how they are doing and he seems pleased. 'Arvos with Brendan and Molly' is now the second highest rating afternoon show on commercial radio. Brendan looks towards Molly giving her an amused clap. She returns the favour as they are a team and it wouldn't work without both of them.

"Thanks, Rowan. Molly and I enjoy working together and this comes through."

"Brendan's right, we make an effort for each episode. But, if there is anything we can improve, obviously we'd like to know about it."

Isabelle answers, "We can always make tweaks if necessary, but why break something that is doing well? For now, you two keep doing what you know best. Ratings can change as audiences can be fickle. Let's enjoy this crest we're riding."

Both Molly and Brendan high-five each other.

The meeting ends with Rowan congratulating them on a job well done. "Keep up the good work."

As they head for the studio after the meeting, Molly says, "Thanks Brendan."

He looks at her quizzically, "What for?"

"For giving me the confidence to do this show with you. I've learned so much."

"Aww, Molly, you're welcome. We make a good team and I've learned from you too."

Molly smiles as they enter the studio. That's the end of their mutual admiration society, it's time to keep working as a team.

AS SHE IS DRIVING HOME HUMMING to the song on the radio, David calls her. "I saw the photos on Samantha's Instagram, looks like everyone had a good time. Did I see Emma in some photos?"

"Yes, she was invited because her boyfriend, Lewis, knows Clay's guitarist."

"Right, how was that for you?"

"Well, at first all I felt like doing was leaving. Then, after she and Lewis greeted us on the dance floor, Emma asked me to sit and speak with her. We're talking again, she forgave me and I forgave her."

"That's fabulous. Molly, you must be pleased all that bad crap is behind you both now?"

"Definitely. We have made a pact to never let anything come between us again. If anything ever does, we talk about it before it becomes a disaster."

"That sounds very adult. Good for you."

"How are you and Naomi going?"

"Well, that's the reason I'm calling you. I'm going to be a dad."

Molly nearly slams on the brakes as she answers, "What? David how fabulous, I'm happy for you both." Jealously rears its ugly head again as David keeps talking. Molly pushes it down, this is David's moment, it's not about her.

"She's three months now and seems to be feeling better. The morning sickness is subsiding. Anyway, I'm about to call Tim, so speak soon, ok?"

"Yes, sure and congratulations again. Bye." Wow, David is going to be a dad. She is happy for him, even though her body is strangled with jealousy. David has Naomi, Emma has Lewis and Molly has ... Bono. She tries to take all this in as she pulls into her carport.

SHE IS in the kitchen when Tim rings. "So, how do you feel about David and Naomi's news?"

Thinking before she answers, she wants to tell him how jealously is creeping in, but she decides to keep their conversation upbeat. "Wonderful. It's great news. David and Naomi deserve to be happy."

"I'm glad to hear that, Molly. I know you still have feelings for David."

"Is it that obvious? I try not to let it show. But David is in my past, he is now a special friend."

"That's one way of putting it, good for you. I was just checking on you and am glad you're feeling ok about it. See you soon." He clicks off leaving Molly with her jealous thoughts. Now Samantha was going to be a mother, David a father, she misses the children at the orphanage even more. She feels like a mother to them and needs to see them again soon.

IT'S Friday afternoon and she is meeting Emma for a drink and a movie in the city. Molly enters the pub at The Rocks that is full of the after-work crowd. She sees Emma waving her over to the bar where she is sitting. They kiss each other hello when Molly reaches her. This is part of their new friendship, they greet with a kiss as it helps them to connect better, it makes their friendship stronger. Molly loves the fact she and Emma are closer than they ever were before, if that's possible.

"Good week?"

Molly picks up her gin and tonic, sipping before answering. "Yes, yours?"

"Fine, the usual."

"So, have you heard David's news?"

"No, what?"

"Naomi is pregnant, he's going to be a dad."

"Wow, that's great. Umm, I mean, it is great, right?"

Molly had filled Emma in on how she still loves David. "Of course! He deserves to be happy. As I explained to Tim, he's my special friend now."

Emma laughs, "Oh right, you keep telling yourself that."

"I have to Emma. There is no future with David, he is happy with Naomi." Emma nods as they click their glasses.

Molly fills Emma in on her next trip to India in a month. They discuss how long she will be there this time. "As my last visit was cut short, I need to stay a year at least. Although, I want to come back for the birth of Samantha's baby, or the christening if they have one."

"And David's baby?"

"Hmm, I'll play that by ear. I'm not sure how Naomi will feel about me being around their child."

"True. Still, being a great aunt is going to be exciting. Another kid for you to spoil."

"This one will be especially spoiled," laughs Molly.

Their conversation turns to how Molly is coping. She is still having therapy to control the demons about her anger at being abducted as well as the accident. She feels that social media has a lot to answer for. Although, both Emma and Evan had told her social media wasn't the issue, it's how people use it. "Yes, but surely the platforms need to monitor what is being posted?"

"Well, freedom of the press and all that. They are improving and placing some restrictions on what can be posted, but this is mainly for serious breaches like terrorist activity. Look, it's great you're coping better Molly, keep that anger at bay and channel it into something good. Focus on the orphanage and use the money from to trust to improve the orphans' lives."

Emma, David and Tim had had a meeting with Molly about the funds. Some had been given to her for her ongoing medical bills, this amount is now in an account Molly manages. She uses the trust now to funnel funds to Tulip Treasures, mainly for repairs and mainte- nance. With the buildings now over ten years old, there was always something to be replaced or fixed. "That's the reason for this trip, I'm going to ensure the money is put to good use."

"Great. Now, drink up. The movie is starting in half an hour."

After having settled in their seats, Molly thinks about how every- thing that has happened has led to her and Emma being better than ever. She remembers how they had clicked in Fiji all those years ago, the fun never stopped when they were together. Emma is Molly's sister in every sense of the word except biologically, had Emma been a male, then she would have been Molly's perfect partner. Wasn't that meant to be David? She chastises herself for thinking of him, he is taken and taken for good now. Picking up her drink, she guzzles it down channelling her thoughts to the movie, a romantic comedy that isn't keeping her attention.

SIXTY-TWO

Molly

SHE IS SITTING in her seat in economy. *Could these seats be any smaller?* Holding a glass of wine, she settles in as best she can with Pete on the floor in front of her. Her prosthetic has become more comfortable, but she takes every opportunity to take it off because she likes to tuck that leg under when she sits. Taking a sip of the wine, she selects a movie to watch before having a nap, which will take her up to when they land in Mumbai.

She had organised with the radio station to do her shows from Mumbai as she had the last time she was away. It worked out well because it is 10.30am in Mumbai when she needs to do the show, and the technical team from the station had organised a good broadcasting set up at the orphanage. The sound technician who came in to help Molly was knowledgeable and professional. Molly didn't have to worry about anything other than chatting with Brendan.

Walking through Chhatrapati Shivaji Maharaj international

airport, Molly spots her driver who is ready to help her with her luggage.

"You are well, Miss Molly?"

"I am thank you. Is everything well here?"

"It is, you will be pleased with the work that has been done at the orphanage."

Molly is looking forward to seeing the upgrades, she has been coordinating all of it with Sharma, Uma and Eeshan via video links for months. Ever since the money from the Trust came through, Molly has been able to put into action most of the jobs that were put on hold due to the pandemic.

When she is comfortable in the car, they drive out of the congested airport carpark. She is thankful every time she visits that she doesn't have to negotiate Mumbai's traffic. This time the weather is behaving itself.

Tulip Treasures comes into view and Molly smiles, she feels so proud of what she and her team have achieved. This fills her with hope for a better future for the orphans they look after.

Sharma is waiting for her as she steps from the car. "Sharma, so good to see you in person again."

"Welcome back, Molly. Here, let me help you with that," she says taking her duffle bag. The driver takes the rest of Molly's luggage to her room.

Molly had noticed a few trucks and vans parked in the carpark, "There are workers still here?" she asks as it is late afternoon.

"Huh, no. Some leave them here overnight, they carpool during the week then take them on the weekends. They won't be here for much longer, the work is almost finished."

"Right, that makes good sense. Thanks for staying here to greet me, Sharma. I'm exhausted though."

"Of course, I wanted to greet you in person. I'll see you settle in then we can meet in the morning. And feel free to sleep in, although the workers may wake you. They are working on the children's back rooms, the ones at the end of the back veranda."

"Ok, thanks for the warning, see you tomorrow." Molly takes her duffle from Sharma and shuffles towards her room. There is a hint of paint and dust as she walks in, she wonders how long ago it was painted. Still, she is exhausted enough to not worry about it. Slipping into bed after changing into an over-sized t-shirt, sleep comes easily to her.

THE NEXT MORNING, she is in the boardroom with her team, the head foreman and two of his men as well as a man she knows of, he is a celebrity of sorts, both in the media and on socials. Sharma introduces him as Kian Bamejee, the CEO of a large chain of Indian hotels. Molly wonders why he is in this meeting but Sharma whispers she will explain later. Sharma is heading the meeting so Molly sits back and listens, all the while taking sneak peeks at the brooding, handsome man who is intriguing her.

As meetings go at the orphanage, this one is a particularly productive one. For once the finances are adequate for jobs to be completed, the weather has been kind to them, and they are on schedule. And Molly is wanting it over so she can speak with Kian.

Sharma is shaking hands with the builders as they file out of the boardroom, the foreman thanking Molly for this opportunity. "Oh, you're welcome. I am keen to see all of your work within the next few days." Molly notices Kian is still seated and walks towards him. Sharma whispers to her why he is still here then leaves telling Molly she will talk to her later.

"I hear they call you *Miss Molly* around here. It's my pleasure to meet you, I'm Kian Bamejee of the Royal Argent Group." His whole face animated with a smile.

Molly laughs, "Molly Edwards, pleased to meet you Kian Bamejee." She stretches out her hand for him to shake but he offers his elbow. "Oh, yes," she says bending her arm, although she feels he's being overly cautious, the pandemic is rarely spoken of now. "So, why were you in this meeting? Have you had something to do with the building projects?"

He asks her to sit next to him before he answers. She gives an inward gasp at how beautiful he is. He looks to be early thirties, is dressed immaculately in an expensive tailored suit and his shoes have a diamond shine. "These builders have worked on my hotels, I came to see the foreman as he wanted to show me his latest work. I was impressed so I asked to stay for the meeting, Sharma was ok with it. You?"

"No, of course I'm fine with it. Did you find the information useful?" She is trying hard to keep this professional when all she wants to do is kiss his amazingly chiselled face.

"Well, I know of their work so I wasn't expecting anything less. But the reason I really stayed was to meet you. Your legacy is what I am interested in."

Molly is mesmerised by his smooth tone of voice, his English is precise with only a hint of an accent, "My legacy?"

"Yes, this," he indicates with both his arms outstretched, "you have placed many years into building this into one of the premier orphanages in India. Somewhat similar to my Group, we strive for excellence in our hotels."

"Umm, well yes, thank you. I am proud of Tulip Treasures and the work we do. My team, especially, Sharma, Uma and Eeshan, is very dedicated. May I offer you a tea? This water on the table has been here for some time."

"If it would be ok with you, may I take you to lunch? I want to speak to you about your future ideas and to know you better."

Molly feels redness on her cheeks. *What is she a teen?* "Well, yes, lunch sounds lovely. I'll let Sharma know." She stands and walks out to find Sharma, more to clear her head rather than to actually find Sharma.

Finding her, Sharma nods and smiles, "Enjoy lunch Molly." She winks as she walks towards her office. Molly turns and walks back into the boardroom. "I'm ready when you are Kian."

Driven in Kian's company car, Molly is ushered into the Argent Mumbai hotel with Kian's hand on the small of her back. Her body tingles at his slight touch. She really is feeling like an obsessed teen right now. Kian is known for dating celebrities, the latest posts Molly had seen on Instagram he was with a young R&B singer from the USA. Her name escapes her, but Molly remembers staring at Kian for some time before scrolling through.

"I hope you don't mind having lunch here, I have a meeting straight after lunch." There is that smooth tone again.

"No, not at all. I haven't eaten here before, I'm looking forward to it." He leads her to a restaurant towards the back of the foyer, which is adorned in black marble, drop chandeliers and a reception desk with flowers dripping down each end of it. The orchids are stunning, the stark white against the black marble finish off the elegance of this hotel. There are more orchids adorning the restaurant. There is no way Molly could ever afford to stay in this 5-star hotel.

As they walk in, Kian is greeted as if royalty and they are escorted to a table near the large window overlooking the hotel's pool and spa area. Once seated, Molly says, "This is beautiful, I've seen photos, but they don't do it justice."

"As I said before, we aim for excellence." When he finishes saying this, a bottle of champagne is brought to the table and the waiter pours them each a glass. "To meeting you, Molly, I have been wanting to for a while." They touch their flutes together and Molly feels the redness glow on her cheeks again.

"Oh, really?" She is trying to sound nonchalant.

"Your reputation is well-known and you are also a bit of an enigma. Your socials show many photos of the orphanage but there is only one small photo of you in the bio. I want to know more about you, Molly, the Australian woman who came to India to help orphans."

And there's the blush growing bigger. "Well, here I am. What do you want to know?" She is trying to make this a light-hearted conversation, but all she wants to do is take this beautiful man into one of the rooms and ..."

"Tell me all about yourself. Even all the bad stuff." He laughs and her body reacts. *Let me lead you to one of the rooms and we can talk later?*

"The About page tells you most of why I became involved in the project, having partied since finishing university, I felt it was time to do something with my life. And I feel I need to know you better before I share my bad side." She laughs and then gulps the rest of her champagne. Thankfully, he laughs too. She is happy he has a sense of humour.

Continuing the conversation in this vein, she learns he has a younger sister who wants nothing to do with the family business. "She prefers to squander her allowance on travelling Europe on the *spoilt brats* circuit."

"Oh, I know about that circuit. I think I worked at many of their parties back in the day. I didn't see you there though?"

"Not my scene, I leave that to my sister. I prefer to work and keep my nose clean. Besides, my parents need someone to run their empire."

It is an empire. The hotels are a family-run business with Kian's father still active in the background. There are forty hotels scattered throughout India as Molly had found out when she looked at Kian's bio. Ten of those were boutique ones especially favoured by celebrities. She imagined this is where he met the ones he has dated. Placing that thought aside, she asks again why he wanted to meet her. "Is it the orphanage you are interested in?"

"I am interested in how it is doing, yes. But more so I am interested in you. Molly, I've watched you from afar, have seen you at events and was devastated when I heard of your accident. It pleases me to see you are doing well."

Ok, where is that room? "Thank you." From anyone else she would have been creeped out by this, but staring into his genuine eyes, Molly is falling into lust. Food being served takes her away from this lust. When did they order?

"I took the privilege of ordering when we arrived. I hope you enjoy this."

The smells of the spices playfully waft into her nose, she is definitely going to enjoy this. As long as she is with Kian, everything will be enjoyable. *Ok, I'm moving way too fast with this.*

She watches on as he helps himself after she has placed her food on her plate. It is nice that they are sharing, this feels like a friendship already.

They chat amicably as they enjoy the meal. Kian had over-ordered and she apologises for not being able to finish. "I am so full, I'm not used to eating this much at lunch. And I'm not used to being with a lovely host such as you either." If he is embarrassed by her comment, he shows no signs of it.

"You are more than welcome. No need to apologise. Now, I will have my driver take you back to the orphanage, I have my meeting and I am sure you have more work to do. I hope to see you again soon." He stands, comes over to her side and taking her hand in his as she stands, kisses it gently. "My personal assistant will send you a date for dinner, I do hope you will be available?" All Molly can do is nod, of course she is going to be available.

All the way back to the orphanage, Molly is scrolling through the socials looking for any evidence that Kian is currently seeing anyone. Although he is photographed with many beautiful women, none seem to be his. She lets out an inaudible squeal, feeling so much like a besotted teenager. *David? David who?*

SIXTY-THREE

The Babies

HIS KISSES DEVOUR HER, she is entranced by him and his touch. Kian has driven her to the airport, himself. He actually drove because he wanted them to be alone. "I wouldn't drive for anyone else. For you, I will always make an exception." He had told her this when she announced she was returning to Sydney to meet her grand-niece. The kiss is tender and loving ... and private. His car has dark tinted windows and as public displays of affection are frowned upon in India, they serve their purpose. "I am going to miss you every minute you are away."

Molly smiles, "Me too. These past few months have been the best times I have had in a long time. You have restored my faith in love. Actually, in life too." They had declared their love for each other a month into their relationship. As they say, "when you know, you know." She pulls away from him with a sigh, "I'm not sure when I'll be back, it won't be too long though, I promise."

"Well, if I miss you too much would it be an imposition if I came to Sydney?"

"What? An imposition. Oh no, not at all, Kian, you are welcome anytime." His formalities were strange at first, but Molly has grown to love his way of speaking. That voice transports her to a place of love she has never known.

"Oh, that's good, because I've booked a flight next month. There are a few things I have to finalise before I can come."

Molly pulls him close again, kissing him with a passion she didn't know she had. "You are amazing. Have I told you that? Send me the flight details. Kian, I can't wait for you to meet everyone I love."

He laughs, the laugh that she has grown to love in such a short time, "I look forward to meeting them. Now, you had better go, you don't want to miss your flight."

She heads into the terminal full of love for him like a love-sick puppy. *How old are you, Molly?*

HOLDING LITTLE OLIVIA, Molly is captivated. Having arrived home two days ago after the longest flight of her life. Well, that's not true, but it felt like it. She was excited to be home but she is missing Kian terribly. Olivia is sound asleep in her arms oblivious to the fact her great aunt is holding her. When Molly arrived at Samantha and Clay's home, a modest apartment in inner city enclave of Surry Hills, Samantha was about to place Olivia into the bassinet but has now allowed Molly to hold her. "She is so tiny. And adorable."

"I know, but she is also a handful. Who knew a baby of a month old needed so much attention?"

"I'm not a mother, Samantha, but I could have told you that given the little experience I have had with Aashvi and the twins at the orphanage. Sharma was in exhaustion mode for the first six months of her daughter's life."

"Oh joy, this doesn't let up for months?"

Molly looks down at Olivia with a sense of motherly-love and with a desire to have her own child. And this needs to happen soon, she isn't getting any younger. "When they're this beautiful it's all worth it, don't fret. Here, you had better take her so I can help you with something, what do you need doing?"

"Really? That would be fabulous, would you mind folding some clothes? The baby's ones I mean."

"Sure, where are they?" Molly is pleased Samantha gives her an easy task to do and when she sees the pile on Samantha's lounge, she is happy to help.

Samantha walks back into the lounge and plonks herself down. "Hopefully she'll sleep for a few hours so we can catch up. You look well, how are things?"

Molly had already told her family and friends about Kian, they have been seeing each other for many months and she is confident this is another long-term relationship. Although she is hoping it lasts longer than the one with David. She loves Kian in a different way than she had loved David, a more spiritual love that is deeper and more profound. This is something she didn't know existed, but she has given herself wholly to him and he to her. They are partners, friends, lovers and spiritual beings all rolled into one. They have much in common like enjoying yoga, meditation and Tantric Sex. Molly smiles as she remembers their lovemaking, the special hours they have spent exploring each other bodies. She is in love with everything about Kian, not just his looks and his money. Especially not his money, she has no interest in it and has kept herself independent by still doing the radio show as well as running the orphanage. Kian had offered to donate, which she allowed him to do through the normal channels. The funds had gone into the pool with every other donation and it's not necessary for her to know anything else about it.

Samantha is staring at her as she hasn't answered, "Oh, right. Things are good, very good actually. Kian is coming to Sydney in a month, he surprised me with this news when he dropped me at the airport. He wants to meet everyone."

"Great, I look forward to meeting him. He really has a presence, not to mention how hot he is."

Molly laughs, "His parents were not too pleased when they met me, well, specifically his mother, but she has come around. And yes, he's hot, he's young and he's mine." They both laugh with Molly snorting. She does this when she is excited.

Molly hears that Clay is away a lot when he's touring and then home for months when they work on new material. So far, it's working out because he hasn't been away since Olivia's birth.

Samantha tells Molly he will leave soon for another tour. "We'll have to wait and see how things go for their next tour, we may need to go with him if it's another long one. The last tour was four months and Clay has said they may want to tour New Zealand and possibly USA."

"Overseas? You'll have to go won't you, but what about your work?"

"That's the issue. I am able to do some organising of events remotely, I will have to employ someone to do the hands-on things while I'm away."

Molly nods and listens to Samantha's concerns. She thinks about her own relationship. How is it going to work when Molly wants to come back home? She has decided to wait until David's baby is born, which is due in four weeks and then return to Mumbai. But at some stage she will want to come back to Sydney. How will their relationship fair by being a long distance one?

HARLEY and Bono are both crashed out on Harley's bed, sound asleep after their long walk to the reserve and back. Molly had come to Emma's home so Bono could have a play date with Harley, this is the first of what will be a regular weekly event while she is in Sydney. Molly and Emma are on the lounge, hot cups of coffee in hand, talking about their respective men. "Those brooding brown eyes had me straight away. And his hair, I thought it was a wig at first," Molly laughs.

"I can't imagine Lewis having hair even though I've seen photos of him with hair. To me, he looks better without it. And Kian, aside from having a healthy head of hair, he is one hot looking man."

"You think so too. Samantha said the same thing and yes, I agree, of course. Anyway, I can't wait until he arrives in three weeks. I'm counting down the days and I hope everyone likes him. I told you he is five years younger than me, right?"

"You did and that's not a problem. Also, what's there not to like? When I've spoken to him on chats with you ... oh that smooth voice, it makes me swoon, I can imagine how you feel."

"Huh, yes, his voice is rather low and sexy. He missed his calling, he should be commentating the cricket or something." They both laugh at this as Molly fills Emma in on how things are going at the orphanage. "Holding Olivia the other day made me think of Aashvi and the twins, they are such a joy to have around. You know, I'm clucky, I think I need one of my own."

"I've felt that when I've spoken to you, you're always talking about Aashvi and her cuteness. You have always had a passion for children, so you should have one of your own."

"Hmmm, I haven't discussed anything with Kian yet."

"The way you speak about your relationship, I don't think he'll have a problem."

"You might be right, but his mother may have something to say about it." Molly had told Emma everything about her issues with Kian's mother early on, how she had made Molly feel uncomfortable and not right for their social standing. This was until Kian told Molly that his mother had come from a humble family, she was being a hypocrite. From then on Molly had stood her ground, which had solicited a modicum of respect from both of his parents.

"His mother has nothing to do with you two deciding to have children. Why is she worrying you?"

"We're still on shaky ground, even though it's better now than when I first met her. But you're right, Emma, it's Kian's and my decision." She puts thoughts of her meddling mother-in-law out of her mind.

MOLLY HAD ASKED Tim to come with her to meet David and Naomi's baby, a boy they named Thomas. She still wasn't sure whether Naomi wanted her around and with Tim by her side she felt some comfort. Besides, she wanted to see David as a father, not that she had any doubt about his capability. He is still her special friend and wants him in her life, especially now she has Kian. Every time she thinks of Kian her body reacts with such love, he has given her life meaning again, the demons are at bay now, something she knows is due to how happy she is.

Arriving at David's home, a place where Naomi had grown up, she still gasps at the size of this stately house, even though she'd been here before.

"Yep, she's a beauty, isn't she?" smiles Tim, "I do a double take every time."

"How do they look after all this? I know David is capable, but this is the size of two homes."

"David told me they have help," says Tim as he knocks lightly on the door. David had texted him not to ring the doorbell in case Thomas was asleep.

The door opens after a few minutes, he's all smiles and accepts the present Molly has in her hand. "Thank you, it's good to see you, Molly."

"You too. Congratulations." Molly sees Naomi walking towards them gingerly.

"Hello." She holds out her hand to shake theirs. "Come in, I'll organise some drinks."

"Oh, please don't, we won't stay long. I'm sure you're busy," says Molly. She knows something isn't right, Naomi looks pale.

"Yes, we came to congratulate you both. A quick hello and we'll be gone." Tim and Molly had discussed this on the way, Molly didn't want to feel any more awkward than needed.

"Nonsense. One drink at least. I'll help Naomi, you two take a seat." David indicates they sit on the chesterfield lounge.

Molly sits next to Tim and wonders how unlike David this place is. Its grandness is nothing like their little home they had together. Then again, time has moved on and people change. The things we do for love, right?

It isn't long when David comes back with bubbly for the three of them and Naomi has a tall glass of water. "Sorry you can't see Thomas today, it's his nap time."

"It's fine, we will meet him another time, David. Naomi, are you ok, you're walking quite gingerly?"

"I'm ok, getting better every day. I had a caesarean as Thomas was too big. David has been a great help." She smiles at him and he holds her hand tighter, they had been holding hands from when they had sat on the chesterfield opposite Molly and Tim. Two chester-fields in one room! This house reminds Molly of Kian's parents' mansion, although not as grand, it is not somewhere she ever imagined David living. As they chat, she notices how David's face lights up every time he mentions Thomas and this reinforces her want of having a baby.

After an hour, Molly says they must leave as she has to go past the station. This is not true, but she is feeling uncomfortable, even though Naomi has been the perfect host. They say their goodbyes and leave, Naomi telling them not to be strangers.

This had surprised Molly until she received a call from David wondering why she had acted the way she did. When she explained that Naomi may not want Molly in their lives, David had laughed. "From what I hear from Tim, I'm your special friend, why wouldn't I want you in my life? Naomi is fine about you, believe me." Molly had cried when she heard this with David telling her all that stuff she thought about Naomi was all in her head and Naomi had always liked her. This bit of news made her day and she decided there and then she was definitely introducing Kian to David and his family.

SIXTY-FOUR

A year later

THE BARBEQUE

MOLLY IS with Emma as they survey the scene. It's a late spring afternoon and Molly is hosting a barbeque at David and Naomi's house. She had wanted to use her own home, but David had laughed and said, "Where are you going to fit everyone?" He had then offered his place, especially as Kian's parents were coming.

"Are they coming in the private jet?" asks Emma who had thought Kian would come to Sydney in this way. Instead, he had travelled business class because he was concerned about the environment. Another thing to love about that man.

"Good question, I'm leaving all those details to Kian. With our situation of this long-distance affair, he looks after all of the stuff at his end and I at mine. So far it has worked well."

"Well, with you going back every four months and he being here in between, you're not apart that much. Although, things will change now." Emma is talking about Molly being pregnant, only just a few weeks yet, and Emma is the only one Molly has told apart from Kian.

"Shh, Kian and I are still working out the finer details. Although, I want to bring our baby up here. Again, haven't discussed any of this yet. And the last person I want to find out before I'm certain this baby is here to stay, is his mother. She doesn't like how we are living in two countries, not that it's any of her business."

Tim walks up towards them handing them both their drinks. "What are you two whispering about?" He hands Molly hers, "Sparkling water, right?" She nods and takes the glass before he can say anything else. Emma helps by answering him.

"Secret women's business, you'd only be bored if we told you." Emma laughs and Molly joins in spurting out her water.

Molly's phone pings with a message from Kian that they are on their way.

Showtime.

"Ok, everyone, Kian is on his way with his parents, so please behave yourselves." Molly had invited her old crew and was pleased when they all accepted the invite. It was great to see Harold, Sophia and the rest of them, even Evan had come along. Some of them hadn't seen each other for years with Molly promising them to keep in touch more often.

She gives Emma a look of sheer terror. Emma comes closer and hugs her shoulders. "You've got this."

KIAN IS INTRODUCING his parents with Molly by his side. She is holding Olivia so her nerves won't take over. By holding the baby close, she feels centred. One of the catering staff calls her over, which she is grateful for. She excuses herself explaining she has to organise things. Walking to Samantha, she hands Olivia over with a kiss to her chubby cheeks. A few minutes later, she asks everyone to sit as the food is being served.

She sits next to Kian who has seated his parents with Tim, David, Naomi and of all people, Harold. Sophia is next to him. This is going to be interesting if Harold brings out some of his not-so-suitable jokes. She whispers her concerns to Kian but apparently David had warned Harold, so he is keeping any discussion appropriate. Thomas, David and Naomi's son, is with their nanny. Yes, David has a nanny, a forty-something year old woman who adores their child. Molly had told David he had come a long way after she had met the nanny at one of her many visits. He had smiled and said Thomas was happy and that's all that mattered. Love makes you do things you thought you never would. Molly knows how that feels.

Her neighbours, Carter and Jacob give her a smile, happy to have been invited. They're sitting with Brendan, who smiles and raises his glass. Carter had said they loved being part of her celebrity lifestyle, something she had scoffed at. Her time as a celebrity died with her TV show and that terrible fight she and Emma had over social media.

The afternoon passes quickly without any incident, something Molly is grateful for. Kian's parents were delightful and spoke with everyone. There was none of the animosity Molly had encountered when she had met them. His parents are the epitome of Indian society, good looking, tall and elegant in both how they handle themselves and what they wear. She had relaxed as the afternoon progressed although she did let out a sigh of relief when Kian took his parents to their hotel as dusk fell. Now she could enjoy her friends and family until late.

When Kian returns, he kisses her and asks, "Are you ok? You seemed a little tense."

"I wanted everything to be perfect for them. It turned out ok, didn't it?"

"You need to stop worrying about them, Molly, they adore you." He hugs her close but she doesn't believe a word he has said. They might like her, but they certainly don't adore her. She wonders how they are going to feel when they find out they are going to be grandparents.

SIXTY-FIVE

The Podcast

AFTER MANY LATE-NIGHT discussions and Molly taking two more trips to Mumbai, Kian agreed that she should remain in Sydney. He is now making arrangements to move to Sydney and setting up a few boutique hotels in the CBD and Parramatta. They will be married in two months at the Opera House. This was on his mother's insistence, she wanted them to have a special place for their special day.

More like she wants to show off to all their rich friends. My future mother-in-law has her own interests at heart, Kian and I don't enter into this. Especially not me.

Molly thought all of this was way over the top but had not argued. After the cool reception they received from Kian's mother post their pregnancy announcement, Molly decided to let this one go. She will pick her battles with her future mother-in-law.

Kian walks into the bedroom towelling his hair after showering.

"She'll come to terms with everything, you'll see. I don't want you stressing about the wedding either, let her do what she wants."

"It's our day, I still want some input." She can't believe they're having this discussion, she is sick of his mother sticking her nose where it's not wanted. "I am only wanting what is best for my son," Kian's mother had said when they were discussing wedding arrangements. Molly didn't even enter into her 'best'.

"Of course you do and so do I. But give her some of the responsibility."

"I insist on choosing the dress. That is definitely my department. And we will have a say in the food."

Kian walks over, his body hard and ready as he drops the towel. He whispers in her ear as he straddles her body, "I love you and that's all that matters." She lets him caress her and allows the stress of the wedding plans to leave her body.

IT WAS Emma's idea they start a podcast about their issues with social media. *Social Mishaps* began with the first episode telling their story and how fighting publicly over social media had hurt their friendship and their careers. With the negative publicity surrounding them at the time, the media scrutiny, the trolls, and the awful things they each posted, it all took its toll. So, now they give tips to listeners on how to avoid the pitfalls of social media. "Keep your posts respectful and social media will work well for you." This was one tip Emma had offered.

After a month, they had a few thousand downloads. This was with Evan's help who was producing the podcast and helping with their social media for the show. Molly and Emma were having a ball bringing the pods to their listeners once a week. With their respective celebrity status now restored to a point, the publicity for the podcast was relatively easy, especially with Molly being able to talk about it on her radio show.

"That's four of them ready and scheduled," announces Evan beaming.

"Great. Thanks for staying back and helping us to finish them," chirps Molly. She looks at the boy who is now a man, she has known him for eight years and considers him a friend. He and Samantha are still close too. Evan moved into radio production after completing his studies and needed something more to do when Molly stopped posting on social media, only leaving the orphanage Instagram account live. He still helps Molly out when she needs assistance, although it's only for the orphanage that she posts these days. When she had asked him to help with the podcast, he had jumped at the chance.

"I'll see you both at the next recording session, let me know the details. Have a good night, ladies." Evan leaves them to it and she is thankful for his help.

"Ok," says Emma who is sitting next to Molly, "You had better book the studio for the next six episodes, we need to have as many as possible prepared before your wedding and the baby's birth."

"Not a problem, I'll book it on Monday, can you be here by five?" Emma nods yes. "And this podcast is a welcome distraction to the wedding, I'm so over it."

"His mother?"

"You have no idea. She is forceful, she gives us the silent treatment if we don't listen, and she moans to Kian about me. Honestly, I'm over her and her antics. I leave it to Kian to calm her. Thankfully, they are leaving the day after the wedding."

"And you have a wonderful two weeks away with your gorgeous husband in the Maldives with no care in the world."

Molly feels the stress leave her body when she thinks about having Kian to herself in paradise, no whining mother-in-law to bother them. "He and I all alone, it will be heaven. By the way, have I mentioned Kian has bought a penthouse in the city for us to use as a weekender?"

Emma lets out a gasp, "A penthouse as a weekender! Is he for real? What's wrong with living in your cute terrace?"

"Nothing. We're not moving out, especially as Bono needs some backyard, but when he has to schmooze prospective investors, my *cute terrace* as you call it, is not appropriate."

"Look at you going up in the world, reaching new heights. You deserve this Molly, I'm so happy for you."

"Thanks." Molly laughs at Emma upping her nose indicating how posh Molly has become. "It's not where I expected to be nearing my fortieth birthday – a handsome, young husband, a baby and a city penthouse." She bends down to attach Pete.

"You're doing so well now, Molly, even Pete the prosthetic has become a part of you."

"I guess so. Being in love has helped me to heal and now I have more responsibilities, the demons that entered my life after the accident are kept at bay. I don't ever want to return to those dark days."

Emma stands and gathers her things, "I'm with you on that one, girlfriend. There were some tough times for me too when you weren't in my life. Look at us now – back together, both in love with beautiful men and working together too."

Molly stands up after attaching Pete and gives Emma a hug, "We're back forever, nothing will ever part us again."

NOAH BAMEJEE, a bundle of dark hair, brooding eyes like his father, and a scream to scare any demon, is born two months after Molly and Kian are married. His grandparents spoil him every time they visit. Samantha, Clay and Tim do too. Olivia is besotted with her little cousin the moment she meets him. David and Naomi love the fact Thomas has someone in his life he will consider family. Emma and Lewis find him a joy and are pleased to be Noah's godparents. He is a much-loved child, something Molly thought she would never have.

Her life has been complicated. She struggles with having no left foot. But Molly can deal with all of what life throws at her because of her gorgeous husband, her family and her friends. This is all she needs.

THE END

ACKNOWLEDGMENTS

This story is part of my past, fictional of course, but the inspiration came from my years of working in television. As my first job, I learned so much about writing and production during those years. The people I met have also influenced the characters in Fame & Other Disasters.

I enjoyed my time in television and being a young woman who was quite naive, I learned many things and these helped me to grow and appreciate all types of people. Creative egos clashed with the bosses ideas, shows came and went, the television industry being a mottled mess of emotions from people of varied talents. I would not change anything about my time during those years.

To my colleague and friend, Mark Drolc, thank you for the cover design, I love the Hollywood star, it really depicts what this story is about. You bring my ideas to life. A big thanks to you as always, Mark.

To my amazing friends who support me regularly, your friendship is also invaluable. And your encouragement to keep writing spurs me on. Also, to all the authors, editors and publishers I have met since starting this journey more than ten years ago, your inspiration and camaraderie has helped me immensely. To my beta readers and two editors on this book, thanks for giving it the polish it deserved.

To my family, you are my rocks. Without you allowing me to follow my passion for writing, my stories would not have been possible. My love for you all is endless.

Fame & Other Disasters is a novel I hope my readers will enjoy for a long time to come. Please let me know what you think by reviewing or sending me an email, your feedback helps me to improve and grow as a writer.

Happy reading,
Maria P Frino

ABOUT THE AUTHOR

Maria has made a career of using words to communicate. Working at a TV station nurtured Maria's love of words. A move to Sydney to study Communications gave her the opportunity to work with advertising & public relations agencies, corporate companies and newspapers.

She has written PR, ads and newsletters for products from food to jewellery, fashion and interiors as well as garden and building products for both traditional print media and digital. When she is not writing website content or as a Senior Reviewer for the online site, Weekend Notes, she works on her short stories and novels.

Her first published story, **The Studio** is a crime short story. **Xenure Station: A Billion Light Years** is Maria's second short story. Both are available on Amazon Kindle.

The Decision They Made and the **Xenure Station Trilogy** are available in print and eBook.

Maria has written many more books and they are all available on her website - www.mariapfrino.com

Maria is also a founding member of **Sydney Authors Inked**, a group of authors dedicated to helping others navigate the writing and publishing industry. This group does free author talks and local authors book festivals throughout Sydney.

Come along if you enjoy reading, writing, and publishing. We talk about all topics related to books, writing, and publishing. You will learn about our experiences, how to avoid publishing mistakes, and technical stuff like Search Engine Optimisation (SEO).

Join us for our events that are published on the Humanitix site. Authors interested in being interviewed or would like to do a talk, please contact us at - sydneyauthorsinked@gmail.com.